Beneath the Dark Water

Smiling Flu Apocalypse Book 3

Len M. Ruth

Ruthless Press

The Smiling Flu Series

Book 1 – *The Unrecovered*
Book 2 – *Rachael's Apocalypse Diary*
Book 3 – *Beneath the Dark Water*

Also by Len M. Ruth

The Pull
Tales of the Doomed

Stay Connected

Get updates, behind-the-scenes notes, and bonus reads in Len's monthly newsletter:
lenmruth.com

Beneath the Dark Water
by **Len M. Ruth**

Publisher: Ruthless Press LLC
Las Vegas, Nevada
ruthlesspress.com
For permissions: info@ruthlesspress.com

First Edition
Publication Date: May, 2026

Chapter 1

Rachael

The bed creaked as I folded it back into a couch. The sound bounced off the walls of our cold cinderblock apartment. One of many in the squat white buildings littering Fort Walters. I stretched and slipped into my jeans.

Cassie stood vigil over the coffeemaker as it burped out its pungent, acidic brew.

When I'd finished pulling on a T-shirt and jacket, Cassie handed me a mug. I rubbed the grit from my eyes, then sipped and grimaced. "Jesus. I might not be into traditional femininity, but I don't want hair on my chest."

Cassie adjusted the crease of her army jacket sleeve. "You're such a drama queen."

"Okay, but I'm not the one in the army. Can't I just sleep in for once?"

"Nope. C'mon. We've got to get your training in before work."

I groaned.

"Hey, you're the one who asked me to help you. Don't be a little bitch now."

I set the coffee on the tiny bar separating the kitchenette from my living/bedroom and struck out with my right fist.

Cassie barely looked up from her cuff folding, blocking me with her left forearm while tapping my knee with her foot, gently, just to let me know she had me dead to rights. "Nice try. Can we go now?"

"Don't call me a bitch." I took a last swallow of coffee.

Cassie reached for the door of our tiny army-issue apartment. "Don't be one."

"You're gonna pay for that."

"I doubt it," Cassie said over her shoulder.

I followed Cassie to the gym, our bicycles clattering over the still-dark streets of Fort Walters. She treated me like a kid sister, which was great as far as it went. But I wanted things to go in a different direction. Cassie just wasn't that way. If I wanted to be close to her, which I did, the folding bed in the friend zone was as close as I was going to get.

The trees stood winter-bare against the slate-gray sky. Dormant, empty, like the depopulated world outside the base. At least the winters this far south, on the border between North and South Carolina, weren't as bad as in DC, where I came from. Still, the January cold bit my nose and cheeks but didn't penetrate the army clothes I bought at the PX. Not the most fashion-forward outfit I'd ever worn, but at least I found pants, shirts, and a jacket that wasn't camo.

It had only been six months since Cassie and I were blasted with radiation and escaped kidnapping by rogue elements of the army. This all happened during an attempted theft of nuclear fuel at the Sea Ridge Nuclear Power Station. After all that, I asked Cassie to teach me to fight.I didn't know that meant: up at oh-dark-thirty for hand-to-hand drills, tactical range work, moving targets.Day after day. Month after month. Every damn morning.

She made me earn every bruise, sprain, and scrape. Now I could hit what I aimed at.

I'm sad to say Cassie was right—she didn't pay for calling me a bitch.But this time, I didn't go down easy.

I moved in fast and clean, got her off-balance with a left hook and landed a sharp elbow that made her grunt, face contorted in pain. I pushed the opening—but let frustration get the better of me, threw too wild, too fast. She blocked, dodged, swept my leg, and had me on the mat with her arm across my neck.

"Keep emotion out of it, Rach, or you'll lose. Come at me calm."

The problem was, I couldn't keep emotion out of it. I liked being that close to her. Liked having her weight on me. Liked feeling her body pressed against mine. Her breath swept my face. Those full lips just inches away... This wasn't helping.

She let me go, and we squared off again. I shook myself and pictured that smug bastard Pearson in his armored carrier laughing at us as we sat cuffed on our bench. My knee went into Cassie's sternum, making her step back. Another kick to her thigh had her hopping like the Karate Kid—until she recovered and dropped me again.

"Better," she said, letting me up.

"Why do we always stop when you win?"

"When you pin me, you can call the shots." She squeezed my shoulder. "Don't feel bad," she added, flashing that wide, infuriatingly beautiful grin. "I'm really fucking good."

And she was.

Her smile still gave me a prickly feeling on my scalp. Butterflies stirred in my stomach. She'd already told me I was like a little sister. I'd have to settle for that.

At the range, Cassie set the target for twenty yards—just about the limit for my little Beretta .380.

The range officer raised an eyebrow.

"Come off it!" I protested.

"Three hits gets you pizza in town tonight," she grinned.

I squeezed one eye shut. Checked my grip. My stance. Lined up the iron sights on my weapon and pictured a face on the target. Pearson.

Conjuring my kidnapper, the mastermind of the plot to steal spent nuclear fuel from the Sea Ridge power station, gave me focus and drive. Pearson, lackey for the deposed President of the United States and his rogue generals. I wondered where they were now. Now that they didn't have the tools to regain control of the country. Probably out looking for new tools to do that job.

I put all that speculation out of my mind, concentrated on the target, and squeezed the trigger.

First magazine? One hit.

Second mag? Three.

I'm not saying I'm a badass.

But I earned that pizza.

Well, there was *supposed* to be pizza. But I'm getting to that.

I hugged Cassie outside the range. Her warm cheek felt so good against mine, fending off the January chill. Her short-cropped black curls tickled my nose. "See you at Carlo's!" she grinned.

"I love you," I blurted. Did she assume I meant it in a sisterly way? Or could she feel the depth?

Her walnut skin betrayed no blush. "Me too."

Fucking soldiers. Tough on the outside, tough on the inside. I couldn't shake the way I felt about her. I tried to push it down. Convince myself that it was just the deep connection between found family. But the way I got a lump in my throat every day when we said goodbye told a deeper truth. The way I wanted her to be the first person I saw when I woke up, and the last person before I went to bed spoke volumes. The way her dark brown eyes penetrated my senses, leaving me stupefied if I stared too long, couldn't be denied.

I made the early shuttle bus into New Hope. On the bumpy ride, I contemplated how my life had changed since my kidnapping and radiation poisoning. Saving the Sea Ridge power plant nuked my chances of ever getting near radiation again—literally. Now I'm cancer bait. It was worth it in some ways. Knowing you saved a huge chunk of the Eastern Seaboard from the threat of a dirty bomb concocted by the ousted President of the United States and a few rogue generals gave me the warm fuzzies for sure. But not being able to use my education in nuclear physics anymore made me super sad.

A depopulated world meant new risks, and new opportunities. The legitimate US government, or what was left of it, formed the Keeper Core—a joint civilian and military organization dedicated to keeping what was left of humanity safe from all the ticking time bombs of the old world. Everything from abandoned chlorine and ammonium nitrate plants that could explode, to unattended oil pipelines, to nuclear power plants that had to be kept cool, even in shutdown mode.

Turned out they were also keeping the history of the smiling flu, and what came after. I got a gig helping with that. Not sure if it was because of my education, or because no one wanted to work with her, but they paired me up with a woman named Sarah Sampson. Man, was she prickly at first. I don't think she was any more thrilled to work with me than I was to work with her.

It's not all bad, though—the record keeping, I mean. One of the people I'm interviewing? Vic.

The unrecovered can't feel pleasure—not since the flu. But Vic's touch lights them up. Makes them worship him. They call him the Prophet. I have no idea what to call him without sounding like a dick—freak? Mutant? Miracle? He can make people feel emotions—rage, euphoria—just by touching their skin. Nobody understands how. The theory is that the smiling flu rewired something in his already-fragile brain.

Sarah wanted nothing to do with Vic, so she handed off the assignment to me. Days of interviews revealed some interesting stuff. Like that he was the only person anyone ever heard of who woke from the smiling flu coma without the antidote. And he had all his normal emotions. He could feel happiness, joy, everything. Not unrecovered at all. And that this fucked-up politician named Dale had taken Vic under his wing, then turned Vic into a cult leader. All the time whispering in Vic's ear about how he gave the unrecovered hope. A reason to carry on. That he was doing good work. But all the while, Vic had become more a prisoner than a prophet.

When I got off the bus on Main Street, I noticed a guy who was comically bad at looking casual lurking in the doorway of the closed hardware store across the street. A trench coat? Come on? He was obviously one of 'The Knights of the Prophet.'

Inside the police station, Clay had his feet up on his old wooden desk. "You're early," he said, setting his mug down.

"I nailed it at the range. Three hits at twenty yards." Bragging. I know, cringy. But damn it, I was proud of my progress.

Clay set his feet on the floor and rose. His dark hair formed wings where it grew from under his sheriff's hat. "With the pistol? Impressive!" His handsome face broke out into a toothy grin. He walked over; the keys jingled on his utility belt like an old west sheriff. I always forgot how crazy tall he was until he stood towering above me. "Let's have it."

He held out his hand.

"But I'm a good shot!"

He brought his hand closer. "No guns in the cell block."

"Clay..."

"It's Deputy."

I tried again. "But you—"

"No *civilian* guns."

"Ugh." I reached down, unstrapped the pistol from my calf, and put it in his hand.

"Thank you. Was that so hard?"

"After the shit I've been through? Yes."

Clay gave me a thin smile. "Okay, Rach. But rules is rules." He put the gun in his desk. "Want me to walk you down?"

"I'm good."

Clay buzzed me in. I went through the barred door and down the lime-green cement steps to the dozen or so cells in the basement. A few drunks or whatever were sleeping it off in the first cell or two; the rest were empty... except the one at the very end.

Inside, Vic's striking green eyes peered at me over his bushy black beard. He sat ramrod straight on the stainless-steel bed that stuck out from the wall.

"Back for another day of prying?" he asked.

Prick. "That's the deal," I said, trying to make my voice hard. "You want to stay in protective custody, you tell me what I want to know."

"Who died and made you top cop?" he sneered.

I took a breath. This asshat wouldn't get to me today. I took my notebook out of my backpack and opened it, pen ready. "Yesterday we were talking about how the unrecovered made you do 'the touch.' Tell me how that works."

Vic looked down at his clasped hands. "No one knows how it works, it just does."

I held in a sigh. Assuming Vic was telling the truth, the irony of a gift like that landing on someone who could barely tie his shoes... "No. I mean, when they make you do it. What happens?"

"They tie me to a chair." Vic stared at the floor, voice low and even. "Line up the unrecovered. Bring them in one at a time. I hold their hand. My skin tingles. I think happy thoughts."

"So they get happy?"

He nodded.

"But you can make them angry, too?"

"Enraged."

"Ever do that to someone in the line?"

"Once." He looked away. "They beat me."

I tapped my pen on my teeth. "Is that why you ran?"

"It drains me. One person, I can handle. But a whole camp? I collapse. And they never left me alone. No privacy. No breaks. Just a tool they passed around."

Oh, he's a tool alright. "But you're a prisoner here."

"By choice. And I don't have to do the touch. Don't have to be drained all the time."

I just couldn't get there. Couldn't believe something, even something as weird as the smiling flu, could change everything science taught us about how people work, how touch works, how emotion works. "You have to admit, all this is pretty hard to believe."

Vic rose, extending a hand to the bars. "Let me show you."

I glanced at the security camera high up on the wall. I'd been warned not to let him touch me. Still, it's not like he could bend the bars by making me happy.

He sighed. "If you're going to write my story, I need you to believe. To understand."

For once, I agreed. "I thought it drained you."

"A quick touch. Not the whole thing like the unrecovered get. They are empty glasses. You have happiness. Your vessel is close to full already."

Made sense. Could all be bullshit, though. Still...I had to know. I rose. Took Vic's extended hand.

The skin on my palm tingled, tickled. Blood rushed to my head. A warm wave rushed over me. I could feel the muscles at the corners of my mouth curling up.

"Let go," Vic said.

My hand. I'd forgotten. It felt so good in his. Like petting a puppy.

"Let. Go." He yanked his hand back through the bars.

I stood there grinning, looking at my palm. An inner well of happiness blossomed in my chest. I hadn't felt this good since the world went to shit. My legs wobbled under me. I went to sit and missed the chair. The whole thing was so funny, I sat on the floor laughing.

Shouts echoed down the stairs.

Then, gunshots, which was ridiculous.

I laughed harder.

Knights of the Prophet raced down the stairs wielding machine guns with those funny banana-shaped magazines.

"Rachael," Vic pleaded, clutching the bar. "Don't let them take me."

"You're right." I giggled. "Let me stop their machine guns with the power of my mind." I burst out laughing again.

"So," one of the Knights said, producing a set of keys, "touching new friends, Vic?"

"Please. Please, no!" Vic squealed, backing deeper into the cell.

The Knight opened the cell door. His friend looked down at me. "Don't try anything."

"Oh," I smirked, "I've already tried things."

The first Knight dragged Vic out of the cell with black rubber-gloved hands.

"I won't do anything for you. No touches!"

"Oh," the Knight said, "I think you will."

Vic dug in his heels. "Not without her." He nodded toward me. "She's going to tell my story. She's the only one who understands me."

"Hey!" My smile faltered. "Not cool, man."

The Knights looked at each other.

"Better bring her," the first one said. "Just in case."

The other guy reached down to grab me.

I held up a hand to block him, but dissolved into a fit of laughter at his bewildered expression. Next thing I knew, they were hustling me up the stairs. In the front office, Clay lay in a pool of blood next to Sheriff Kyle. Both dead.

My euphoria slipped. I struggled free, trying to make my way over to the unmoving cops.

Something cracked against the side of my head.

The lights went out before I hit the floor.

Chapter 2

Sarah

Sarah woke before dawn to get the fire going and warm the house before she woke Penny. Koontz, her German Shepherd, and King, her pit bull, padded by her side, ready to go out for their morning constitutional. Dickens, her black Lab, still lay in bed with Penny, keeping the child warm.

Electricity hadn't come to this neighborhood since the pandemic. Sarah chose a house far from town because she missed the quiet, simple life of her Montana ranch. She hadn't thought it through. How much firewood she'd need to keep herself and her foundling daughter warm. And though South Carolina's January chill was nothing compared to the frigid Montana winters she was used to, it still demanded heat to keep her two-year-old daughter cozy.

No time for coffee this morning. Not if she wanted to catch Rachael before she started another interview with Vic down at the sheriff's office.

Sarah kissed the top of Penny's head and set the toddler down on Nate's porch. The child's unique, sweet, clean scent lingered in her nose as she straightened and held out a hand, refusing the coffee mug Nate offered. "Don't want to spill it in the truck."

Penny wrapped her little body around Nate's leg. "Daddy!"

Dickens, Sarah's black Lab, took the opportunity to bathe the child's face with his wide pink tongue. His brothers, King the pit bull attack dog, and Koontz the German Shepherd watchdog, looked on with disapproval. Sarah reached down and gave the K-9 companions at her side a quick pat. She would never have made it through the pandemic and collapse without her three fuzzballs.

Nate pushed the steaming cup toward Sarah a second time. "I made it just the way you like it."

"This again?" He'd been trying to woo her since they met on the reservation last year. And she'd been telling him she was asexual and couldn't be wooed. Still, he'd basically adopted Penny. And she'd grudgingly accepted his choosing the house next to her when they landed in the survivor's colony. Not that she didn't love him. She did, of course. Nate was like the little brother she never had. And the way he was with Penny, so patient, so giving, made her question her own parenting. But Sarah needed space from *all* people, except Penny. She missed the solitude of her sprawling animal rescue ranch in Montana.

The idea of neighbors was all new to her, and she didn't much care for it, adoptive little brother next door notwithstanding.

"What? It's just coffee." He gave her his signature goofy half-grin.

Sarah accepted the cup. The hot bittersweet concoction woke her mouth and mind alike with a taste almost forgotten. "Holy shit, Nate! Where'd you get cream?"

"The new guy on the edge of town has a couple of cows. I traded him a for some venison. *Cream's* easy. I'm worried about where we're going to get *coffee* once the food warehouse empties out."

Penny hugged his leg. "Daddy? Jess and Davie?"

Nate tousled Penny's hair. "They'll be here soon, sweetie."

Sarah took a big gulp of coffee, swallowed too fast, coughed, and said, "you're a regular daycare."

"Yup." Nate tucked his hands in the pockets of his jeans, leaving the thumbs out, tapping a nervous rhythm on the denim. "Worked out a trade with each family." He paused. "You know, *you* could pay me."

"Dads don't get paid to watch their kids."

Nate shook his head. "What's the world coming to?"

"Destroyed by a global pandemic." Sarah took another big swallow of coffee.

"Oooooh yeaaaaah." Nate freed a hand to tap it on his forehead. "I almost forgot." He fixed Sarah with a sardonic grin.

Sarah took one more gulp and handed the mug back to him. "Thanks for the java, but I've got to get to town. I want to catch Rachael before she goes in to talk to the Prophet."

"Rach-a?" Penny asked, tugging on Sarah's pant leg.

Sarah bent down, bringing her eyes level with her daughter. "I'll tell her you said hello. You're staying here with Daddy today."

A soft "woof" at her side brought Sarah's eyes up, scanning. She patted Koontz absently. "What is it, boy?"

Dickens stopped licking Penny's hand to circle in, jealous.

King stood at attention, nose pointed at the sound.

The rhythmic thump of an approaching helicopter cut the air. A big twin-rotor chopper flew low over the treetops like a dull-green, moldy banana.

"What would make them burn fuel for a chopper?" Nate asked, not taking his eyes off the sky.

"There's some shit going down somewhere," Sarah said.

"Shit," Penny mimicked.

Sarah sighed, kissed Penny, and stood.

"That's a bathroom word, Penny," Nate said. "Don't copy Mommy's potty mouth." He returned his eyes to Sarah. "Why don't you go to work before you get her drinking whiskey and smoking cigarettes?"

"Na-na-na na na-na-na," Sarah sneered, duplicating Nate's cadence.

"Nice. Real mature. Aren't you like a million years old?"

"Fu—"

Nate held up a finger.

"Have a fu—n day today, Penny," Sarah said, tousling her daughter's hair. To Nate she said, "fifty-two is the new thirty." She banged down the porch steps and advanced across the too-tall lawn. "Bye, Penny," she called. "Mommy loves you!" A soft, warm rush filled Sarah's chest every time she said those words.

"Bye, Mommy."

Strange to think that less than a year ago, she'd found the girl buckled into a car seat with two dying, unconscious parents in the front. When she'd rescued Penny, she vowed to find somewhere safe to leave the child. Somewhere the nameless little girl wouldn't have to endure the same fate Sarah had in the foster care system. Then, mile by empty, ruined mile through what was left of America, Sarah realized there was no place safer than in her care. And with each nap the child spent curled up against Sarah's warmth, with each feeding and diapering, Sarah fell in love. She named the foundling Penny, after Sarah's mother. And to the surprise of everyone around her, Sarah became a doting, affectionate mom. Now, she couldn't imagine her life without the cheery, adorable little girl.

Winter sun dappled the debris-strewn suburban South Carolina roads. Goosebumps rose on Sarah's arms. The light flannel over a cutoff AC/DC shirt was a poor choice this morning. But the second-summer January air roaring in through the truck's open window smelled crisp and clean. Gone was the smell of sorrow and death that had pervaded the previous fall. Sarah piloted the truck around stalled cars and downed branches, constant, powerful reminders of capital-B, Before.

At the edge of her neighborhood, Martha looked out the window of a little white cape home, radio in one hand, binoculars in the other. In the days before the smiling flu, she was probably the neighborhood busybody. Now, she was a vital link to law and order in a world without telephones. Martha kept tabs on the neighborhood and radioed the cop shop if she saw something out of the ordinary. How they kept her from reporting every squirrel, Sarah had no idea. Martha gesticulated wildly as Sarah passed. No way was Sarah stopping to hear every detail of Martha's morning routine. It took the woman half an hour to say hello. Sarah gave a half-wave as she passed, never letting off the gas.

Sarah let out a frustrated huff as she got out to clear a fallen tree limb from the street. The army had bigger fish to fry, and the civilian government had its hands full keeping the bare minimum of services and infrastructure going. Clearing far-flung neighborhood streets would just have to wait.

On Main Street, soldiers in tactical gear ran among the buildings. Wrong. Sarah slowed.

Deputy Winslow descended the steps, gun drawn, head on a swivel, scanning the area. When he caught sight of Sarah, he waved frantically.

Sarah drew the truck up next to him.

"The Knights came for the Prophet—"

"Did they—"

The deputy nodded. "They got him."

"Rachael?"

"We tried to stop them. Kyle and Clay were shot—"

Sarah had trouble hearing Winslow over the sudden roar of blood in her ears. "What about Rachael?"

"They took her too."

"Where'd they go?!"

"We got a call from—"

Sarah's heart pounded. "Where. Did—"

"Listen! We got—"

"Damn it! Where—"

"Martha just reported gunfire! We're looking at multiple attacks!"

The bottom fell out of the world. "Penny!" Sarah stomped on the pedal, peeling out in a cloud of smoke.

Winslow shouted an unintelligible admonition.

Sarah was barely conscious of him as she wheeled the skidding truck around, popping the curb. The back tires caught traction. Dickens cowered in the passenger footwell. Sarah launched from the smoke cloud, narrowly missing an approaching Humvee.

In the back, Koontz let out a plaintive bark. King was a rock. The pittie crouched, feet planted, ever ready for whatever came next. When Sarah nosed the truck onto Honeysuckle Ave., another Humvee blocked her way as it weaved around the obstacle-strewn road. She couldn't get around the wide olive drab machine, and the driver wasn't helping.

A soldier popped out of the top, waving her back and motioning her to slow down.

She did neither. She knew these were the good guys, rushing to confront whatever was happening in her neighborhood, but nothing could stop her rushing to Penny. Nothing.

Humvee guy brandished a machine gun.

"Shoot me," she muttered, trying again to pass. Downed tree by the blue house in two blocks. At this speed...

She juked back behind the rolling green roadblock.

Army guy in the top of the truck shook his gun.

The house on the corner of Crestwood. No curb. Clear, short-cropped lawn. She didn't know the people who lived there, but the lawn was evidence someone did. The Humvee would probably stay on the street. Probably.

And...Yes! The Humvee slowed at the corner.

Sarah gunned the pickup catty-corner into the driveway and across the lawn. She slammed off the curb on the other side, getting more air than she expected. A hard yank on the wheel kept her from hitting the burned-out car on the far side of the street. The skid slowed her enough that the Humvee was right up her ass as she poured on the power coming out of the turn. Koontz got his legs under him again and barked furiously at the Humvee.

The dappled sunlight she'd enjoyed just minutes before took on a harsh white-out quality. Time slowed. Sarah recited a single-word mantra. "Penny, Penny, Penny..." She leaned forward over the wheel, propelling the truck toward her daughter by force of will and internal combustion.

Nate's door stood open.

Sarah skidded the truck to a halt.

Someone lay on the porch.

She pulled the gun from the glove box. The dogs ran alongside her as she raced across the lawn.

Blood pooled around Nate's motionless chest. A jagged hole in his shirt told the story.

Silence.

Sarah bent to feel for a pulse.

Dickens licked Nate's face. No reaction.

A soldier tapped her on the shoulder.

"There should be three kids," she whispered.

He nodded and gestured his squad forward.

Poor Nate. She should have been kinder to him. Much kinder. He was a good man. A good father. A good friend. No. Good didn't cut it. Nate was amazing. One of a kind. And she'd loved him the best she could, which in hindsight, was pretty crappy. Sarah stroked Nate's hair, then followed the soldiers. She'd have to grieve later. She needed to find Penny.

The woman in front of her waved her back. Sarah flipped the soldier off.

Sarah's foot crunched on broken glass. She stepped around an upturned chair. King made the move with her, brushing her leg. The attack dog was all business, plunging into the chaos with single-minded ferocity. Behind her, she could hear Dickens whining softly at Nate's side. She couldn't do it. Not now. She had to find Penny. There'd be time to grieve for Nate later.

"Clear," a woman's voice drifted down the stairs.

"Clear," someone called from the hall.

By the time Sarah got to the middle of the room, the soldiers reentered.

"Deceased female upstairs, front bedroom," one said.

Bile rose in Sarah's throat. "Female?"

"Adult," the soldier clarified.

"No kids?" Sarah asked.

Silence.

"The basement?"

"The house is clear," said the soldier she'd spoken to on the porch. "They're not here."

"Cabinets?"

"I said it's clear. Feel free to take a look."

"They didn't pass us," Sarah said. She hadn't heard or seen another chopper on the way back home. And the neighborhood was blocked on all sides by the wreckage of the last hurricane through these parts, except the road to town. "There's only one street out..." Her words trailed off as she pictured the backyard. Penny playing in the grass, and... the overgrown fire road.

Sarah ran.

"Lady, wait!" the soldier shouted behind her.

The dogs raced with Sarah to the truck. Images of Penny superimposed themselves over Sarah's consciousness. Her hand shook as she turned the key.

Chapter 3

Mike

The needle's stab was nothing to Mike. He closed his eyes, willing the medication to work. To have some effect. A search of his mind and his feelings revealed the sad truth: nothing. No joy, no hope, no reward, just the black sea of despair. But that wasn't all. The yawning mental chasm full of dark water on which his consciousness floated hosted all the unrecovered. When they drew close, walking by on the street, or sharing a meal, traces of their minds tickled at his. Just a slight touch, enough to keep breathing, eating, and putting one foot in front of the other in a world devoid of happiness. Even now, with no unrecovered close by, Mike knew they were there. Ripples on the dark water told him he wasn't alone.

The only sounds disturbing the quiet of Mike's room were his breathing and that of Dr. Carl Parks.

Dr. Parks withdrew the needle from Mike's liver-spotted arm, placed a cotton ball on the dot of blood, then guided Mike's hand to hold it. "Anything?"

"Still nothing," Mike said.

"It may take some time for the tao to have any noticeable effect."

"But you're confident it will?" Mike wished he had the capacity to like the man. Dr. Parks, like himself, pushed on with little hope of reward or happiness. It must be intolerable for this man to spend so much time among the dour unrecovered.

"Well, I'm confident you won't get Alzheimer's. That's what this medication traditionally treats."

"Might be better," Mike grumbled. "And what about the other part of this? The connections between all the unrecovered. The synchronized screaming when one of us wakes from the flu coma? The Prophet...."

"That's harder to study. At least not with the staff and equipment available these days." Dr. Parks grew silent. Then he started out of his woolgathering, saying, "We've lost so much."

"Not as much as the unrecovered." Mike knew what he meant, of course. He meant society. But Mike figured spending fifty years locked in an agonizing catatonic state earned him the right to say what he wanted.

"Of course," Dr. Parks said, busying himself putting his things back in his medical bag. "I'm sorry."

"We're all sorry," Mike said. That much was true. "So, no theories on the synchronization? The way we *needed* to gather together and live in the same little dorm building on this little college campus instead of spreading out into a town or neighborhood the way the immune do? What about the mental awareness of the others? The black water?"

"There is no medical explanation that I can find. That's not to say there isn't one, but it's beyond what I have the means to test for."

Mike tossed the cotton ball into the trash. "No bullshit. What do you make of it?"

"I'm a man of science," Dr. Parks said. "What you're talking about...is beyond me."

"Are you saying it's...what? God?" Mike looked out the window into the sunny southern morning, studying the way the tree branches waved at him, trying to believe.

"An unknown psychotic effect of the smiling flu treatment, perhaps." Parks wouldn't meet his eye.

"That's bullshit, and we both know it. If Vic is to be believed, he never received treatment, and he's got the largest effect of all the unrecovered."

Carl raised his eyes to meet Mike's. "Vic?"

"The Prophet," Mike sneered. Just the word made him sick. Vic was a nasty little piece of work who'd randomly been given the keys to the kingdom. "I'm not used to hearing him called that," Dr. Parks said.

"He's a stupid little shit. Dumb as a box of rocks."

Dr. Parks straightened, holding his medical bag. "He was smart enough to run away from here and lock himself in the New Hope jail."

"He'd have been smarter to keep running. Now Dale and the other unrecovered know exactly where he is." Dale. The new de facto leader of the unrecovered. If Vic was a nasty piece of work, Dale was his maker. Puppet master. Dale was the worst kind of person, smart, cunning, and power-hungry. "How long do you think they're going to sit around while the source of all their happiness rots in jail?"

Dr. Parks raised an eyebrow. "You aren't including yourself?"

Mike shook his head. "I don't partake of Vic's pleasures. I did once. Afterward, it only made the despair worse. The touch of the other minds is enough to sustain me...for now." Sampson paused. "As patient zero, and the oldest of the unrecovered, I feel a sense of duty to them. I need to keep my mind clear."

He wanted to say more, but not here. Not within the thin walls of the dormitory. He rose.

Dr. Parks smiled. "You've got the clearest mind of any septuagenarian I've ever met."

Sampson rubbed his bad leg through his khaki trousers. "Fifty years in a coma will do that to you. I'm a walking mummy."

"No more cane?" Dr. Parks nodded at the place Sampson rubbed.

"No. I'm getting around quite well these days. Care to walk with me?"

Dr. Parks looked uncertain. "I should go see my other patients."

"You should walk with me. Supervise my exercise."

"Something on your mind?"

Mike held a finger to his lips.

Dr. Parks nodded. "I guess I could use a chance to stretch my legs before I settle into a day of appointments."

They stepped into the linoleum-clad hall. Sampson pulled the worn, pine-paneled door shut behind them. He held the wrought-iron railing as they descended the wide concrete steps onto the cracked asphalt walkway leading away between the ivy-covered brick buildings. The grass on the quad grew tall. Sampson cut across it anyway.

"I'm not sure this whole 'touch of the Prophet' thing is what's best for the unrecovered," Mike said.

"I'm sure it isn't," Carl replied. "But who am I to say they can't take what joy is left to them in this world? A person without pleasure or gratification is every bit as dead as those who died of happiness from the flu. It's the same, just opposite. Without hope or reward, we just lie down and die. No reason to eat or breathe."

Sampson stopped in the middle of the quad, as far as he could get from straining ears and prying eyes. "I'm living proof that isn't true."

Dr. Parks switched his bag from one hand to the other. "But how can you be sure the others feel it as strongly as you do? You had many years of smiling flu coma. Most of *them* only had a few months. How do we know it wasn't as much time as it is severity that caused this phenomenon?"

"They feel it," Sampson said. "They told me so." He ran a hand through his thinning gray hair. "When we woke from the coma, in Washington, I was...like their shepherd. Their leader. Now, with Dale and Vic, I'm all but useless. If I don't go along with whatever they say, the Knights will do me harm." He cast his eyes furtively around the campus. Here and there, a lone figure walked between the buildings; some, the Knights, walked with guns slung on their backs.

Dr. Parks nodded. "The tao will work. We've just got to give it time."

Mike shook his head. "Hubris."

"Maybe." Dr. Parks put a hand on his hip. "I might be a young doctor. And this may not have been my area of expertise before the smiling flu, but it is now. No one, I guarantee, no one is going to outwork me. From the moment I wake up every day until the moment I go to sleep, I'm working on reversing the aftereffects of the smiling flu. And I think this anti-tau immunotherapy is very promising. Well, if the smiling flu encouraged tau buildup in the pleasure centers of the brain. Which seems likely. And also...I'm all you've got."

"That much we agree on."

"I'm going to check in on Jamie and Aella. Want to join me?"

Want was an odd choice of words. It implied hope. That part of his brain, if it were still alive, slept, as if still in a coma. "Okay."

They crossed the lawn and walked along the paved path, crossing the entrance road by the gate. Outside the locked iron bars, a solitary figure stood vigil.

"I can't believe he still comes and stands out there every day," Dr. Parks said.

"Ed still has hope, and nothing else to occupy him."

"If you're going to worry about someone doing something crazy, worry about that one," Dr. Parks said. "Why won't Jamie and Aella see him?"

"Ask them yourself," Sampson replied. He knew why, but explaining the desperate hopelessness to someone who wasn't unrecovered was too complicated.

"Doctor Parks!" Ed yelled. "Mister Sampson!"

Sampson ignored him.

Dr. Parks turned his head Ed's way, but didn't break stride.

"Doctor Parks, tell the guards to let me in! I have to see Jamie and Aella! I have to see my family! Please!"

"That's not in my power, Ed," Dr. Parks called back.

"Please tell them I'm here! Tell them I love them!"

Dr. Parks nodded.

"Shut up!" one of the Knights guarding the gate said, waving his Kalashnikov, "or I'll come out and shut you up."

Ed went silent.

It wouldn't be the first time he'd received a beating at the hands of the Knights. Sampson didn't like the Knights. Though since the smiling flu, it was hard to point to something he did like. The very word 'like' was in the same bucket as 'want'—motivations his flu-damaged brain couldn't experience.

Their steps drew them away from the road by the gate and in between a row of buildings that, in another lifetime, housed fraternities. Here, a few buildings down, Aella and Jamie perched in their accustomed positions, knees drawn up under them on porch chairs like a couple of dispassionate gargoyles.

Mike and Dr. Parks ascended the wide wooden steps onto the sweeping southern porch.

Lost in their internal worlds, Jamie and Aella didn't react to their presence.

Mike knew what they were doing. He could feel their minds touching his own, seeking out what little connection they could find on that placid mental sea of dark water. They probed, searching for something he didn't have to give—joy.

"Jamie? Aella?" Parks whispered.

It took a moment for Aella to turn her eyes to the Doctor. "Dr. Carl."

"How are you feeling?"

Her eyes fell, returning to their wide, vacant state. "The same."

"No change at all?" Dr. Parks insisted.

"That's what the *same* means," Jamie said without moving her eyes. "Do you have any idea yet why Aella hasn't recovered, but all the other children have?"

"Well," Dr. Parks cleared his throat. "I wouldn't say recovered—"

"They're not here," Jamie said. "They smiled, and then they were moved to New Hope."

"Almost all the children are suffering long term emotional aftereffects, depending on their age, and the severity of their exposure to—"

"So the answer is no. You don't."

Mike felt bad for Dr. Parks. That emotion, at least, was still in his repertoire.

Footfalls on pavement broke the horrible silence. "Hey!" a Knight shouted, brandishing a machine gun. "Come with me, now."

"I'm a doctor—" Carl began.

"I didn't ask you shit. Follow me. All of you. Now!"

"What is this?" Sampson asked.

"This is me telling you to get your ass off the porch before I shoot it off."

Jamie and Aella didn't say a word. They put their feet on the old planks and rose as one.

Mike turned. He knew better than to push the patience of the thugs Dale dignified with the title 'Knights.'

"What the hell?" Dr. Parks whispered.

"No idea," Mike said.

"Hurry up!" the guard shouted.

"He's seventy—" Dr. Parks began.

The Knight raised his rifle toward the doctor, butt first.

"I'm Mike Sampson, patient zero, in case you forgot. And this is the doctor that's been treating all the unrecovered. So pipe down and show a little respect."

The Knight lowered his gun and his voice. "Hurry up. All of you."

The Knight ushered them down the street and around the corner, into a waiting bus. Many unrecovered were already nestled in the green Naugahyde seats.

Dale boarded the bus. Sweat glistened on his forehead and dripped from an errant hair of his comb-over.

"Where are we going?" Jamie asked.

Dale smiled ruefully and shook his finger at her. "Someplace where we can all get happy."

Chapter 4

Rachael

I woke, head pounding, on the seat of a passenger van. A plastic wire tie's hard edge cut painfully into the flesh of my bound wrists. I knew there were videos of how to break out of this style of cuff. I wish I'd watched them. I felt myself grinning. Actually grinning. And even though I was bound, kidnapped, and surrounded by armed goons, I felt pretty good. How was that?

Then I remembered. The touch. I'd let Vic show me his mystical power. The one that drew these assholes to risk their lives to break him out of prison. I got it now. At least a little. I mean, I didn't have to live without happiness, like the unrecovered. But feeling this intense joy and inner well-being, I knew if I had easy access to Vic, I'd do anything to feel this way again... and again... and again. It was like the best pot anyone ever smoked, except, it didn't feel chemical. I was just happy. Simply, deliriously, happy.

There was no way for me to tell if the fuzzy-headed feeling came from Vic's touch, or from getting cracked on the head. The interplay of pleasure from the touch and pain on my skull. I...

We hit a bump. I lost my balance. Next thing I knew, I was lying sideways in the seat, giggling in the lap of a Knight of the Prophet.

"Well, hello, frisky little lady." He grinned down at me, all stubble and long tangled hair. He stank.

Gross.

I did my best to get back into a sitting position. And even though I knew what the disgusting man was thinking, I giggled as I struggled upright. A small, quiet voice deep inside told me this wasn't funny, but I laughed anyway.

I had a hard time remembering what I was supposed to be doing. My head throbbed. My mouth was so, so dry. I should be pissed. Should be fighting. But the patterned sunlight filtering through the overhanging trees warmed my face in the most delicious way. My brain felt foggy. Like I was somehow experiencing the world from inside a glass of the most delicious juice. The thought made me giggle again.

The van stank of old sweat, and a sharp tang of something else. Adrenaline? Testosterone? Gross. I know it doesn't work like that, that you can't actually smell those things, but the thought made it real in my mind. I almost gagged.

Around me, the Knights of the Prophet sat, guns ready, all smiling. Vic sat a couple of seats in front of me. His head lolled. I guessed some of the Knights couldn't wait for 'the touch' and had tired him out.

We drove through backstreets and backyards. Someone cleared obstacles, fences, and cars from our route in advance. They must have been planning this the whole time Vic was hiding out in the jail. I smiled. Yeah, if I counted on Vic for my happiness, I'd have planned this out too.

There was a part of me that stood arms crossed, tapping its foot in my mind. Pissed, I was so damn happy. It reminded me of the time I smoked a blunt with my college roommate. Vic's touch made me feel the same way. Kind of happy and giddy. *Fight!* my mind said. I made a conscious effort to drop my smile, take in my surroundings. I took a couple of deep breaths and let them out slowly. *Focus on the tactical situation.* Tactical sounded like testicle. I grinned again. Damn it. Focus!

We were on a dirt road in the middle of a forest when the van came to a stop. The Knights got out. The one next to me tugged my arm, half-dragging me with him. Just a little ahead, a yellow school bus idled.

Weird place for a school bus. We walked toward it, leaving the van behind, doors open.

"You're going to kill the battery," I said. "The dome light..."

Why would I say that? Yeah, 'the touch' made me feel stupid, unable to focus. I remember not liking that feeling when I smoked that blunt. That's why I only did it that one time.

Come on, Rachael, the voice in my head said. *Now!*

I yanked my arm away from the Knight holding me and started to run for the trees.

"You idiots!" someone shouted. "Get her!"

Dead leaves and sticks crunched under my feet. Branches scraped my face. There was no place to hide in the January forest. No leaves on the trees. My breath steamed into the sun. The world spun crazily as I zigzagged through the brush.

Footsteps behind me.

A hand squeezed my shoulder.

I tried to run forward.

The hand didn't let go.

I fell over backwards.

The Knight, the same one who'd been sitting next to me in the van, grabbed me by the armpit and hauled me to my feet. "Come on."

"Let go!" I tried to shake him off.

He just hooked his arm tighter in my armpit and hauled me back toward the bus.

I wished I were bigger, stronger, and struggled.

He dragged me to the bus and hauled me up the steps.

"Go!" someone shouted.

I turned.

It was Dale.

I'd seen him before. Knew who he was. Who didn't know Dale, the real leader of the unrecovered? The one Vic told me about when I was writing down his story back in the jail. Dale wasn't much to look at. Pudgy, balding, with mean little eyes.

"Watch yourself, Rachael," he said. "You're only along because Vic has a thing for you." He gave me a very sinister grin.

Gross, gross, GROSS!

"And if you don't play ball..." Dale raised an eyebrow. "...you're not much good to us alive."

"Who's us?" I asked.

Dale winked and whistled, *Hail to the Chief*.

"The President?"

Dale didn't answer. Didn't need to. Was it just that morning at the range I'd wondered what that defrocked idiot was doing now? Looking for a new tool to regain power? What better tool than the only man who could make the unrecovered happy? That would lock up the unrecovered vote, if there was ever another election. That thought almost made me laugh.

The Knight tossed me into a seat about halfway back as the bus started rolling.

Be aware of your tactical situation, the voice in my head said again.

The stoned feeling finally started to fade. I looked around. Just a couple of seats ahead on the right, I saw Mike Sampson and Dr. Parks whispering.

Behind me, kids were crying. Kids! I turned in my seat to get a better view.

The bus hit a bump, bouncing into the air. I hit my head on the window. Through the pain, I saw a Knight holding a squirming Penny, Sarah's daughter.

Any residual high left in my brain cleared. I still felt a queasy, happy feeling, but my brain, my thoughts, were my own again. I had to get Penny. Get out. Get away. Bring her back to Sarah.

Chapter 5

Sarah

Sarah released the key when the truck roared to life.

"STOP!" a soldier shouted from the porch.

The sound buzzed in Sarah's ear, searching for connection. She was too far gone. Her truck thumped across the side yard, headed for the forest in back, and the old disused road leading into the deep woods. The dogs braced themselves for another rough ride. Dickens curled up in the passenger footwell. King and Koontz stood on the pads she'd secured to the truck bed ages ago.

Deep, wide tire tracks made a circle in the grass at the edge of the wood. They'd come this way, turned around, and left with the children. She saw Nate's lifeless face in her mind. No time to grieve. There was only Penny now. Her old Ford bumped along the track between the trees. The dogs scrambled to keep their feet.

Half a mile along, a pickup truck sat on the trail, blocking the way. Its rear tires were flat, its hood, up. The cab and bed appeared empty. A deliberate roadblock. Could be someone lying on the seat or tucked up against the tailgate? That thought brought another. There could also be a contingent behind the raised hood, or in the trees. Sarah reached for her gun. It wasn't there.

The twisting knife of fear stabbed her chest. She turned. The gun lay on the floor beside Dickens. She'd just thrown it on the seat when she left the house. Stupid. Emotions were the enemy here. If she wanted Penny back, she'd have to summon all her wushu training. Summon her calm. First, situational awareness. If there were people in the truck or in the woods, they weren't shooting. Her move.

Sarah closed her eyes. Three box breaths. In through the nose. Hold. Out through the mouth. Better. After wiping her sweaty palms on her jeans, she bent down and picked up the pistol. Sarah left the truck door open for Dickens, then approached the pickup on the balls of her feet, muscled legs bent like a coiled spring. She popped up, gun first, and peered into the back of the truck.

Empty.

Koontz padded up beside her, tail at half-mast. Work mode. He sniffed the air but made no sound.

Probably no one around then. Sarah gave his head a grateful pat before advancing to the cab. The front tire sat on its rim, too. Sarah crouched under the driver's rolled-down window. Same maneuver. Pop up, gun at the ready, but not so far from her chest an attacker could grab it.

Empty.

She scanned the trees. No sign of anyone.

The rumble of a motor on the track behind her brought her up short. Sarah dropped into a crouch.

A Humvee. The army.

She waited, just to make sure it wasn't a hostile force.

The truck stopped. Soldiers piled out. Same ones from the house.

She started to break cover but thought better of it at the last instant. That was a good way to get shot. "It's Sarah. I'm coming out."

Sarah rose, staring down the barrels of four machine guns.

"Jesus, lady..." one of them said.

No one needed to point out that the trees were too dense to get her truck or the Humvee past the abandoned Chevy.

"We need to get that roadblock moved," the driver of the Humvee said.

"No shit, Sherlock," Sarah replied. A glance into the engine compartment revealed missing spark plug wires.

"And put it where?" another soldier asked.

Every second they wasted took Penny further away.

"This road empties onto route sixteen about a mile down," Sarah said.

"Everett, Levy," the soldier on the passenger side commanded, "proceed on foot and wait at route sixteen. Vaughn, let's go."

Two soldiers advanced toward Sarah at a trot. The others got into the Humvee and backed down the fire road.

Sarah tracked the running soldiers, then swung her gaze to the retreating Humvee. The chances the Knights, or whoever, were stopped in the forest somewhere ahead were slim. She got into her truck. The dogs followed.

Arm on the back of the seat, Sarah reversed down the dirt track until she was nearly bumper to bumper with the retreating Humvee.

The army driver knew his shit. When the trees opened out into her backyard, he jerked the wheel, peeling out of the way and spinning his machine toward the street.

Sarah had the advantage. She knew the neighborhood. There were no fences here in the civilized southern suburbs. Sarah cut across the backyards of the next two houses and bumped down onto the street.

A helicopter thumped overhead, streaking away to the west. Sarah made the twists and turns at high speed. Dickens cowered in the passenger footwell, whining each time the truck knocked him against the door. Sarah cast a glance in the rearview mirror. Koontz and King were faring little better, digging their claws into the dog beds she had fixed to the truck.

She knew every downed tree and stalled car on the road. By the time she reached the other end of the logging road, the soldiers were jogging along the verge toward her.

She slowed and pulled up alongside.

The soldier shook his head. "They turned onto the road this way."

"You sure?"

"Muddy tire tracks on the pavement."

The Knights were headed for the campus. The unrecovered colony. "Hop in."

An approaching motor.

Sarah glanced in the mirror.

The Humvee.

"That's our ride," the soldier said.

Sarah yanked the steering wheel. Koontz and King dropped to their haunches. The tires squealed across the road, pointing her truck toward the unrecovered. She stomped on the pedal.

The orange needle of the speedometer bobbed and weaved, boxing with 100. And still, the road disappeared under her with agonizing slowness. Each time she braked for a bend in the road pushed Penny further away. When she chanced a glance in her rear-view, it showed only blacktop and trees. Even the reassurance of the army was behind Sarah now; she was just too fast for the Humvee to keep up.

When at last a curve revealed the campus road ahead, Sarah's heart sank. The gate, which the unrecovered always kept closed, locked, and guarded, stood open and empty.

"Sarah!" Ed emerged from the treeline at the edge of campus and jogged along the outside of the fence.

Sarah's stomach turned, just a little. She didn't really like Ed. Though he'd helped her with Penny when Sarah was a new mama, something about him always put her a little on her guard. He was...off. But, she'd fuck a werewolf to find out where the Knights of the Prophet, had taken her daughter.

"They tried to kill me!" Ed yelled.

She doubted that. The Knights weren't the brightest tools in the shed, but they knew how to point a gun. Nate....

"Where?"

"Right here at the gate—"

"Where did they go?"

"I don't know—"

"Which. Way." The man was obtuse.

"Sarah—"

"They have Penny. Tell me—"

"Out the west gate—"

Sarah stomped on the gas. She didn't care if she ran over his foot, or any other part of him.

"Hey!"

And he was gone, behind her.

The college's brick buildings whizzed by on either side of her.

A gunshot cracked the glass and thumped into the passenger door. They'd left someone behind, presumably to slow pursuit. It wouldn't slow her. But the adrenaline it added to her system brought a bit more order and clarity to her thoughts. What if there were more resistance ahead? What if the sniper had been a better shot? Who would go find Penny? And who would care for the child when she was found? That brought icy fear to Sarah's pounding heart.

And then the Humvee was behind her.

Ahead, a bus sat parked across the west gate.

"Fuck, fuck, fuck!" Sarah swerved at the last moment.

The Humvee stopped, spun, and rolled down a walkway between buildings.

Sarah followed.

They came to a smaller gate, meant for pedestrians, but in grand Southern style, its wrought-iron arch towered over the pavement, and the bollards meant to stop vehicle traffic lay on their sides, sawed off. The Humvee squeezed through, sparks issuing from its sides. Sarah followed in her slimmer F250. King and Koontz went airborne for a moment as the truck smacked onto the road on the far side of campus.

There was no sign of the unrecovered, tire tracks or otherwise, yet the Humvee turned right and sped off on the directive of unknown intelligence. Sarah had no choice but to follow.

After a mile or so, the grunt she'd spoken with at the end of the logging road popped out of the top and waved her back.

Sarah ignored him.

Again, he waved his rifle.

Sarah reached for her gun and held it up.

The soldier shook his head and gave up shooing her away.

Penny, Penny, Penny. This was taking too long. Pictures of her child flashed through Sarah's mind. Cuddles on the couch. Penny's first tentative steps in Nate's kitchen. Her first word, "Ma-ma," and the realization this foundling meant her, Sarah. She was the only mother Penny knew.

The Humvee turned suddenly onto a dirt road.

Sarah jammed on the brakes, overshot, backed up, and then, followed.

She heard the shots and the thumping of the helicopter. The stink of cordite replaced the scent of pine. Tendrils of smoke drifted across the road, then grew so thick Sarah had to slow.

She almost crashed into a soldier crouched behind the Humvee. "Get down, goddamn it!" he shouted as she climbed out of the truck. "The enemy is beyond the smoke."

"Penny!" she shouted into the swirling gray-white clouds.

A bullet hissed past her ear.

Chapter 6

Mike

Swirling smoke took Mike into fever-dream memories. Back into the white-hot mists of pleasure and pain where he resided for so many, many years. He did his best to shake it off. The sounds—guns, bullets, shouting—pulled his mind another way. The forest surrounding the bus became a jungle superimposed on reality. Mike's hand squeezed for a rifle that wasn't there.

"Head on a swivel, soldier…" a voice from long ago said.

As Mike scanned the bus, his eye caught on a Knight holding…Penny. That…that was his granddaughter, he realized. Named for the wife he'd unwittingly widowed when he went to Vietnam. Penny was the only family besides Sarah he was ever likely to have again.

Too many thoughts at once. Too confusing. Muddy. He had a granddaughter. Was…was that joy? After all this time, he didn't recognize the feeling. Could barely name it. Better. And Penny. From the second he'd woken from the smiling flu coma until a moment ago, he'd felt only anger and despair. Now something new blossomed.

Mike's senses sharpened. He snapped back to reality. The newfound feeling of well-being vanished.

Penny sat screaming her little head off in the Knight's lap.

The Knight was speaking to Penny, but Mike couldn't make out the words over the confusion.

"Head on a swivel, soldier..."

He scanned the bus, looking for threats. They were all threats. All these Knights with guns and no brains.

"Get this fucking bus moving!" someone shouted.

"Shut up or get out and help clear the road!" another voice said.

Mike turned back to Penny again. And again, something stirred in his mind, reaching a tendril toward his heart. The name of his wife, long dead. Yet there was a kind of hope there, like a creeping, tiny flicker of joy. He put his mouth to Carl's ear so he could be heard above the chaos of battle. "It's working."

"Huh?" Carl turned to him, eyes wide as saucers, fingers white-knuckle-clenched to the seatback in front of him. "What's working?"

"The tau. I think it's working."

"Now?! You're telling me *now*?!" he hissed.

Everyone on the bus not armed ducked down in their seats.

The boom of gunfire echoed through the bus. Glass shattered.

The child screamed and cried in the hands of the struggling, impatient Knight. It had been fifty years, but Mike remembered when Sarah was a toddler. It took all his will to stifle his fatherly instincts. If he showed any interest in Penny as family, his standing with the unrecovered, specifically Dale, would suffer. And that damaged relationship could spell real danger for Penny. Well, more danger than Penny was already in.

Across from him and a little to the rear, Rachael stood. Sarah's friend, insofar as Sarah *had* friends. A Knight caught sight of her. What was her plan? Rachael turned toward the back of the bus.

Mike cursed his old, slow body. He cursed Dr. Silva, the man who'd stolen his life. He may not be able to fight for his granddaughter, but he could aid Rachael, if that was her intent.

Rachael, his daughter's friend... Penny, named for his wife, Sarah's daughter... the war... the spark of joy. The bus spun around him. Something moved under the surface of the mind-water. Something... needed. Something... dark, terrible, wonderful.

The darkness closed in on him. Cold, black water lapped at his floating consciousness. He could feel the other unrecovered there, bobbing on the surface, mind touching mind. Holding on.

Down into the darkness... Where the water had only been a mental image, an impression, now Mike felt it. The sensation of touch. Of cold, so, so cold, and wet. He let his mouth open under the surface. Let the water fill him. It filled his body, bringing the cold of death... and something... else. Was this dying? Was that why the unrecovered floated only on the surface? Did each of the joyless living understand on an implicit level that to succumb meant death?

Gasping, choking, blackness engulfed him. The cold, sharp and stinging, stabbed him. His legs lost sensation, becoming blocks of wood. He sank down and down into the blackness.

"Mike?!"

Mike's eyes snapped open. The shaking came from Carl's hands on his arm.

"MIKE!"

And then... Mike coughed.

Black water spewed from his mouth. It spattered the Knight in front of him, who'd risen to intercept Rachael.

The Knight fell. His gun clattered into the aisle between the seats. The man stared up at Mike, eyes wide in terror.

A massive fit of coughing produced more water from Mike's lungs, dousing the downed soldier. Black, viscous liquid ran in streams from the Knight's face, through his scraggly blond beard, before pooling on the rubberized floor of the bus.

Spots formed at the edge of Mike's vision as he struggled for air. Struggled to clear his body of the liquid that had no right to exist in the physical world.

Below Mike, the Knight's mouth made little circles of terror, at first soundless. But as Mike's coughing subsided, the sound grew...

"No...No...NO! NO! NOOOOOO!" And then the man's saucer eyes widened. The scream died in his throat. He sat up, mucus running in gooey streams down his face, dripping, blackening his tattered shirt. He grinned. "Yes. Yes! YES! OH FUCK YES!"

Mike gasped, sucking in air.

Carl tried to push past him.

Mike leaned forward, blocking Carl's exit from the seat. Intuition told him not to let the doctor render aid. Even as he struggled to regain his breath, he fought to keep Carl from touching him. "Don't," Mike gasped, "touch him."

Chapter 7

Rachael

When the bus stopped, we were in the middle of bum fuck nowhere. A chopper thumped overhead. The Pines. A little outdoor church where, according to Vic, the Knights sometimes take folks to have the Prophet do the touch. It was like some kind of jacked-up church service.

A distant voice on a bullhorn shouted for the Knights to surrender. My heart slammed against my ribs. Be cool. I closed my eyes and concentrated on my breathing, like Cassie taught me during our fighting lessons. I heard her voice in my head. "Lesson one, control your breath. Control your emotions, or you'll lose every time."

Three long breaths. I opened my eyes.

The Knights started holding the kids in the windows like human shields. I've never wanted to kill anyone more in my life.

I got out of my seat. My stomach flipped like I was going to barf. Head throbbing from where I'd been cracked and knocked out, I crouched along the aisle toward the back, where some asshole held Penny in the window.

Someone screamed behind me.

"No, no, NOOOO!"

A Knight lay on the floor, clutching his chest. Sampson coughed black shit onto the guy.

No time to wonder. I had to get Penny. To get out.

No one was paying any attention to me. They were all focused on what was happening behind me, or the chaos outside. The windows were opaque with smoke. I duck-walked along, hands cuffed in front of me. In the last row, the greasy, long-haired Knight held Penny in front of his sunken chest. She was screaming. Her cries echoed in my spinning head.

Focus, focus. Almost there. Then I stood, raised my foot, and kicked the guy's knee out from under him.

Penny fell onto the seat. Her pale eyes met mine. She lifted her arms and called my name through her tears. "Rach-a." That's how she always said it.

I tried to shoulder her guard aside and make a grab for her.

The guy got his legs under him.

I moved against the back door of the bus so I could kick again without the guy falling on Penny and hurting her.

"Rach-a!" Penny yelled, trying to clamber off the seat.

The guard was quicker than I thought, swinging his gun hand around and thumping me in the chest with the butt of his pistol.

I fell against the emergency door release.

The door opened.

I fell out.

It all happened so fast.

Two shots from behind me. Bang, bang.

The Knight's chest exploded. He fell out of the bus on top of me, spraying me with gore and pinning my cuffed hands under him.

Return gunfire exploded out of the bus.

"Rachael!"

"Cassie?" I called, frantic.

I glanced back at the bus. I could still get Penny with the guard down, maybe...

A hand grabbed me, pulling me and the dead thug on my back. "I got you," she said.

I bucked and twisted, trying to shake off the corpse. He fell free.

"We have to go!" Cassie shouted over the barking guns.

God, it was good to see her wide, dark eyes.

"I have to get Penny."

Another Knight appeared at the back of the bus in the swirling smoke, firing over our heads in the direction Cassie had come.

"You're gonna get us both shot!" Cassie turned.

"We have to get Penny."

Cassie yanked me forward. "We're no good to her dead. They're not gonna hurt her." She led the way through the sulfur-smelling mist.

"You don't know that!" I crawled toward her.

A canister of billowing smoke landed on the pine needles next to me. The noxious stink filled my nose and mouth, gagging me. I crawled on, following the soles of Cassie's boots ahead of me. A tire appeared in the swirling cloud on my right.

Cassie turned behind a Humvee.

"Here." She put her hands under my arms and helped me to a sitting position behind the truck. Bullets thumped into the other side. Seeing my bound hands, she pulled a knife and cut me free.

"Thanks!" I shouted as more bullets slammed into the far side of the Humvee.

"How many?" Cassie asked.

"Kids?"

Cassie shrugged. "Bad guys. But yeah, kids too."

I closed my eyes, picturing the inside of the bus. "Six. Two at the back, two at the front, and a couple in the middle."

"Six kids?" she asked.

"No, bad guys." I counted the kids in my head. Penny, her friend. Aella and two more unrecovered girls. "Five kids."

"People total?" Cassie asked.

"With the unrecovered adults, maybe forty."

Cassie made a bunch of hand signals to someone I couldn't see.

More bullets from the bus peppered the Humvee.

I cringed, covering my head.

"It's armored, and they're slightly above us," Cassie said. "The bullets can't get under and can't go through."

"Give me a fucking gun!"

"Are you kidding, Rach?" she shouted. "Stay here and keep your head down."

I grabbed her sleeve. "Where are *you* going?"

"To save some kids!"

I didn't let go of her. "I love you!"

She hesitated but didn't look away. "I...love you too, Rach." Then she disappeared into the smoke.

And I was alone.

After a minute, I poked my head high enough to look through the window of the Humvee. I figured it was armored, so... didn't matter. I couldn't see anything through the smoke. Another round of bullets plinked off the metal. I dropped back down.

All around me, people shouted. People screamed. The chopper cut the air with a constant whump, whump, whump.

A big, booming explosion lit up the clearing. My world closed in. I felt myself on the pavement outside the hotel pool, back by the Sea Ridge power plant. This battle morphed into the one I'd barely survived only a few months ago. I was there, in the forest behind the Humvee and on the pavement by the abandoned gas station, all at the same time. I couldn't make sense of anything. The world spun around me in the smoke. I screamed for Cassie. And screamed. And screamed.

Someone dragged me back, away from the bus, behind a Humvee. They shook me.

"Rachael." A voice cut through the sounds and images racing across my mind. "Rachael!"

"S-Sarah?"

"Yes. Get your shit together. These people need to talk to you."

I looked up to see a bunch of army people gathered around me. "Where's Cassie?"

No one said anything.

"Where's Cassie?!"

"Do you know where they were going?" Sarah asked.

"Where's Cassie?!" I screamed.

"Screw this," one guy said. He grabbed my arm and hauled me to my feet, frog-marching me to where a woman with a red cross on her helmet crouched over a figure on the ground.

"Cassie!" I dropped to my knees.

The medic had her hands laced together, doing compressions on Cassie's chest. And not far from those hands... a blood-soaked bandage on Cassie's neck.

"Damn it!" the medic cursed. She quit pumping.

"No!" I yelled. "No! Keep Going!"

"Rachael..." Sarah's hand gripped my shoulder.

I shrugged her off. "Move!" After shoulder-checking the startled medic out of the way, I started doing compressions myself. "One, two, three...."

"Rachael...." Sarah said again.

"Fuck off. Five, six, seven. Help me, goddamn you!"

"She's gone," the medic said.

"NO!"

"Rachael," Sarah yanked me to my feet. "She's gone. The Knights got away. They took Penny. I need to know where they're going, and I need to know now!"

I sagged. "I don't know where they're going."

Chapter 8

Sarah

Sarah paced back and forth in Colonel Harding's office. He'd told her to sit several times. "This is insane," she said, turning on her heel by the dusty metal blinds. "We've got to go after them. Go after my daughter!"

"There are more kids in New Hope, which has just suffered a three-pronged attack in which two-thirds of its law enforcement officers were killed. We have to set up a perimeter. We have nuclear power plants, pipelines, chlorine manufacturing plants, and a hundred other threats that could make it so there will never be another child in this area... ever. I simply don't have the personnel to chase the unrecovered. We'll get the word out on the airwaves to all the bases. They'll be on the lookout too, and will do what they can."

"My daughter—"

Harding inclined his head—conciliatory, but unyielding. "Was in more danger when we tried to engage the unrecovered. We're burning precious chopper fuel, and have sent a couple of squads out, but that's all I can do."

"Not good enough," Sarah said.

"I agree," Rachael said. "Not. Good. Enough. Not for Cassie. And not for the other soldiers who gave their lives to stop the unrecovered."

"*You*," Colonel Harding snapped, "don't get to tell *me* a god, damn, thing, about what's good enough for *my* soldiers. I'm sorry for your loss, but a soldier's duty—"

"I guess we're done here," Rachael said.

Sarah wasn't done. She had a lot more to say. She drew a breath, but exhaled again. Nothing she said would move Harding to further action. She wasn't going to change his mind with emotional pleading for her daughter.

Rachael stood, opened the door, went through, then turned back. "I don't know which one of you I say this to..." she looked from Sarah to the Colonel, "but I quit." And then she was gone.

Sarah stood there for a moment, then said, "I'm going to get my daughter back. I quit too." She made for the door.

"Wait."

She did, turning back to the Colonel.

"What are you going to do if you find them?" Colonel Harding asked. "They killed several outstanding soldiers. Took down a helicopter."

The black clouds of malice in Sarah's heart cleared long enough for her to acknowledge the Colonel had a point. No words came.

Harding nodded. "My men will fix you up with a radio. It will put you in contact with the nearest base, wherever you are in the country. If you find the unrecovered, call for help. Don't go charging in like some kind of action-movie vigilante."

Sarah wanted to punch him for that one. Maybe drive a kick into his forehead.

"Sorry." Harding must've read it on her face. "I know you're tough. Been through a lot. My people are tougher, and now, some of them are dead. Take the radio. Ask for 'almighty.'"

"That's a bit high-handed, don't you think?"

The Colonel waved a hand. "It's an homage to—"

"I don't care."

Colonel Harding rubbed his neck. "You're a real pain in the ass, you know that?"

Sarah shrugged. "I get that a lot."

"*Your* call sign is Vengeant."

"You know I'm a librarian, right? That's not even a word."

"Do you want the radio, or do you want to argue over semantics?"

Sarah closed her mouth.

"Good." The Colonel tugged at his sleeves. "Now get out of my office."

As she ran into her house to grab a few things, Sarah didn't look at Nate's place. Didn't let her eyes wander over there. Didn't turn her head. But the act of not looking conjured in her mind the images from which she shielded her eyes. There'd be no police tape. Not these days. Not anymore. But there'd be blood, and signs of violence. And... signs of Penny, and Penny's absence.

The dogs followed her through the open door.

Tamping down the lump in her throat with a mountain of hatred and malice, Sarah went first for her guns, then for some warm clothes for herself and Penny. Crossing the mountains in January was no joke. That's where she assumed they were headed. Into the hollows of the Smoky Mountains.

Dickens sniffed at the comforter on Penny's bed and gave a soft whine.

That did it. A sob, like a soft bark, burst from Sarah's throat. The world melted behind saltwater lenses. Sarah sagged to the floor, burying her face in the Lab's fur as sorrow and grief overtook her. Images of Penny. The ghost sensation of her daughter's little arms around her neck.

"Noooo," she grimaced. Dripping tears and snot mixed, making her mouth saline and bitter.

Outside, an engine approached.

Sarah rose.

Metal crunched. The engine, motorcycle most likely, cut out abruptly to the screech of rending metal.

Silence.

Sarah pulled her pistol, stepping from room to room, cover to cover. Now, a door frame, a peek around the corner. Now crouched behind a divan. Koontz and King kept in step with her, Deadly. Silent.

Footsteps on the porch.

Sarah leveled the pistol. She cursed herself for leaving the door open in her haste to fetch supplies and leave.

A shadow fell into the living room.

Sarah checked the safety. Red is dead.

Dickens trotted heedlessly across the open space, wagging his tail.

Sarah lowered the gun a notch. The Labrador must know the person.

"Hey, buddy," Rachael said. "Why is your fur wet? And... sticky. Ew. Where's your grumpy old mom?"

"You almost got shot," Sarah called, annoyed. She rose, flicked the safety on, and tucked the pistol into the waistband of her jeans. "What do you want?"

"Oh," Rachael said. "I'm sorry."

Sarah wiped her face with embarrassed, too-quick motions. "What. Do. You. Want?"

"I thought we should ride together."

"Ride?" Sarah knew what Rachael was asking, but making her spell it out bought Sarah more time to consider. Right now, she leaned strongly towards 'no.'

"You know. To get the unrecovered."

"Get?"

"Kill," Rachael said.

"What makes you think I'm going to kill them?"

Rachael frowned. "Come on. You're Sarah Sampson, an infamous bad ass, and...they have Penny."

The mountain was back in Sarah's throat, making it impossible to speak for a moment. Then, she managed, "you're just a kid. A liability. I'm going after a group of bastards with big fucking guns. This isn't a field trip to Disneyland."

A shadow crossed Rachael's face. "Don't underestimate me."

"You're wasting my time. Every minute we talk, they get further away."

She pushed past the young woman, down the steps, and onto the lawn. That's when she noticed the motorcycle had crashed into the back of her pickup. "Where'd you learn to drive?"

"The apocalypse," Rachael answered.

"Stay home. Stay safe."

"Oh, I'm going—with you or alone. But we'd be better together." Rachael grabbed her elbow.

Sarah shook herself free. "No. Your motive is revenge. You're a loose cannon. You could get Penny hurt. I can't allow that."

"If it wasn't for me, you'd have no idea she was still alive. Plus, I tried to save her, which is more than you did..."

Sarah's nails bit into the flesh of her palms or her clenched fists.

Rachael held her hands up. "I-I'm sorry. I didn't mean that..."

Sarah nodded toward the crashed motorcycle. "Get that piece of shit off my truck."

Chapter 9

Mike

The bus lurched forward. People jumped on.

"Go! Go! Go!" shouted a Knight who threw himself inside and cranked the doors shut behind him.

Sharp twinges of pain rattled Mike's old bones as the bus bumped down the dirt track.

At Mike's feet, the Knight covered in black mind fluid reached into his pants and produced a throbbing erection, all the while shouting, "Yes! Oh, yes!"

"Restrain that man!" Dale shouted between bursts of gunfire. He elbowed his way toward the fallen man among the confused Knights and unrecovered, stepping and straining to see what was going on. "And gag him. NOW!" He glared at Mike as the Knights closest did Dale's bidding, producing an orange extension cord, and binding the guy. Someone shoved a bandana into the goo-covered man's mouth.

And all the while, the guy alternately fought to get his hand around his cock.

After another withering look at Mike, Dale turned and made his way back to the front.

The Knights dragged the exposed, struggling man up front with Dale.

The gunfire ceased. Their pursuers must have backed off. It didn't take a genius to figure out why. The kids. They couldn't risk firing into the bus. Hostages, plain and simple.

"What the fuck was that?" Carl asked after things calmed down and the bus bumped along another old logging road.

Mike's eyes rose a notch past half-mast. He tried to shake himself out of the intense drowsiness that overtook him after vomiting the black goo. "I—I don't know." But, somehow, he did. Or suspected he did. Whether it was the tau, or something beneath the black water in his mind, Mike couldn't say. But for sure, he felt *better*. His heart and mind weren't quite so heavy. And the Knight's reaction—pure bliss, could not be mistaken for anything else.

The doctor pushed Mike off his shoulder every time Mike's head sagged into sleep. Whatever had happened with the black fluid in his lungs and the euphoric Knight of the Prophet, it had taken a lot of energy from Mike. All he wanted to do was lie down and sleep for a thousand years. But there was no way he'd get the chance. They'd have to stop soon, and it was a sure bet when they did, Dale, the Prophet's puppet master, would be there and demand to know what had happened on the bus.

Mike himself was very, very curious about the nature of the Knight's... what? Affliction? The upcoming confrontation with Dale filled him with dread and diminished any lifting of his spirits expelling the black goo brought. If the black goo brought happiness to that man the way the Prophet's touch did, then Mike was in grave danger. Dale would either enslave him, the way he did Vic, or outright kill him. If another besides Vic, The Prophet, could bestow happiness on the unrecovered and Dale wasn't in control of it, then Dale could lose control of all of them. The man was a humanoid serpent and certainly wouldn't accept Mike's assurance that he didn't know what happened, either. Moreover, Mike feared him. Well, not so much Dale as his absolute control over the Knights of the Prophet. Each Knight had been hand-selected by Dale for their violent tendencies, low IQs, and responsiveness to clap-trap gibberish speeches. In the before times, many of these were ex-cons, fanatics, or both. At least that's what Dr. Parks had said on more than one occasion.

Each time Mike turned his gaze toward the back of the bus where Penny and the other children sat, the Knight guarding them stared daggers at him.

The urge to test this new ability nearly overwhelmed Mike. He watched a head movie of marching to the back and spewing the black happiness-water all over the Knight and taking his granddaughter away. But the movie always ended with him and Penny being shot or pushed out the back of the moving bus. The second scenario was more favorable, but probably still fatal for a septuagenarian and a toddler.

All day, the bus moved along a series of dirt roads followed by short stints on pavement, then back into the woods. Freshly cut trees, newly mended log bridges, and orange painted blazes marked the way. This was a long-planned operation. How had Dale kept it secret? In a community as small as the unrecovered colony, there was no way to mask the massive drain on personnel it would have taken to prepare these roads. How were they doing it?

When the day began dying and light faded from Appalachia, the bus drove into a hangar-like building, and Mike's question got the beginnings of an answer. Military. Just a few, but with armbands bearing the seal of the President. So, the President's unrecovered faction had thrown in with the Knights. Made sense. Dale's background was in politics, and the hand that held Vic's leash could be a valuable political ally.

Several other buses rested inside the massive public works structure. Mike, Carl, and the captive children were hustled out of the bus and held by a silent Knight at gunpoint while all around them, people were busy setting up tents and sleeping bags.

The world darkened.

When Mike swam out of the depths of unconsciousness, he heard Carl's voice.

"You can't just hold us here like this," Carl said. "He's in his seventies. He needs proper rest."

Mike found himself lying on the concrete floor, head in Carl's lap.

The Knight leaning over him said, "You're wanted. On your feet."

"He's sick," Carl protested.

"Then help him up. Dale wants to see him."

With Carl's help, Mike rose shakily to his feet. He leaned heavily on the doctor.

"Move," the Knight said.

And so, they made their slow way across the crowded floor with Knights in front and behind.

Around Mike, among the rusted snowplows and salt trucks, the unrecovered huddled around butane stoves or hid in tents pitched on the cracked concrete. What unnerved Mike was that two hundred or so people lived in the unrecovered colony outside New Hope, and there were double that number of people here. And, in the center of it all, the Prophet sat cuffed to a chair while the unrecovered lined up to receive their daily dose of happiness—the touch.

"This is bullshit," Carl said. "He can barely walk!"

"Don't make a big deal, Doc. Dale just wants to have a little chat," the Knight holding Mike's arm said in a voice indicating he'd watched too many mobster movies.

The Knights led them into a large tent, by family camping standards. In it, chairs formed a semicircle around a small desk featuring a kerosene lantern, a stack of papers, and behind it, Dale.

Jonathan, the blond, scraggly-bearded head of the Knights, leaned over Dale's shoulder as the little warthog traced a line on the map with a pudgy finger. He straightened as Mike reached the center.

"Ah, Mike. Oh, and the good Doctor Parks, a fortuitous bonus. Glad you could join us." He pointed at the map without taking his eyes off Mike.

Jonathan reached over Dale and folded the map. Instead of the hard, dead eyes Mike expected to see, when the henchman's gaze met Mike's, his brow furrowed. There was moisture there, and sympathy maybe? Sorrow?

"Sooo," Dale drew the word out while he rifled through a stack of papers. "Ah," he selected a scrap from the pile and examined it in the lamplight. "What the fuck did you do to Kyle?"

He raised his eyes to Mike, staring expectantly.

Mike shrugged.

Dale made shameful, tutting sounds. "From what I'm told, this is some magical new ability, akin to Vic's."

"I don't know what you're talking about," Mike said. "I got sick from the bumping and adrenaline from the battle. I don't know what happened to that guy."

"Well, you vomited black goo on Knight Harris, at which time he fell screaming on the floor. Then, you coughed up more of the black gunk. Knight Harris screamed 'Yes, yes, yes' and pulled his dick out."

"Too much coffee," Mike said. He was a bad liar. He knew it. Dale knew it. "The guy must be some kind of pervert."

"Are you familiar with Occam's Razor?" Dr. Parks cut in.

"Of course," Dale said.

Mike wasn't surprised. Dale had the pedigree of patina that grew in the Ivy League, wrapped around a wannabe dictator.

"It states," Dr. Parks went on, "that all things being equal, the simplest explanation of a phenomenon tends to be the correct one."

"You would have us believe that Mike vomited on a Knight, and at the exact same time, the Knight found happiness and tried to whack off in the thick of battle?"

"A psychotic break," Carl said without missing a beat. "Isn't it more likely that after a very stressful kidnapping, one man lost his mind and another vomited?"

"My people—" Dale began.

"—are not medical experts," Dr. Parks interrupted. "I was right there. I've seen it, in Iraq, and Afghanistan. I know what it looks like, and I know the often sad outcome."

Dale steepled his fingers. "My understanding is that Mike prevented you from examining Mister Harris."

"He—"

"I panicked," Mike cut in, strengthening Carl's narrative. "I couldn't get my throat clear. Couldn't breathe. I needed his help."

Dale turned to the Knight in the corner. "What do you think, Stephen? Can you feel his mind?"

"There's something different about him," the Knight nodded toward Mike.

"He fainted. He's sick and dehydrated from vomiting," Carl said.

Dale ignored Carl. He turned in his seat, looking at Stephen. "Oh?"

"I should feel his mind. Feel his proximity on the surface of the dark water. And...I do, but not the normal way. It's like he's far away. He should be close. Should be right here. But he isn't."

Dale rolled his eyes. "Eloquent as ever, Stephen."

"We're very hungry," Dr. Parks said.

Dale looked from the Knight, Stephen, to the doctor.

"And tired," Mike added, hoping to muddy the waters and get food and rest.

Dale held up a hand. "There's something else strange..." He rose, walking a line that took him past both Mike and Carl.

Mike's stomach tightened as Dale bored into him with beady black eyes. "You haven't asked for the touch. All unrecovered do. But not you. Vic hid out in that jail for a long time. Everyone else is desperate. But Mike Sampson, the oldest and hardest hit of the unrecovered, isn't asking. Just chilling. Cool as a cucumber. Why?"

Mike's heart raced. He fought to keep his breathing even. Keep the fear from reaching his eyes. "I don't like being dependent on you and your lackeys for my joy."

"Bullshit," Dale said.

Mike tried to make himself as still as a stone.

"Let me show you something." Dale inclined his head, and the Knight behind Mike and the doctor gave them a shove toward Dale.

Dale raised the flap at the back of the tent. Kyle sat on the canvas floor, hands tied in front of him, and to his thighs, allowing him access to his crotch, but not the freedom to move in any other way.

Kyle's hand grasped his uncircumcised penis. A mix of blood and semen coated his hand and ran down onto his jeans.

Dale spun on Mike and Carl. "He's beaten his bishop bloody and raw. And every time we try to remove the gag, he just starts yelling 'oh God, yes, thank you, yes!' Now how do you explain that?"

Mike opened his mouth, but no sound came.

"I already have," Carl said.

"All right," Dale sighed. He nodded to the Knights holding Mike and Carl. "Get them set up with a meal and sleeping bags, but don't let them talk to anyone else, and don't let them out of your sight." He made a shooing motion with his hand.

The guards led Mike and Carl from the tent, steering them toward the smell of beef stew somewhere in the middle of the building.

Mike desperately wanted to talk to Dr. Parks, alone. To compare notes. He had so many questions. Was the distance the Knight mentioned because the tau was working? What about the black water and the other Knight? Was that the tau, or something else? He needed to talk it through, but first he'd have to ditch the guards. That would take some doing. Though most of the Knights were dullards and zealots, they were dogged and relentless.

The soup line featured silent, smiling unrecovered, fresh from their touch with The Prophet. And though Vic was an unpleasant little piece of work, he wasn't evil. Mike sympathized with the man. He knew how much the touch drained Vic. So much in fact that Vic lived like a dairy cow, providing the milk of happiness, then returned to his pen.

Was the softening in his chest sympathy? Strange. Was this more of the tau at work?

Because the freshly pleased unrecovered stood, bowls out in silent inner reverie, there was no babble of mixed voices in which Mike could steal a quick conversation with Carl. He got his scoop of lackluster stew and sat on the sleeping bag the Knight pointed him to. Across from him, Dr. Parks sat blowing into his steaming soup, staring at Mike over the lip of his bowl.

Mike scanned the room, looking and listening for some sign of Penny, Aella, and the other kids. From his vantage point on the floor, with so many tents, buses, piles of sand, salt, and the highway department trucks, there was no way of telling.

When they'd finished their meal, the Knight took their bowls back to the makeshift kitchen. As the man retreated, he cast furtive glances over his shoulder.

"Do you think it's the tau?" Mike asked, trying to keep his lips from moving too much.

"Do I think what's the tau?" Dr. Parks whispered.

"The black goo. The masturbating guy."

Carl reared back and frowned. "That's not how tau works. That's not how anything works."

Mike looked at his aged, liver-spotted hands. "It's how something works."

"Are you shitting me?" Carl hissed. "You really think you did that?"

Mike swallowed. "I know I did. You really believed what you told Dale?"

"Hey, shut up," the Knight said, standing over them.

Carl stared at Mike, wide-eyed.

They sat in silence.

There was nothing for it. Maybe Mike could wake the doctor and hash this out when he got up for his 4 am. bladder break. Oh, the joys of age! Mike's joints popped and crackled as he zipped himself into his sleeping bag on the hard concrete. At least the building was reasonably warm between the mass of humanity and the cooling engines of the buses. Mike was tired. He fell asleep to the tick of cooling metal and the smell of hot grease in his nose.

Pain woke him. A sharp poking in his shoulder. Mike opened his eyes to the tip of a work boot. A Knight towered over him. The ragged denim and flannel clad man held Penny. "Get up."

Chapter 10

Rachael

Dickens laid his head on my lap as Sarah drove. I rubbed the soft skin under his chin, grateful for this small connection as a giant chasm inside me, aching and empty, yearned for a word or a touch from Cassie. The tree-laden hills of the Smoky Mountains passed by in a blur. As the sky overhead darkened and turned vermillion, the shadowed arboreal spaces gathered themselves together and became the battleground where Cassie died.

"I love you..." Cassie's final words echoed across the whole world.

Holes between the trees became holes between Cassie's ribs.

I love you... echoed in my head.

Dickens whined.

"Hey," Sarah said, squinting into the sunset.

I looked down and realized I'd been squeezing Dickens's neck. "Sorry, buddy."

"You've got to keep your mind in the game," Sarah chided. "We can't afford to miss anything."

"It's getting dark," I managed. The lump in my throat made it difficult to choke the words out.

Sarah leaned in, her nose almost touching the windshield. "I can still see."

I snorted.

Dickens whined again.

I tried another angle. "It's been hours since the dogs had a pee."

"Don't tell me how to take care of my dogs."

Dickens stood and turned, putting his ass in my face while licking Sarah's.

"Et tu, Brute?"

Dickens kept going.

"Shit. Okay, fine."

I didn't like his butthole so close to my nose, but anything to get Sarah to pull over. At that point, we'd been at it for several hours, only stopping to examine fresh tire tracks in the detritus covering the once busy roads.

The apocalypse had its advantages. Sadly, the lack of modern plumbing wasn't among them. With no running water, regular bathrooms were gross now. Peeing in the tall grass by the roadside gave me the creeps ever since I had to watch that lecture on Lyme disease back at Fort Walters. Every time we stopped to cop a squat, all I thought about was deer ticks crawling up my cooch.

Sarah caught me wiping at my legs and picking through my pubes.

"Will you cut that out? It's too cold for ticks. Look," she pointed at a patch of snow near the tree line. Obviously, it wasn't the first time she'd caught me doing that. Hey, we all have our little things, right?

I pulled my pants up, but the damage was done. I had no idea how high up in the mountains we were, but the January air let me know we weren't on the coastal plain anymore. My thin flannel wasn't doing much against the chill. All I wanted to do now was get back in the truck and crank the heater. I stomped my feet on the blacktop. The warmth was already draining from the boots I got at the PX.

Sarah sat on the tailgate, watching the dogs trot this way and that, sniffing and pissing in the tall grass along the road.

"So what's the deal?" I asked, parking my butt beside her.

"What deal?"

"I mean, how are we going to do this? It's too cold to sleep in the bed of the truck. And you said yourself, if we drive through the night, we'll miss a track or a clue."

Sarah nodded. "Or a trap." Then, she just sat there, staring at the dogs. The woman was impossible.

"So?" I asked, rubbing my arms through my overshirt.

"Yeah, okay." She didn't move.

"Ugh!" I stomped back to the cab.

A minute later, Sarah got in and started the engine.

We just sat there.

"I..." Sarah started when the silence got thick, but she didn't say anything else.

"Sarah," I whispered. I felt a little better and more sympathetic with the roaring heater blasting my goosebumps away.

She turned to me, tears streaming down her face. "I don't know what to do. They have my baby!" She wiped her face with her arm. "Do we keep driving through the night? What if we pass them and don't know it? We don't know where they're headed. What if they turn off or change directions? How am I going to get Penny back? How will we find them?" She turned away, dissolving into an ugly cry.

Sarah's sudden and unexpected emotions triggered my own, again. The lump in my throat made it impossible for me to offer her any words, which turned out to be fine because what the hell was I going to say? I realized I'd been leaning on her like some kind of martial arts guru. An emotional pillar. Like Sarah was a rock I could cling to. Like she'd never have doubts, or depression. As if she were some immovable stone. And now that she was having a breakdown, a moment of vulnerability, I found myself angry at her. And I knew that wasn't fair.

"I wish I had something smart to say..." I sucked in a sob as Cassie's face flashed across my mind. Tight black curls framing freckles and bright eyes. "I want to find them, too. Find Penny. With...with Cassie gone, you and Penny are...all I have." Deep breath. "And I want to kill every last one of those fucking monsters."

Sarah wiped her eyes with the backs of her hands. The dashboard lights cast greenish horror movie shadows on her face. "I feel that. Don't think for a second that thought doesn't cross my mind. But what would it cost you? You'd be just like them. A monster. If Penny and I are all you have, and you want a connection with us, know that if you go on some rage-fueled revenge killing spree, I won't let you anywhere near us. I've been down that road. I know where it leads."

That hit me in the gut, hard. "I—"

Lights hit the side of Sarah's face. Headlights. Behind us.

"Shit!" she said.

I pulled the Beretta from my ankle holster.

Sarah nodded and drew her pistol.

We got out and hunkered down by the grill, putting the bulk of the truck between us and the approaching interloper.

The headlights grew brighter. Hard to tell in the glare, but it looked like another pickup.

The truck pulled up behind us.

Rustling in the grass next to me caught my ear. I turned in time to see King disappear. The pit bull was earning his chow today. Beside Sarah, Koontz growled.

Someone got out of the other truck.

"Sarah?"

"Ed," she grumbled, and I rolled my eyes.

"It's just me, Sarah," Ed called.

"What do you want?" she asked, rising.

"I thought we could travel together, just like old times?"

I stood and followed Sarah to the back of the truck. Ed stood there, breath steaming in his truck's headlights. A sliver of moon rose behind him.

Sarah put a hand on her hip. "As I recall, in the old times you traveled with me because you got your other traveling partner killed."

Ed grabbed his chest. "That's not fair!"

"No," Sarah said, "it sure as shit isn't."

"I can't control what other people do," Ed said. "Erica's death wasn't my fault."

"It kind of was," I said.

Ed's head snapped to me. "What the fuck do you know about it?"

"I read Erica's journal. You were dead drunk. Passed out. The rest, Sarah told me. She found Erica, blown up," I said.

He pointed at me. "That would have happened whether I was there or not. And I haven't touched a drop of alcohol since that day."

"So," Sarah said, "you admit it is at least a *little* your fault?"

"Are we gonna stand here and argue, or are we gonna go get our kids back?" Ed patted a holstered gun at his side.

"You got a plan?" Sarah asked.

Despite the emotions still raging through my system, I hid a smile. Sarah might be a cross between a stone and a cactus, but God, what a great role model for empowerment.

Ed folded his arms. "Yup."

Chapter 11

Sarah

Sarah's arm twitched. She shooed away the impulse to raise her pistol and shoot Ed. Why? She'd just given Rachael the speech about becoming a monster, and here she was, close to losing her shit. Projecting—that's what the therapist called it all those years ago when Sheriff Ralph took her in. It wasn't so much that she feared Rachael becoming a monster. No. Sarah was afraid that she herself had *already* become a monster. Afraid that once she got Penny back, she'd kill them all and lose Penny. Not because anyone would take the child away from her, but because once you do something like that, there's no redemption. No humanity left.

"My plan?" Ed put a hand to his chest. "Is anything better than running off half-cocked with no supplies and no way to track the unrecovered."

Sarah shifted her weight and cocked her head. "Are you saying *you* can track the unrecovered?"

Ed gave a little triumphant smile. "Not me, and not exactly..." He nodded toward his truck.

"What the fuck..." Sarah started walking.

"Hey, wait!" Ed chased after her.

Rachael's footsteps followed.

"Let me explain..." Ed protested.

In the passenger seat of Ed's truck, Jamie sat half-mummified in bandages. She'd been beaten within an inch of her life.

"I didn't..." Ed began.

"Don't. Move," Rachael said.

Sarah glanced back to see Rachael pointing her gun at Ed, arms extended and braced, out of Ed's reach, and keeping her clear of the crossfire. "Good girl," she whispered to herself.

The door gave a loud creak as Sarah pulled it open.

Jamie turned, focusing one hemorrhaging eyeball on her. "Help me."

"What do you need?" Sarah whispered.

"Help me get Aella back," Jamie said.

"Goddamn right," Sarah said. "Did he do this to you?"

Jamie looked confused. "Who?" She turned her head and winced. "Ed?" A feeble frown and another wince. "No. Dale's goons. The Knights."

"Why?" Sarah asked. She'd thought the unrecovered were a cohesive unit. One mind, linked by some ill-defined psychic connection and the need for The Prophet's magic happy touch.

"I don't know," Jamie said. "All they said was, where we're going, you can't follow."

"Weird talk for a bunch of feeble-minded ex-cons," Sarah said.

"Dale's words," Rachael said, holstering her gun. "That's how he talks, or at least, that's how The Prophet represented him when I was interviewing him."

"Can we just call him Vic?" Ed asked. "All this prophet talk pisses me off."

"Me too," Jamie coughed.

Sarah nodded. "Can we do something for you? Find a place for you to lie down?"

"No. Keep going, just take it easy on the bumps. My ribs might be cracked."

"Ed seems to think you can track the unrecovered," Rachael said.

Jamie nodded. "That many minds. I can feel them, if I'm close enough."

"Do you feel them now?" Sarah asked.

"No. But they're heading west, right? So, at some point, if we keep moving, I should."

"There's a lot of ways to go west," Sarah said. "How close do you have to be?"

"I don't know." Jamie focused her blood-red eye on Sarah. "I've never been this far away from them. Not since I woke from the smiling flu."

"Are you okay with the traveling arrangements?"

Jamie's eye flicked to Ed, then back to Sarah. Her mouth drew into a thin line.

"Ed," Sarah said, "take a walk."

"Oh, give me a fucking bre—"

Koontz, who'd been standing at Sarah's side, took two steps toward Ed and growled.

Ed held up his hands. "Okay, okay Koontz. Just don't forget I took good care of Penny too, once." So saying, Ed retreated up the road a bit and watered the grass.

"So?" Sarah asked Jamie.

"It is what it is." Jamie's face betrayed no emotion.

Sarah marveled once again at how weird it was dealing with the unrecovered.

"We have a lot to talk about," Jamie said.

Sarah didn't follow. "We do?"

Jamie shook her head. "Ed and I."

Sarah didn't want any part of this. She couldn't imagine what it was like to be unrecovered, and to have a husband that wasn't. And then there was Aella. The little girl who'd shot and killed Dr. Silva, the man responsible for the smiling flu. But Jamie's daughter had also killed the same Dr. Silva, inventor of Laetanol, which had saved so many lives, including Sarah's, from suicide.

Sarah rubbed her forehead. "So, you're the only one of us who has the slightest chance of tracking them. How do you want to do it?"

"Not much to do," Jamie said. "We follow the interstate—"

"No." Sarah shook her head. "They knew where and when to hit in New Hope. They had the back gate ready. Dale planned the shit out of all this. We won't find them on the interstates. The army is likely to look there, anyway. No, they'll use the secondary roads where they can disappear."

"That'll be slower," Rachael said. "They're choked with cars, debris, abandoned roadblocks, wrecks...."

"Can I come back yet?" Ed called.

"No!" the three women yelled in unison.

"Fuck sake," Ed muttered loud enough for them to hear.

"You're going to pay for that later." Rachael winked at Jamie.

"That account has been closed a long time," Jamie said.

Rachael's smile dropped. The unrecovered didn't do humor.

"If it's slower, I have a better chance to feel them with my mind," Jamie said, picking up the thread of conversation.

"And if they've got the way cleared, like they did in New Hope, they'll be easier to track," Rachael added.

"Okay. We keep to the secondary roads, searching, but moving west. Rachael and I will look for physical signs. Jamie, you'll concentrate on finding their minds."

Jamie and Rachael nodded. Good. They'd accepted her lead. Ed could go piss up a rope. She sighed. But he had helped when she'd first found Penny. It was just... Sarah didn't like him.

The cold crept into her clothes.

Rachael rubbed her arms.

"We're gonna need a bigger vehicle. Something we can all sleep in," Rachael said. "Keep warm."

Sarah gritted her teeth. Her eyes fell on her trusty pickup truck. "Goddamn it."

Jamie reached out and clasped Sarah's arm. "I feel something." Her thin fingers bit Sarah's flesh like a hawk's claws. "Someone's coming."

Chapter 12

Mike

The Knight led Mike to the tent where Dale had interviewed him just a few hours before. Penny looked at him over the Knight's denim-clad shoulder. Her eyes drooped with sleep; her pupils dilated. Drugs. A murderous rage simmered in Mike's gut. They were drugging his granddaughter.

Inside the tent, Dale perched in an easy chair that hadn't been there hours before. The Knight set Penny on Dale's lap.

Her sleepy head lolled onto Dale's chest.

"She's beautiful," Dale said. "Such intelligent blue eyes. Don't you agree?"

Mike stood mute.

"No words of praise for your granddaughter? Tsk, tsk, tsk."

"She's nothing to me," Mike said. He hoped the lie would protect the child. But, after the words left his mouth, he could see how they could also get Penny killed.

"That's a shame for both of you." Dale stroked Penny's hair absently. "I had hoped bringing her along might keep you focused on your role among the unrecovered. And perhaps make you more forthcoming about what you did to Kyle."

"I didn't do anything."

Dale lifted Penny off his lap and held her out to the Knight. "Why are you being so difficult?"

The child's eyes opened to half-mast then closed as the Knight received her, holding her awkwardly to his chest.

Dale rose and approached Mike. Days of sparse gray stubble stood out on his haggard face. The smell of old sweat hit Mike just ahead of Dale's tuna breath. "They all look up to you...well as much as the unrecovered can look up to anyone." Dale circled Mike, hands behind his back. "You're their de facto leader. And then you do... whatever you did to Kyle."

"I'm not—" Mike began.

But Dale cut him off. "—stupid. And neither am I. So let's not pretend that. You are the unofficial leader of the unrecovered and you gave Kyle happiness...of a sort."

"No," Mike tried again. "You're the leader."

Dale waved a hand. "Oh, they tolerate me because I hold Vic's leash. If Vic's touch is the drug, I'm the dealer. I tried with the whole 'prophet' thing, but Vic just isn't smart enough or charismatic enough to pull it off, making the Knights necessary. And now this." A Knight in the adjoining area of the tent raised the flap, revealing Kyle again. He sat, tied to an old kitchen chair, his hands restrained away from his sex this time. His eyes bulged, pleading. And that strange smiling flu smile, the one billions died wearing, defiled his lips.

"What did you do?" Dale rose and approached Mike, hands clasped behind his back.

Mike held Dale's eyes. He might be physically weaker, half a lifetime older and dependent on Dale's goodwill for food, shelter, and the safety of his granddaughter, but he wasn't going to knuckle under for this half-baked Napoleon. Already, Mike's mind searched for chinks in Dale's armor. Weaknesses that might someday bring about Dale's downfall.

"Did you know the Germans have two words for power?" Dale asked, returning Mike's stare.

"Probably more," Mike said.

If this micro-rebuke had any effect on Dale, the man gave no sign. "Let's concern ourselves with two for the moment. *Macht* and *Kraft*. Macht is the power to make something happen through sociopolitical power. It's reflexive, automatic. Kraft is the power to make something happen through force of personal will and skill. Incidentally, it's where we get the words craft and crafty. You," Dale extended a finger toward Mike, "are crafty. As such, you've carved out a little Macht for yourself among the unrecovered.

"But," Dale went on, "I have built a *lot* of Macht through Vic, and, I blush to say," he put a hand to his chest, "no small measure of manipulation. But no matter how hard I push, no matter how addicted the unrecovered are to Vic's dopamine dispensing touch—"

Mike wasn't at all sure that's how 'the touch' worked, or what it did, but this wasn't the time.

"—you still hold sway over them. Like a tick I can't get rid of, no matter how many matches I touch to your head. And so, my plan to go west and find the source of the smiling flu and do our own research, well, it's a tough sell without you. And now this," he waved a hand at Kyle. "They're out there whispering that *you* have the touch too. Is that what this is? Are you holding out on us? Denying your people happiness?"

"He doesn't look happy to me," Mike said, and instantly regretted it. It was tacit confirmation that he had done something to Kyle. He didn't understand it, not fully. But he could *feel* it. Whatever part of his brain the smiling flu killed was coming back. And whatever that black stuff was that came out of him, had done this to Kyle. Had made the man, what? Some kind of sex fiend?

Dale returned to his easy chair.

Mike's legs ached. He didn't let his pain or the jealousy of Dale's soft chair show on his face. The advantage of having gone through the shit Mike had was his ability to internalize discomfort and present a stone wall to the world.

"And so," Dale resumed, "enter your granddaughter, Penny."

"Adoptive granddaughter," Mike corrected. He knew it was a dangerous game. And he hadn't had time to sort the new feelings creeping through his mind: caring for Penny, the need for Sarah's approval, and forgiveness.

Dale frowned. "Nevertheless, harm to the child will also destroy your relationship with your daughter."

"I'm unrecovered," Mike said. "There's no motivation for me to repair that relationship. No reward. You know this."

"But what if it turned out that you killed the girl, then turned the gun on yourself, perhaps? It wouldn't bother you to have your estranged daughter forever think of you that way?"

Mike made himself a rock. A slab of standing granite. This feckless warthog would not get Mike to betray his burgeoning emotions. He stood mute.

"You will resume your normal rounds. Talk to the people. Reassure them that this is the right thing. A way to get their happiness back."

"Is it?" Mike asked. He didn't believe a word of it. He only wanted to hear how Dale would answer the question.

"Of course it is." Dale's faux grin wasn't meant to fool Mike, but to menace him. Again, Dale held his gaze.

Mike refused to break the spell or tip his hand by glancing at Penny. If he could talk to the other unrecovered, maybe he could work out an escape plan. And with the help of Dr. Parks, find a way to get the other unrecovered on tau. That had to be the answer. Had to be the key to whatever was happening to him.

"I need to hear you say you'll do it," Dale said. He glanced at the Knight holding Penny. "Your granddaughter is counting on you."

"I'll do it," Mike rasped around the unexpected lump in his throat, "on one condition."

Dale raised a finger. "You're in no position to be putting conditions—"

"—Doctor Parks stays with me."

Dale closed his mouth and dropped the finger. "Huh...."

Mike's feet ached with fatigue. He shifted his weight while Dale stared off into space, considering.

"Why?"

"He's their doctor. The unrecovered. He's been there since the beginning."

"I'm not buying what you're selling." Dale rose from the easy chair again and began pacing back and forth in front of Mike. "None of it. Not your reason for wanting the doctor with you." He ticked the points off on his fingers as he paced. "Not your bullshit about having nothing to do with Kyle smiling and compulsively pounding his pud when you threw up on him. And not your assurances that everything's fine with you, even though the unrecovered can't feel your mind the way they used to." Dale halted in front of Mike, nose to nose. "You can have your doctor friend with you. And I'll have my new little friend with me." He inclined his head, indicating Penny. "But my bullshit detector is off the scale with you. One toe out of line, one hint that you and the doctor aren't giving this plan your full-throated support, and, well, maybe Penny and I won't be such good friends after all."

"Can I go back to bed now? I'm old and tired."

They stared at each other. "Fine," Dale said, turning away and then resuming his seat.

Mike turned to go.

"Mike?"

His shoulders sagged. He twisted to look at Dale.

"Regardless of what you may think about my methods, understand that I'm doing all this because it *is* in the best interests of the unrecovered."

"The unrecovered don't need you, Dale. And they don't need Vic's touch."

"I'm afraid we'll have to agree to disagree there. And remember what I said about my little friend." He waved at Penny in an exaggerated game-show host motion.

Mike turned to go again. Then stopped. Without turning around, he said, "The thing about living half your life in a coma, is that the events before that are fresh. Basic training, Vietnam, killing—it's all so... fresh in my mind. My body might be old, but, I wonder if I'm still just as good at it? I wonder if what I learned there still applies?"

"And what would that be?" Dale sounded amused.

Facing away, Mike didn't have to hide the smile that touched his lips. "Victory is measured by the body count."

Chapter 13

Rachael

I adjusted my grip on the pistol for the tenth time in as many seconds. The damn tall grass prickled my belly through my clothes and provided no insulation from the cold, frozen ground. Sarah was off to my right, lying low, sighting the pickup where Jamie sat.

Jamie had told Sarah the direction she thought the stranger was coming from, and Sarah turned the truck around to face that way.

I squeezed my eyes shut, trying to acclimatize them to the darkness. With both trucks shut down and the headlights off, only a sliver of moon lit the night.

I still didn't know who was coming, but we'd decided to leave Jamie in the truck. She was too hurt to run off and hide. We practically had to bludgeon Ed to get him to agree to leaving her as bait for whoever was coming. He lay in the tall grass on the other side of the road, positioned ahead to keep Sarah and me out of any crossfire.

Dickens nuzzled my side, trying to get his furry black nose under the hem of my sweatshirt.

"You cold too, buddy?" I whispered.

"Quiet," Sarah hissed. "They're coming. Look to the east."

A faint shadow picked its way along the roadside with agonizing slowness. A rhythmic sound echoed among the lifeless, leafless trees. The tap, tap, tap of a cane on asphalt. As the figure drew closer, I could see it was a bulky man in a fedora with something clutched under his arm.

"Hello," he called as he neared the trucks. "I mean you no harm."

"Prove it," Ed called from the far side of the road.

"You cannot prove a negative," the man said.

He had a heavy Middle Eastern accent.

"You're unrecovered," Jamie called.

"As are you," the man replied.

"Show us your hands," Sarah called.

"How will you see them?" the man asked.

The truck's headlights flicked on in a dazzling blast of light.

The man arched back, shielding his eyes. He was old, hard for me to say how old. In his sixties, maybe. Silver stubble stood out on his wrinkled cheeks in the harsh light.

"Drop the cane!" Sarah yelled.

"Please. It's fragile. An antique."

"Damn it," I heard Sarah grumble. "Cover me, Rach."

"Got you," I said.

She rose and approached the man. "Set your cane on the hood of the truck and lift the flaps of your coat."

"As you say," the man said. He tottered to the front of the truck, still shielding his eyes. Then, very gingerly, he laid his cane on the hood and reached down.

"Slowly," Sarah said, sidestepping her approach to avoid my line of fire.

"I'm but an old pilgrim, you understand, a refugee of sorts." He raised the flaps of his sport coat.

I couldn't see any weapons, but his clothes underneath the coat were a mix of bulky layers. Which explained why the old guy wasn't freezing his ass off in just an old black blazer.

"What about the scarf?" Sarah asked as she closed in one step at a time.

"You think I'm hiding something under my shemagh?"

"Are you?" Sarah asked.

"My cold neck," the man replied, clearly annoyed. "I am Asim El-Shaer. A teacher, erstwhile author, and poet. I am no danger to you."

"Said every bad guy ever," I called.

Asim nodded. "Yet you are the ones holding guns to me."

"What are you doing walking out here at night? You've got no supplies. It makes no sense."

"My vehicle broke down several miles back," Asim said. "Can I please put my hands down and lean on my cane? These old bones are tired."

"Why didn't you just sleep in your car?" I asked, rising from the grass.

Asim turned to face me. "That is a good way to freeze to death, young lady. Best to keep moving in the cold and sleep when the sun warms the glass."

He had me there.

"My cane?" he asked.

Sarah sighed. "Go ahead."

"Where are you headed?" Ed asked, breaking cover and crossing the road.

"That is a long story. The short version? West."

"Why?" Sarah asked.

"Please," Asim begged, "if you could share the heat of your vehicles, I'll tell you everything you want to know, and perhaps some things you'd rather not."

"That sounds ominous," I said, walking over to them. "I'm all for heat, though."

Dickens, always up to make new friends, approached Asim slowly, tail low between his legs.

Asim said, "Is he friendly?"

"To a fault," Sarah replied.

Asim extended his arm toward Dickens, who licked it. "Dogs are the joy of the world," he said.

"What now?" Ed asked.

"Jamie," Sarah called. "What do you think?"

"He's unrecovered. I can feel his mind on the dark water. But it feels different somehow. I can't explain it."

"Try," Sarah said.

"What your friend struggles to explain is that I exist on that plane, but I'm not beholden to it. Protected from the ravages of despair."

"Well," I said, "that's weird, and it explains nothing."

"I'm protected," Asim asserted, "because I know what it is. I know the darkness. The dark water. And... what lies beneath."

"Like hell," Ed muttered.

Asim tapped his cane on the pavement. "Exactly."

Chapter 14

Sarah

Two thoughts warred in Sarah's head. The first was that she didn't like surprises, strangers, men especially, and would just as soon leave this old guy by the side of the road. The second was that she didn't want this weirdo at her back. But the promise that he had some mysterious intelligence couldn't be overlooked. If what this man knew could help her find Penny, then she had to explore the option. Either way, standing in the cold wasn't doing anyone any good.

Sarah tucked her pistol away, sighed, and rubbed her temples. "Okay. Rachael and I were getting ready to call it a night, anyway. Next place we come to, we'll hole up and get warm for the night."

"I am eternally grateful for your assistance," Asim said.

"You'll ride with Rachael and I," Sarah turned to Ed. "You following us?"

"Yeah, but, why the hell is he going with you?"

Sarah grabbed Ed's elbow and walked him back toward his truck. "Two reasons," she whispered. "One, both Rachael and I are trained fighters. He makes any kind of funny move, and he's between a black belt and a military trained—"

"Rachael isn't really—"

Sarah let go of his elbow and waved for him to shut up. "And two, I want to know how the hell he ended up out here."

"So do I," Ed whispered.

"And I'll tell you when we get there."

Sarah walked back to the others. "King, Koontz, come."

Rustling in the grass announced the arrival of her protection detail from the shadows.

Asim raised an eyebrow. "Three dogs."

"They're more trustworthy than people," Sarah said.

"Indeed."

"Let's go," Sarah said.

Dickens bounded toward the cab of Sarah's pickup, wagging his tail.

"Not this time, buddy," Sarah said. "There's no room at the inn. You're in back."

Dickens let his tail drop. He might not know the words, but he knew the tone.

Rachael protested Sarah's instruction to sit in the middle until Sarah whispered, "I need you to cover him. Keep a tight grip on that pistol and keep it in your lap."

Rachael nodded. "I got you."

The heat brought pins and needles to Sarah's icy hands as the vent directed its air onto the steering wheel.

Rachael's teeth chattered. "I need some better f-f-f-fucking clothes.""We all do," Sarah agreed. And then to Asim, "You seem warm enough."

"As you say, layers," Asim said. "And much walking."

"You really came all this way on foot?""My car broke down miles back."

"Why take the risk? No food. No winter coat. Doesn't make sense."

"Because I've seen what's coming," Asim said. "And someone has to speak for the ones nobody's listening to, you understand?"

The man might be strange—but he wasn't wrong.

Sarah took the next exit off the highway. Instead of the usual gas stations and hotels, there was nothing but a sign indicating that the next town was several miles away. The hardwoods lining the road gave way to a pine forest. Occasionally, dirt and gravel tracks left the road and vanished into the trees.

"There!" Asim said.

Sarah hit the brakes just past a gravel road. "What?"

"A woodpile." Asim pointed. "There will be a house not far away with a chimney."

"Let's hope no one's home," Sarah said. She backed the truck up and shut off the lights.

Ed's headlights, which had been painting the back of their heads, went out too.

Just beyond the woodpile, the trees opened up, revealing a small house in the woods, dark and still.

Sarah and Ed cleared the yard first, then broke the glass on the back door and cleared the house, going from room to room. No bodies, but evidence of a hasty departure; rotten, petrified food on the table, and bedroom trash baskets full of soiled tissues. Smiling flu. Maybe the inhabitants had gone to seek medical help. They'd never made it home.

By the time everyone sat in the country living room around a roaring fire, the night was getting old. The dogs lay at Sarah's feet, far enough that the occasional popping log didn't send sparks into their fur, but close enough to enjoy the warmth.

Asim's head nodded to his chest.

"I'm sure you're tired," Jamie said. "But I need to know what you know."

Asim looked up, his eyes shining with intensity. "Yes. Yes, you do."

Chapter 15

Mike

Mike glanced over his shoulder at the towering mountain of a minder Dale had saddled him with. The scraggly-bearded man stood head and shoulders above anyone else in the hangar-like building. "How much of that shit do you have with you?" he whispered to Carl.

The doctor applied a small square of gauze to Mike's arm, then straightened. As he did, the plastic tote of supplies he sat on creaked ominously. "Enough to treat you for a few weeks. Do you feel it?"

"Yes," Mike said. He wanted to smile. Felt the muscles at the corners of his mouth tugging. But that smile, surrounded as they were by the unrecovered, might be the kiss of death for Penny, not to mention Carl and himself.

"That's all you've got for me? A yes?" Carl frowned at the needle, then cast his eyes around the highway department structure full of people and buses. "No place to dump this needle."

Mike's jaw tightened. "What do you want me to do, sing the smile song from Annie?" The words came out harsher than he meant them.

"But you can feel a change? Joy?" Carl insisted as he snapped the syringe and needle into a plastic case.

"I do," Mike whispered. And then, noticing an approaching Knight of the Prophet, "Incoming."

"You're both to come with me," the ruffian said. The pimply-faced young man, not a day older than twenty in Mike's estimation, put a hand on his hip.

Carl rose and offered a hand to Mike.

"For Christ's sake, Doctor, I can get up off a crate on my own," he growled. But the loud crackling of his knees and ankles as he rose took the punch out of his indignation.

The Knight's blond curls bounced as he led Mike and Carl through knots of unrecovered. Some smiling from a recent touch by Vic, others whispering mutinous assertions. What was clear to Mike as they made their way through the space—there were way more people here than lived at the New Hope unrecovered colony.

They weaved their way in and out of people, rolling up sleeping bags and loading supplies onto the buses. They juked right around a mountain of rock salt as tall as a bus stood on end. Above them, men worked with shovels, cutting a crude switchback path up the tower of salt. Behind it, Dale, the Prophet, and Aella stood, flanked by Knights.

Dale motioned them over. Next to him, Vic looked drugged. His eyelids barely made it to half-mast, and he wobbled on his feet. A Knight held him by the armpit, presumably keeping him from collapsing. "Mike and Doctor Parks. We're all here then. So, I'm going to go up and give a little speech. I'll introduce each of you. You'll come out, wave, and come back down. There are no speaking parts for any of you. Understood?"

The Knight shook Vic. "Boss axed you a queshun."

Mike assumed Vic was exhausted from performing the touch on his faithful, but it could also be something Dale had given the man to keep him docile.

"Uh?" Vic looked up, rolling his head until his dark, dilated pupils found Dale.

"You going to be a good boy?" Dale sneered.

"Yuh," Vic said, then his head lolled.

"How about you, Mike?" Dale asked. "Are you with the program?"

He wanted to know where Penny was. Wanted to make sure she was alright, but he didn't want to show too much concern. Best to skirt the line, keep her alive without giving Dale carte blanche to make him dance like a puppet on a tangled string. "Where's the child?"

"She's fine, as long as you do what you're told." Dale raised an eyebrow. "Will you?"

"Yeah, fine."

"Doctor Parks?"

"I won't lie for you," Carl said.

"Just smile and wave for now," Dale smiled. He turned to Aella. Her brown ringlets held just enough moisture for Mike to note she'd bathed. "Ready, kiddo?"

"Ready," Aella replied, with a trace of the Prophet-induced smile on her lips.

"She's coming down," Dale said. "Touch her again."

Vic could barely speak. "I'm worn down. So tired. Nothing left to give."

"Just a bump. You can do one more little bump." Dale grabbed Aella's hand and placed it in Vic's.

"Ahh," Aella smiled. "It's like cupcakes under my skin."

Mike's jaw clenched a degree tighter. Partly because of Dale's use and abuse of Vic, and partly because Aella was freshly showered. And that made him wonder about the circumstances. If Dale were doing anything untoward with the preteen, Mike would murder that shitty little toad with his bare hands.

Vic collapsed into the Knight's arms.

"Fuck!" Dale said. "Jonnie, the coke."

The Knight who'd been following Mike around as his minder stepped forward, producing a small baggie of white powder.

"Ken, get his attention," Dale said.

"Dude, I'm holding him up."

"Dude? *Dude*?" Dale huffed. "Jonnie...."

"I got you, boss," the shaggy mountain said. He slapped Vic in the face.

Vic's eyes opened.

Jonnie held out a lump of white powder balanced on the meat of his fist between thumb and forefinger. "Sniff." He poked Vic's other nostril closed with a sausage-sized finger.

Vic snuffed the powder. His eyes opened three-quarters. The Knight holding him hauled him to his feet.

"There," Dale said. "That's better. Now, on with the show." He held out a hand. A Knight placed a megaphone in it. Dale climbed the switchback path up the salt hill and stood at the top. "People!" He waited. "Friends! Unrecovered!"

The unrecovered cheered. That was wrong. Incongruous. All these joyless humans... cheering? The sound hit Mike like the gong of a cracked bell with a bent clapper. It took him a few moments to figure out that's why Vic was on the verge of death. Dale got the crowd good and liquored up on dopamine before the speech.

"Look at all these smiling faces!" Dale raised his arms triumphantly, flicking his fingers upward in a sign for more applause. He got it. "And there's so much more to come. If you're new, if you've traveled from afar to join our quest, our movement—welcome! I'm Dale, assistant to..."

The Knight who'd been holding Vic gave him a shove. "Get your ass up there, smile, wave, and come back down...or else."

Vic stumbled forward, struggling up the salt hill.

Dale gesticulated like a game show prize model. "The Prophet!"

The crowd cheered.

"His only mission is making you happy again!"

More cheers.

"But there are so many of us now, and it tires him out. Go take a rest, Your Happiness."

Dale lowered the bullhorn and whispered something to Vic, who, hearing it, turned and shambled back down the salty trail. "But that's why we're here, isn't it? To work on getting our Prophet some help and getting you all happy again. That's the whole point of this quest. We're going back to the start. Back to the beginning—"

Mike thought about the recordings of Hitler's speeches, Stalin, Mussolini, demagogs, building castles of populism and rhetoric. It made him sick to his stomach.

"—back to where the smiling flu emerged. We're going to get some real answers. We're going to make some real progress, and we're going to make each one of you your own prophet!"

The crowd cheered.

"What if you could share the joy of recovery with all the unrecovered you meet? It will make you feel so, so good." Dale offered a big stage wink. "So powerful, eh?"

The crowd cheered like drunken revelers at a rock concert.

"Let's introduce you to the folks who are going to make all this happen for you...."

"Go." Jonathan commanded. But then, in a whisper, he added, "sorry about this." Then, he pushed Mike toward the loose, salty path winding up the hill.

Mike's feet dug into it like sand. He lurched forward.

"Hurry up, old man," Dale hissed from the top of the hill. Then into the bullhorn again, "Here's the man, the myth, the legend, someone who spent fifty years in the grips of the smiling flu! If he can do it, you can too..." Dale drew out Mike's name like a boxing announcer. "Mike Sampson!"

Mike reached the top.

Dale grabbed Mike's hand and raised it over his head as if he'd won the match.

The crowd cheered.

Dale lowered the bullhorn. "Wave, damn you," he snarled between clenched teeth.

Mike waved.

"Good. Now get the fuck out of here." Dale held the bullhorn to his lips again. "And here's something you didn't know—his doctor, the one who administered the cure—"

Mike, halfway down the hill, paused and stared up at Dale. Silva? Was he talking about Mike's first doctor, Anthony Silva? The *first* one who'd administered the cure, also the accidental creator of the smiling flu itself?

"—Doctor Carl Parks is on our side. He's here with us, working hard to get you all smiling again. Come on up, Doc!"

Mike shook his head, trying to clear the myriad of emotions the thought of Silva evoked. He passed Carl where the salt pile met the concrete. "You've got to be kidding me."

"We play the game until we find a way to win," Carl said behind gritted teeth, then trudged to the salty top and waved at the euphoric crowd.

Mike stood behind the salt mound, surrounded by Dale's entourage. He watched absently as the Knights tied Vic to a battered kitchen chair attached to an upright two-wheeled dolly. Jesus.

He'd tuned out of whatever crap Dale spouted on top of the mountain, but then he saw Aella, Dr. Silva's killer, standing at the foot of the path up the sodium podium.

"We've got one more big surprise for you. The next person on our team is your modern patient zero. She's the first person to get the smiling flu since Mike Sampson. The first person to contract the modern smiling flu outside the lab. And, *AND*, this strong, brave, twelve-year-old girl killed the smiling flu's creator. She single-handedly avenged all of you and your loved ones. Please welcome, Queen of the unrecovered, the preteen with a pistol, a one-woman crusade for justice, A—ella Harrrrgrave!"

Dale clapped his hands wildly and gestured for Aella to stand beside him.

The crowd went nuts.

Mike's stomach turned.

Chapter 16

Rachael

The fire popped and crackled behind its protective screen, sending dancing shadows across a room with ugly brown floral furniture and taxidermy fish on polished wooden plaques adorning the walls. I had an unsettling feeling of unwelcomeness, of otherness. Like the home's former inhabitants wouldn't accept me based solely on the color of my skin. The type of people who would work security and follow me around in stores. The silent, insidious version of racism.

My gaze fell on Asim. Where this home's former inhabitants would follow me and give me the stink eye, they might just shoot someone like Asim, clearly from the Middle East, and not from 'Murica. Yet Asim seemed perfectly at home, snuggled down in an easy chair, cane between his legs in the firelight, Dickens laying at his new friend's feet.

"You must hear me out," Asim was saying as the dancing flames sent monstrous shadows playing across his leathery face. "What I'm about to tell you will seem incredible in the truest sense of the word."

He looked at everyone, each in turn. When his eyes fell on me, I gave him a slight 'go ahead' nod. The dark water, the unrecovered, the smiling flu, the stories about them all screaming in unison as another woke from the flu's coma — it was all incredible. Why should new information make any more sense?

Asim rubbed the stubble on his chin. "I was—am—studied in the sciences, but more than this, I am a spiritual man," Asim raised a finger, "but not a religious one. The distinction is important. Religious people are consumed with dogma, canon. I am consumed with a quest for the truth at the intersection of spirit and science."

"Go on," Sarah goaded.

"Please," I added. I was tired and not in the mood for his overdramatic bullshit. But Sarah could be a little overly gruff.

Asim nodded. "As you say. The problem with modern medicine is that it treats humanity as a machine, a biological machine, a psychological machine. But there is a third part. A part that is not a machine. The spirit."

"Oh, come *on*," Ed said.

Asim patted the air in front of him. "Please, hear me out. There is some recent evidence of the spirit, measured in the brains of the dying. Activity after death, things of that nature. We treat the smiling flu as dead. Done. You get it, your brain overproduces dopamine, you go into a euphoric coma, and you either get medical help and remain in a dopamine coma, or you die."

"Or get the cure," I said.

Asim's watery eyes bored into mine. "Is it, though? There is an antidote for the coma, but the damage is done. We don't know the long-term effects. What if the smiling flu isn't done? What if there is a second stage of the disease?"

I wasn't necessarily buying the spiritual thing Asim was selling, but this part… a second stage…. I sat up.

Dickens looked at me and thumped his tail on the floor in a single wag.

The firelight danced across Sarah's face, casting deep shadows across her eyes. "Keep going."

"What if the brain wires new pleasure pathways? That's what the brain does in accident victims who learn to walk again. Who learn to speak again. What if the second stage allows us to feel joy again, wired through a different pathway… the pathway of the spirit?"

"Phhhttt," Ed snorted.

"The evidence is in my smile. My manner. I have some small measure of my joy back. And you," he gestured to Jamie, "can feel the difference in my mind on the dark waters. No?"

"I can." Jamie leaned forward on the couch. "You said you knew what was under the dark water…."

"I do. Or some minor part of it. It is the second stage. Close your eyes. Reach down under the dark water with your mind. Gently. Not too far. What do you feel?"

Jamie closed her eyes. "It's… sick. Ugly." She opened her eyes. "I don't like it."

Asim nodded. "No. Nor should you. It's the ugliness of the modern world. It's the malevolence of spirit. The endless need and consumption. More food, drink, drugs, shopping, nicotine, sex, all of it. It is *need*. The brain is rewiring itself. The lack of dopamine, and the craving we trained into ourselves through modern life, have infected the spirit, leaving us bereft."

I shook my head. "This all sounds like bullshit."

"You are young." Asim gave me a sad half-smile.

No shit, Sherlock.

"I come from Atlanta. From your C-D-C," Asim pronounced the letters slowly, giving each weight. "I was among the few taken into the infectious disease center there. Before the building went into lockdown. And so, I was among the first few to receive the original antidote. The one that brought the smiling flu victims out of the coma." He paused, shifting the cane back and forth between his legs. "I am among the few who have yet progressed to what I think is the second stage of the disease."

"You *think?*" I asked.

"I have only..." Asim looked at the ceiling, searching for words. "...anecdotal evidence. At the end, there was no electricity there. No way to run the tests and machines. And even then, as I say, science can't reach all the way into affairs of the spirit."

"You're saying this is a spiritual disease," I supplied.

"Precisely, that." Asim agreed.

Asim stared down at me with dark, sad eyes. "What happened at the CDC was terrible. Monstrous. And I think there is no other explanation." Asim fell silent. He looked off into the distance, eyes unfocused.

"What happened?" Sarah prodded.

"I don't like to remember," Asim said, still staring into the shadows. He sighed. "It starts with nausea. A drowning feeling. As if mind and body are sinking into those terrible dark waters. It's as if all the negative thoughts I ever had were made manifest. I became, for a moment, the agent of terrible evil. Evil that dwelt in me. Evil that dwells in us all. Cutting someone off in traffic. Any intrusive thought of revenge or wishing someone ill. I like to believe I'm a good person, as we all do. But we all have these thoughts. We don't act on them, of course. We push them down. Push them aside. But it seems they never leave us. Stored in some dark corner of the mind...."

"The dark water," Jamie whispered.

Asim nodded. "I believe this to be true."

"So, what happened?" Sarah asked again.

"All those thoughts, made manifest in mind and body... when the second stage strikes...they come out."

Ed slapped the arm of the couch. "What happened at the damn CDC!"

Asim stared down at his gnarled hand. His knuckles went white.

"By the end, we were living like rats in a cage. Segregated from the ruined world by steel doors. The doctors kept trying to reverse the effects of the post-antidote victims."

"The unrecovered?" I asked.

"Yes. We were human pin cushions, each receiving different pills or injections. The doctors studied their samples in old-fashioned microscopes by the light of battery-powered lanterns. And then the first of us felt...unwell. My friend, Porter. He vomited unexpectedly. It came on him suddenly, and in a rush. Black viscous bile, like motor oil, sprayed everywhere. A young doctor by the name of Hardwick came into contact with it. Ugh..."

Asim produced a handkerchief and wiped his eyes.

I felt sorry for the old man. We'd all been through so much. So much loss. I saw Cassie in my mind. My soul hardened. Of course, this was important, but what I wanted from Asim was intelligence on how to defeat the unrecovered and kill Dale.

On that score, I hadn't learned shit.

"It took only seconds for the infection, whether physical or spiritual, to transfer to the young doctor. He was a man of loose skin. His arms and neck showed the stretch marks of someone who'd been obese. Of course, we were all on meager rations. Small meals of freeze-dried food, you understand. When the vomit hit Doctor Hardwick, he tried to wipe it off, but it spread over his skin. And then... I..." Asim drew a deep breath. "His eyes changed. He ran from the room. I was concerned for my friend. When I tried to assist Porter, he only waved me away. And gave me a little smile."

"He was unrecovered?" Sarah asked.

"Yes. But not the doctor, you understand. Hardwick never contracted the smiling flu. Never got sick. Never had the antidote. And yet when he came into contact with Porter's vomit... he changed."

"Changed how?" Ed asked.

"We found Hardwick in the cafeteria. He'd taken a fire ax and destroyed the locked door to the pantry...." Asim wiped his face again, as if trying to clean an internal image from his eyes. "He found the sugar. It covered him. He shoved fistful after fistful into his mouth, cramming it in until he choked. This was a doctor, you understand, a man of science, control. And he shoved the white crystals into himself. Gagging, chewing, and pouring again, like a starving dog."

"What happened to him?" I asked, vengeance momentarily forgotten in the face of this new horror.

"They tried to reason with him. Tried to restrain him. He fought with the strength of many men, clutching the sugar to him, consuming it while fending off the other doctors. By the time they got control of him...." He fell silent again.

"What?" Sarah asked.

"They sedated him, strapped him down. He screamed and raged for more sugar. He went into convulsions. The doctors tried emergency surgery, but it was too late. His stomach had burst, and he'd metabolized enough to kill him."

"Because he touched that other guy's puke?"

"As you say," Asim nodded. "He was... the first."

"The first?" Sarah asked.

"Another man, Petrov, the safety officer, tried to clean up Porter's sick. He went in with a full suit. Biosafety Level Four, you understand—positive air pressure, full decontamination protocols. He only managed to spread the black goo around. No chemical available in the facility could wash it. It was like glue."

"What happened?" Jamie asked.

"Even with the most stringent decontamination protocols, a few hours later, they found Petrov dead. He'd gotten a hold of some sedatives from the pharmacy lockup, crushed up the pills, and snorted them. His was the most humane death. At first, we thought perhaps he was affected by Hardwick's death. And then another unrecovered became ill and vomited. Suddenly. Just like Porter. And again, because there was no warning, a staff member came into contact with the black bile. And again, that woman died."

I wanted to ask... and didn't.

"How?" Ed asked for me.

"Let's just say, excessive self-harm," Asim said. "Doctor Musa was found with deep cuts all over her body. The blood.... Please. No more." Asim mopped his face.

"Everyone here has a loved one in the hands of the unrecovered...." Sarah said and turned to Jamie, eyes wide as saucers.

"Am I…" Jamie paused, then drew a breath and began again. "Does it happen to all the unrecovered?"

Asim fixed Jamie with a knowing stare. "In time, I think, yes."

Ed leaned away from his wife, recrossing his legs.

"Why hasn't this happened to any of the other unrecovered?" Sarah asked.

Asim said, "We were the first to receive the antidote, you understand. Test subjects. We were treated a month before anyone else."

"How long ago?" I asked.

"About a month," Asim said gravely. "But I have not yet told you the most terrifying detail."

"*What?*" I blurted.

Asim turned to me, his face ashen. "What happens when an unrecovered person comes into contact with the black goo…."

Chapter 17

Sarah

Terror clouded Sarah's mind. Panic for Penny. Her baby was in the clutches of Dale and his twisted, unrecovered Knights. And now, this hedonistic vomit virus.... Mental images of her little girl covered in black goo, running around eating sugar until her stomach exploded, or worse. Her stomach churned at the thought of the next bombshell revelation Asim might drop.

Ed nearly shouted, "What *happens* when the unrecovered come into contact with the black puke?"

Asim held Ed's eyes for a moment. "They exhibit all the symptoms, you understand. The same compulsive behaviors of those who never had the smiling flu, as I've described. But the psychic connection between the unrecovered seems strengthened by contact with that vile substance. I've only seen it twice. But each time, the victim, that is to say, the person who touched the bile, took on the hedonistic impulses of the unrecovered who vomited in addition to their own latent desires."

"You're going to have to spell that one out for me, Doc," Rachael said.

"Let's say that my suppressed impulse is gluttony, as was poor Doctor Hardwick. If I vomited and an unrecovered with a proclivity for violence touched it, that person would be an uncontrollable maniac for both food and murder, killing and eating their way through the world until they ate themselves to death, were killed in turn, or turned their violent streak on themselves."

"A gluttonous berserker," Ed said.

"Shit," Rachael whispered.

"How sure are you about all this?" Sarah asked, looking for a way to punch a hole in Asim's story. Make it not be true.

"The events at the CDC happened as I have described. After the first few cases, we didn't bother trying to decontaminate the area. Simply closed that room. The few survivors eventually found themselves compelled to leave. As for the consequences of the unrecovered coming into contact with the stomach effluent, I only have two cases on which to base my conclusions. One quite personal...and recent."

"Your car didn't break down," Sarah said. She'd suspected something about that part of his story seemed off.

"Yes...and no." Asim looked at his hands. "I was traveling with the last of the people from the Infectious Disease Center in Atlanta. We were following the unrecovered, basing our directions on where we sensed the gathering of minds in the west. That's when I became ill."

"You got your sick on someone, didn't you?" Jamie asked, her voice trembling.

Asim nodded. "Oma. My wife." His lip trembled. A tear ran down his cheek.

Sarah's heart dropped. The world was a shitshow. How could she raise Penny in such a place? Maybe they'd all be better off dead. Everyone.

No one spoke.

Asim stared into the fire, avoiding everyone's eyes.

"To know your worst, deepest, darkest inner demons were only seconds away from being visited maniacally, irrecoverably, on the only person left to you in this world.... I pulled my pistol. She nodded...."

Sarah's skin crawled and itched. The thought of the scene in Asim's car....

"Your own vomit had no effect on you, though?" Ed asked.

Asim's lip trembled. "As you say, it had no effect on me. I changed my clothes... and burned the car."

"Are you still dangerous? Will you get sick again?" Rachael asked.

Asim gave Rachael a soft, sad smile. "There is no instance of it happening twice to an unrecovered person. But that isn't to say it couldn't. No testing has been done. You understand, it is as much an affliction of the spirit as of the body..."

He cleared his throat.

Sarah jumped, rearing away from him.

"Sorrow," Asim said in a choked voice, "not vomit. I feel fine... physically."

"And spiritually?" Rachael asked.

"Losing my wife has had the same effect on me as the smiling flu. There is no joy in the world. I feel only the overpowering need to reach the unrecovered and warn them before.... I want to save as many as I can."

"We have a radio," Rachael blurted out. "The army gave it to us to call in the location of the unrecovered when we found them. We've got to warn them!"

In that moment, Sarah both hated Rachael for betraying their secret lifeline, and loved her for her dedication to humanity. A dedication *she* didn't feel. Sarah cared only for Penny's safe return. But that feeling of love for Rachael—that was something new. A spark of something she'd only shared with a tiny handful of people in her fifty-one years. And maybe that meant there was hope for her beyond motherhood.

Asim shook his head. "They know. The CDC was in contact with them."

Sarah's fists clenched. Her heart raced. They knew. The bastards. They let her and Rachael go out to confront the unrecovered with nothing but a radio. Let Penny suffer—maybe die—if the unrecovered holding her went into stage two.

"Why wouldn't they do anything?" Rachael demanded.

No one spoke.

Sarah rose. Her anger needed a place to go: the radio. "I'm going to find out."

Asim nodded. "Do not expect them to be forthcoming. Men like that will not discuss their motives with outsiders—especially on an open frequency."

They all followed Sarah outside. She dug behind the seat of the truck for the radio.

Her heart pounded her my chest. Sarah tucked her hands under her arms against the cold.

The army's response, after hearing a shortened version of smiling flu stage two, was maddeningly curt and succinct: "We know. Report when you have found the unrecovered. Keep this channel clear. Almighty out."

"Well," Rachael sighed, placing the radio back behind the truck seat. "That was a colossal waste of time."

Sarah wanted to scream, to shout, to tear her hair out. "I don't understand why they wouldn't act. Why won't they try harder to save Penny?" She took a deep breath, trying to focus her anger on an action that might actually do something.

"It's terrible," Asim agreed. "There could be many reasons. How much fuel and manpower do they have in this broken world?" He gestured around them with his cane. "And stage two is barely a month old. There is no vaccine. No antidote."

"I bet this was their plan all along," Ed said. "Do nothing and let stage swo take care of the unrecovered. The problem solves itself. And if a few civilians get caught up in it—well, too bad."

Asim muttered, striking the icy ground with his cane. "How do you Americans say? Collateral damage?"

"We have to go." Sarah stood, squaring her shoulders. "Now."

Chapter 18

Mike

Mike stood dazed behind the giant salt pile as Dale finished whipping the euphoric crowd into a frenzy. In the milling group of Dale's entourage, he spotted Aella. The limp he'd managed to shake since waking from the nearly lifelong coma returned as he made his slow way over to the girl. "Where is your mother?"

The Prophet-infused light in her too-wide pupils dimmed. "I-I don't know?"

Mike scowled. "What do you mean? What happened?"

"Um, well, Dale came. And he said he was going to make me a queen of all the unrecovered. But mom said no. And then Vic gave me the touch. And...I haven't seen her." She looked down. And then a moment later, back up at Mike. "Have...have you seen my mom?"

The touch of the Prophet acted like marijuana in the minds of the unrecovered sometimes, especially the younger ones. Dale knew this... and exploited it. Rising anger boiled up inside Mike's chest. "No, but I'll find her."

"Mister Sampson," Aella clasped Mike's arm. Her nostrils flared under wide, terrified eyes. "Do you feel it? Do you...."

"Feel what?" Mike's heart pounded. Aella's unexplained fear was like a contagion, flowing through her hand into him as if Dale's plan had already come to pass.

"Something is... *coming*," she whispered.

"I-I don't..." Mike caught sight of Dale making his way toward them. Goons flanking him. "I have to go." He pulled his arm free. The fight-or-flight instinct gripped him so hard that he cast about, looking for a way out of the building. His eyes alighted on a door not far off at the back of the space, away from the crowds and the entourage. The uneven scraping footsteps of his shoes on cement served as a testament to the unfair advancement of age. Inside, he still felt twenty-five. Outside, ugh. It wasn't fair. He banged through the door. It took a moment for his eyes to adjust, even from the dim lantern and headlight atmosphere inside.

A red coal burned in the darkness, hovering at shoulder height. The stink of tobacco filled his nose. The silhouette of a tall, shaggy figure resolved itself out of the pitch-perfect blackness of a country winter night.

"Smoke?" The faint chuffing of paper on paper accompanied the question.

Mike squinted to see the proffered pack in an outstretched hand, a filter protruding. Without thinking, Mike took it. No sooner did he have it in his mouth than a sputtering flame appeared. On the other side of the tiny fire, Jonathan's huge, shaggy countenance flickered in the orange glow. Mike hid his surprise and touched the tip of his cancer stick to the fire, drawing the smoke into his lungs.

They puffed in silence.

The shapes of the forest slowly resolved in the meager starlight, becoming shaggy shades of gray pines.

"Made me sick," Jonathan said at last.

"Hmmm?" Mike pretended to be less aware of the presence of Dale's chief enforcer than he was.

"The speech," Jonathan said. "Shaking you, the doctor, and the girl in front of the crowd like that. Other things, too."

"Uh-huh."

"The way Dale treats Vic, and this whole thing with making more Prophets, using the kids."

Mike kept silent. All he could think was that this was some sort of trap Dale had laid for him. That he'd directed Jonathan to confide in him, to get him to declare his treasonous intentions.

He coughed. The cigarette was a bad idea. He'd smoked in his old life. It was the sixties. Everyone smoked. But now, well, fifty years in a coma didn't do his lungs any favors, not to mention the rest of him.

The giant man next to him nodded. "You don't trust me. I get it. Smart. I wouldn't either. Not sure how I can prove I'm on your side." He drew a long pull on his cigarette and let it out slowly. The smoke swirled in front of the stars. "I guess when the chips are down sometime, you'll know."

Mike drew a shallow lungful of smoke, then sent it out into the night. He wanted to trust. Lord knows he needed an ally.

"People don't think much of me," Jonathan said. He spoke as compelled to let his speech make a hole in the night. "Big dumb ex-con. I'd probably think that too. Hell, I *did* think that. The world trains poor young men to believe their place is fixed. Settled. You work a crappy job, drink beer, raise more brats to do the same. They told us in school we could be anything. But our fathers, mothers, and older sisters told a different story. Couldn't get out of the mine, or our shitbag little town." Jonathan let out a derisive snort. "And now here I am. I'm out. The world is over, but I'm still working a shit job for some asshole trying to get high, to eke out a tiny fucking shred of happiness every now and then. Tell me, what's different?"

"Nothing," Mike said. "But you don't have to work for Dale."

"You got a magical happiness elixir in your pocket?"

tau. Mike wanted so badly to tell Jonathan. It would feel good to help the man. And that good feeling, even the promise of it, was impossible without the tau. The risk was too great. "No." Maybe there was a way for Jonathan to prove he wasn't buying into Dale's program. Maybe the shaggy giant could help him and Dr. Parks unravel this whole thing. "How many children does Dale have?"

"Far as I know, Dale doesn't have any—"

Mike ground out his cigarette and turned to the big man. "How many kids is he planning on using in his experiments?"

"Oh. I only know about the ones from New Hope. Six from there, counting Aella. But they're coming in from all over. Dale put out the word to unrecovered groups up and down the coast. He put this whole thing together on a spit and polish. Meeting places. Having everyone split up and take different routes. Clearing the back roads. I've even heard whispers that there's a rogue element of the army allied with the former President. So is Dale. That's the rumor anyway. The legitimate army might get a carload or two, but the unrecovered will reach Destination, Idaho. Dale made certain of it."

The whole thing turned over in Mike's mind. Destination, Idaho—that's what Dale meant by back to the beginning. Where it all started. Fort Johnson, Aella, the whole smiling flu outbreak. "What was all that about, making everyone their own prophet?"

"Far as I can tell," Jonathan said, crushing out his own cigarette, "Dale figures there's still some of that virus out there on the Hargrave farm. And he figures maybe if he cracks some people on the head, gives them brain damage like Vic, he can make more people like Vic."

Mike gaped. "That's insane."

"I tend to agree with ya. Whole thing's nuts."

"What does he want with the children?"

"Ain't no little ones in the unrecovered camp. They all got better and moved to town with foster families. The way Dale figures, if the brain damage happened to Vic when he was a kid, making him, I dunno, acceptable to the brain changes that gave him this weird power, maybe he can do the same to some kids. Have to be young, resilient brains...."

Penny. Dale was going to corrupt Penny. Beat her brains out in the hopes he could make more prophets to control. His granddaughter. The girl named after his widowed wife. Mike's fists clenched. His heart pounded. His limbs shook with nearly uncontainable rage. "I'll fucking kill him."

"Yeah, ain't no one ever called me a good guy, but braining kids for a science experiment, that shit's fucked up. But I need Vic. Understand. I can't do anything to screw up my easy access to happiness. Not now. Not like this. Without that, I got nothing."

Mike dug his fingernails into his palms to keep from attacking this man who'd just shrugged off the imminent maiming of his granddaughter. Jonathan's forthright attitude impressed him and went a long way toward building trust. But he had to admit, maybe Jonathan was only telling him exactly what Dale wanted him to know.

He drew a breath and let it out, thinking of Carl's words: *We play the game until we find a way to win.* "Who else knows the routes, the plan?"

"Each group knows their route. Their rendezvous. I doubt most of them even know Destination is the ultimate target. We better get back inside before they wonder where we are. And," he shrugged against the starlight, "I might have to fib to keep us both out of trouble."

"Fib?"

The door burst open.

A skinny, dark-haired Knight peered out.

Jonathan grabbed Mike's arm. "Caught him out here. Maybe making a break for it."

Mike tried to shrug off the big man's iron clutch. "Where would I go?"

"Dale's looking for you," Dark Hair said.

"Which one?" Jonathan asked.

"You."

"Come on," Jonathan said, pulling Mike toward the door.

"I can walk on my own, damn it."

Jonathan let go and ushered him back inside.

On the black water, Mike drifted further and further from the minds of the unrecovered around him. He could still feel them on the periphery of his consciousness, but the close connection, the one that kept people getting up and feeding themselves absent the brain's reward system, had abandoned him. Loneliness, the same kind he'd felt when he first stopped screaming after he woke, enveloped Mike.

Something moved under the dark water. Something great and terrible. A malevolent, malignant leviathan slithered through the blackness underneath Mike's consciousness. A chasm opened in Mike's stomach. Dark, churning filth roiled inside him.

Mike woke with a start. He was barely able to lean over and empty his stomach on the cement without soiling himself. All the darkness and putrescence of the vile world exited his body in a viscous stream. Heaving, panting, gasping, he fought desperately for oxygen. Spots formed at the edge of his vision. Blackness closed in.

"Mike!" Carl exclaimed. The doctor was kneeling a few feet away, rolling up his sleeping bag.

He mustn't touch it. Must not help.

Mike held up a hand, keeping the good doctor at bay.

The black bile soaked into the cracked cement. The reek of stomach acid and rot filled the air.

"Don't," he gasped. "Don't come close. Don't touch it."

Sounds filtered into his consciousness. The noise of four hundred morose unrecovered gathering up their sleeping blankets and bedrolls surrounded him. No one spoke. Just rustling despair.

"It's..." Mike sucked in a breath. He lowered his voice. "It's like on the bus."

"I don't understand," Dr. Parks whispered back.

"Water," Mike gasped.

The doctor handed him a bottle.

Mike drank and gathered himself, shaking off the physical horror. When his breathing calmed, he told Carl about his dream. Then, about his interaction with Aella and her assertion that something was coming. Although in his waking mind, he felt distant from the other unrecovered—he knew Aella was right. Something was coming. He felt it too.

"I don't know what to say," Dr. Parks said. "My instinct is to tell you that it was just a bad dream caused by a sour stomach."

"An underdone bit of potato?" Mike asked. "We're in a Dickens novel now?"

"Where we are is surrounded by the stench of your sick. Can I help you get cleaned up?"

Mike shook himself. Cast a glance at the Knight standing watch. The man appeared to be ogling a blond girl stretching not far off. He turned back to Dr. Parks. "It's like on the bus. Don't touch it. Don't go near it, and don't let anyone else touch it."

Carl frowned.

"You don't believe it. What I did to that guy, Kyle, on the bus. You don't think I did that."

"I'm a medical man. And while I can't explain the mental side of the unrecovered, this mass hallucination about black mind-water, the synchronized screaming when you all woke... What happened on the bus doesn't fit any kind of pattern. I must say, given the state of things, I can't rule out the possibility, but I'm afraid I'm going to need more—"

"If you touch that shit," Mike pointed a finger. "You'll get your proof, and you won't be sane enough to figure out what to do about it."

"How do you know?" Carl asked, still frowning.

"I just do." He felt it. Felt the evil rising off the concrete, masked in the stench of bile. Whatever that stuff was that came out of him, it came straight from hell. And since he'd purged, he felt better—well, more able to feel reward and love for Penny and Sarah. Sarah, his little girl, now in her fifties. It wasn't fair. "If you've ever believed a word I said, believe that shit does what I say it does. It's not the good kind of happiness. Don't touch it." Mike's bladder ached. "I need to take a piss."

The doctor nodded. "I'll pack your things."

Mike looked down at the speckles of vomit on his sleeping bag.

"Leave them."

Jonathan, who was their Knight guard this morning, wagged a finger at the doctor. "Don't talk to no one while we're gone. You'll get me in trouble. That'll make me real angry, Doc. You copy me?"

Carl made a wry face. "Copy."

As he walked toward the door, Mike took in the scene. No one smiled. Dale must have Vic in seclusion this morning. Probably their precious Prophet had exhausted himself from administering the touch four hundred times. Mike wondered how long before some idiot tried to cut Vic open and pull the touch out by hand.

Mike limped through the frosty grass carefully. It wouldn't do to slip and fall on his ass. His breath steamed into the pale dawn air. The bitter chill bit into his old bones.

He relieved himself of his burden and returned to the door.

Jonathan stood outside the door, smoking. He betrayed no hint of the previous night's confidences. "I got this," he said to the Knight who'd led Mike outside. Then he opened the door and followed.

"He's building his own stinking kingdom," the doctor muttered as he sat on his bedroll.

"I would have thought that was obvious," Mike said. His back ached. His neck ached. His everything ached, especially the parts that cracked when he moved them. He groaned and stretched.

Carl motioned to Jonathan. "He shouldn't be sleeping on the ground. Not at his age. Certainly not in January."

"I shouldn't be sleeping on the ground at *my* age," Jonathan said, "but here we are."

Mike gave the doctor a wan smile. Doctor Parks was a good man. Truly good. For someone to be Black and gay, to suffer the mistreatment Carl surely had, and still help others, not just as a doctor, but as a person... it awed Mike. Dr. Parks took good care of him.

And then, he thought of Sarah. He'd never taken care of her. Not really. Her mother did all the heavy lifting when Mike was around—the changing, the feeding, the bathing. Hair, nails, all of it. But oh, Mike had doted on his little girl just the same. How she used to laugh when he lay on his back and hoisted Sarah onto his feet, yelling, "Fly, super girl, fly!"

A tear crept down his cheek. He brushed it away.

Carl stared down at the drying puddle of puke. "I feel like I should get a sample."

"And do what with it? I fucking told you. Don't touch it."

The doctor sighed. "Yeah."

The first of the bus engines started. The roll-up door at the far end of the highway department building rose, clanking loudly on its chains. A bus roared away in a cloud of black smoke.

"Twenty-minute intervals," a voice whispered behind him. "Don't turn around." Jonathan's voice. "We don't know what satellite capabilities the army still has, but Dale doesn't think they can re-task them into geosynchronous orbits. If they managed to track us, they'll get one vehicle if they're very, very lucky. And they're all going in different directions to start."

Mike's mind raced. "Can you get us on the bus with the children? With Aella?"

"Maybe, but that's Dale's bus. The Prophet's bus. Seats are tight, and they'll watch you like a hawk. I'm going to shove you now. Make it look like I'm rushing you."

A breath later, Jonathan yelled, "Hurry up!" The warning helped Mike keep his balance.

"Unless you have another doctor, it might be handy to keep me close to the children," Carl said without looking up from the ties on his bedroll.

"I'll put it to Dale that way," Jonathan winked. "If I get you on that bus, what are you going to do?"

Chapter 19

Rachael

I don't remember falling asleep. When I woke, I was nose to nose with Dickens by the dying embers of the fire. At least I was warm. Before we settled in, we raided the redneck's closets. Mostly we got woodland camo stuff. Not that I was ever a fashionista in the before times, but woodland camo? Ugh. And the woman who lived here was a lot wider than me, so I had to cinch the lined pants around me with a too-long belt I cut a hole in with a hunting knife. At least the guns weren't locked up, so we were all armed to the teeth. I'll give that to the bumpkins.

Something nudged the back of my knee.

I rolled onto my side.

Sarah stood over me, hands in the pockets of her new camo parka, poking me with her boot. "First light," she said. "Let's go."

I sat up. Sarah and I were alone in the room.

"Time to see if anyone froze to death during the night," Sarah said.

"Cheery," I grumbled. "Good morning to you, too."

Sarah stood in the hallway entrance and bellowed, "Asim, Jamie, Ed, let's roll. Daylight's burnin'. Our daughters are counting on us."

I was kinda pissed at her for waking me up, but if it were my kid, yeah, I'd be a nightmare. I guess she wasn't doing that bad. That got me thinking about my own shit. Cassie. She'd been killed before I could know if there was any chance she'd ever think of me as anything more than a sister. Though I guessed it didn't matter. I would always love her. And that part of me that crushed so hard on her, that part, was murderous. I watched head movies of me blowing Dale's brains out, seeing his body crumple and fall, a shocked expression on his face.

Dickens got up while I was woolgathering and licked my face.

"Yeah, buddy." I patted his head. "Time to go kill some bad guys."

"I'm hungry," Ed said, rubbing his face and shambling into the living room.

"Heads up," Sarah called.

Ed caught the can of Spam she tossed him.

"Eat in the truck," she said.

My stomach rumbled, but not for Spam. "I fucking hate the apocalypse," I muttered.

We all found something to munch on. Before, I would have gagged at the idea of eating peaches out of the can, especially for breakfast. But now, well, it was a delicacy. I mean, when would any of us see fresh fruit again? We were living in a frozen, dead world.

An argument broke out outside. After siphoning the gas out of a Taurus in the driveway, we stood gathered around the trucks.

"It's too dangerous for you to ride with Jamie," Sarah said to Ed. "What if she..."

"Progresses to the second stage," Asim supplied. "Sarah is correct. The danger is great, you understand."

"She's my wife," Ed said.

"So was my Oma." Asim looked at the ground and smashed a patch of ice with the tip of his cane, shattering it. "I put a bullet in her yesterday." He fell silent, then looked at the steel-gray sky. "Oma..."

Sarah glowered at Ed. "Don't be a jackass." She shook her head. "Rach and I are leaving."

The first flakes of snow fluttered down from the sky like bits of instant potato.

Sarah looked up, then at the dogs, then at the back of the trucks. "Shit."

Asim nodded. "The vehicles are impractical. Not enough seats. Any supplies we take will freeze."

"Yeah," Sarah said. "I know."

Ed rode with Sarah and me. The dogs got nestled down in the piles of sleeping bags and supplies in the back of her truck. I had to sit in the middle. Again.

The heat brought blessed relief and pins and needles to my frozen fingers. We'd divvied up the winter gear we found in the house, but the woman who lived there had small hands, and the knitted gloves I got pinched my fingers and didn't do much for the cold. I'd have to check how they worked with my pistol.

We rolled slow, mostly so the dogs in the back wouldn't freeze, and partly so we wouldn't miss any signs of recent travel on the roads. The thing about those big buses the unrecovered were using was that they left tracks, even in frozen mud. Weeds had grown in the cracked roads before winter killed them. Any passing vehicle would crush them.

We spent a lot of time in the next town we came to. And we got lucky. Someone had already broken into the car dealership. In fact, there was a brand-new Mustang crashed into the side of the building with a frozen body in it.

A guy a little younger than me, flu grin still on his face, half hidden by the deployed airbag. Idiot.

It took some time, even with the key safe door hanging crooked on its hinges. We gathered up the keys still in the safe and those scattered on the floor around it, then stood in the parking lot next to pickup trucks with toppers, clicking the fobs.

I argued that we should be looking for RVs, but Sarah said they were too big to get down the logging roads and used too much gas. As if a big pickup truck were a lot better. But I got where they were coming from. I figured Jamie could quarantine in the back of one truck, Asim in another.

"What about the dogs?" I asked. "Asim said they never got the mess from the stage two puke clean. What if he or Jamie pukes on them?"

"As I say," Asim said, "I have not seen anyone expel the evil twice. I think my risk is lower, you understand. I *think*."

"You're riding up front, anyway," Sarah said. "I need you to guide me."

I grabbed Sarah's elbow. "Can I talk to you?"

"There's no *time*," Sarah said.

"I will begin moving your things to the new truck," Asim said.

Sarah huffed and followed me into the rows of cars. When we got out of earshot, she turned. "*What?*"

"Why are we taking this guy with us?" I asked. "How do we know that shit about the second stage of the smiling flu is even true?"

"We don't," Sarah said. "But there's something different about him. Jamie said so."

I didn't get it. She was after Penny, and I was after revenge. Lugging this old guy around the country was going to slow us down. Give us another mouth to feed. "Old people are...slow," I said. "Why burden ourselves by dragging around some old guy with a crazy story?"

"Two reasons," Sarah said. "If he's telling the truth, then maybe he's got some other nuggets of wisdom he hasn't thought to share. My intuition tells me he might be more help later on. But here's the other thing, and I want you to think about this." Her eyes bored into mine. "If we leave this old guy here in the snow and go on some half-cocked Rambo killing spree, we'll become what we're fighting against. Even if we rescue the kids, we'll become what we hate."

"But I don't want—"

"Fuck what you want, you selfish little shit. What would Cassie want for you?"

My fists clenched. "Oh, that was low."

"I don't care."

"Fine. I'll get my own fucking truck and—"

"Think it through, Rach," Sarah said. "You can barely drive. And without Jamie and Asim reaching out with their minds to find the other unrecovered, how will you find them, alone? And even if by some miracle you do, what then? You're just one person with just the little bit of training Cassie gave you. What are you going to do? March into their camp with your little Beretta and kill them all? Keep reloading? Even if I let you take the radio and you do call in the airstrike, are you just going to let them bomb all those kids? My kid, Penny? Aella? Is that how much you care about anyone else but yourself?"

I opened my mouth, but no words came. I hated her. Hated her for being right.

Sarah gave a curt nod, reading my face. "Now go get your ass over there and help Asim get the stuff moved. We've wasted enough time, and I'm friggin cold."

"Come on," Ed shouted. "What're you guys *doing?*"

Sarah turned and mumbled under her breath, "*That guy* we could leave here."

When we got back to where the others were loading the new trucks, Jamie grabbed Sarah's shoulder. "I feel them. A group. Not far."

"Unrecovered?" Sarah asked.

Duh. What else would she feel like that?

"Quickly," Asim said. "To the west."

Chapter 20

Sarah

Sarah got the dogs settled in their new home as fast as she could. She gave the disappointed Dickens a quick kiss on the top of his head as the Lab made his way into the back seat of the crew cab. "Don't look at me like that," she said, shutting the door. "I need Asim up front to help guide us."

In their haste to get going, there was no more argument about whether it was safe for Ed to ride with Jamie. stage two or no, they had to catch up to the unrecovered, and Jamie needed to be where she could tell Ed where to go.

Rachael sat in the backseat with Dickens, arms folded, pouting.

Asim climbed into the front seat, a large book under his arm in addition to his 'spiritual' tome.

"You know how to use a gun?" Sarah asked him.

"*Please.*" He gave a faint smile. "I grew up in Mosul."

"Good," Sarah thrust the rifle at him.

She fired up the truck and sped out of the dealership, not looking in the rearview mirror to see if Ed was behind her.

"Which way?"

"Ahead," Asim said. "West."

But there was no way ahead. Just the hardware store across the street.

"I need to know which way *on this street?*"

"It doesn't work that way," Asim answered. "It's not a map. It's a *sense*, you understand."

"Left," Rachael said. "The interstate goes west."

"They won't *take* the interstate," Sarah snapped. "We've established that."

Ed honked.

Sarah checked her mirror. Ed had his left turn signal on. Maybe Jamie had a better sense of direction than Asim.

Sarah turned onto the road and pulled to the side, letting Ed take the lead with a wave of her hand. It hurt her soul to do it.

Ed shot past, kicking up snow on the disused street.

"We need a damn map," Sarah said, cranking the wheel to follow Ed's truck.

Asim drew out the big book.

Sarah glanced over. An atlas of some kind. Thank fucking God. "Rach, navigate."

Asim handed the book to her.

Blessedly few stalled cars barred their way on these country roads as they made their way west. Only patches of snow and the brown winter-dormant stalks of weeds inhabited the roads. The sun was only a faint outline behind the gray curtain of clouds. For a while it looked like it might come out, but now fat snowflakes dotted the windshield with gathering intensity.

"This would be a lot more useful if I knew where the hell we are to start with," Rachael said.

"There," Asim pointed. "A sign. Damn my eyes, I can't make it out."

"Rocky Point Road," Rachael said. "What state are we in?"

"Tennessee," Sarah and Asim answered at once.

"I'm losing them," Asim said. "They're getting further away."

"Go faster!" Rachael shook the back of Sarah's seat.

Sarah pounded the steering wheel. "Cut it out! When *you* learn how to drive, then you can tell *me* how to drive."

"*Really?*"

Sarah glanced at Rachael's hopeful expression in the rearview mirror. "No."

She gave the truck a little gas despite the curving, weed-choked country road, overtaking Ed. Her stomach churned. What if Penny was with this group? The thought of her daughter dumped fresh adrenaline into Sarah's veins.

"Yes, that's it!" Asim said. "We're getting closer."

Sarah wheeled around a blind corner and had to jam on the brakes. Ahead, a white van teetered on the edge of a ruined bridge fording an icy creek. Smoke rolled lazily from the tailpipe.

"Look around," Sarah said.

"Are they still inside?" Rachael asked.

Asim raised the rifle. "They're close, but I don't know exactly where."

Ed got out of his truck and approached Sarah's window. "Where are they? Jamie can't tell, exactly."

"We don't know," Asim said. "And that's a good way to get yourself shot. Get to cover."

Sarah gave a half-smile. So, it wasn't just her. "I thought you were smarter than this?"

"I went to Northwestern, not Annapolis," Ed shot back.

"Get behind the truck," Asim suggested. He opened his door and climbed out slowly, aiming the rifle between the gap between door and truck.

"Dogs, come," Sarah said, opening her door.

King knocked Rachael in the head as he squeezed between the narrow windows of the bed cap and truck cab. The giant pit bull leaped over the center seat and out Sarah's door. His tanned fur blended into the dead leaves on the shoulder. Sarah caught a glimpse of the stalking dog, picking his way carefully among the trees, before she lost sight of him. Good boy.

Koontz came after, more graceful, bounding out of the truck to stand at Sarah's side. And Dickens, true to form, stood on the driver's seat, staring at her, panting and wagging his tail as if the whole thing were a trip to the dog park.

"Do we go up to the van?" Rachael asked. She'd opened her own door and stood behind it, careful to keep her line of fire away from Asim.

Cassie *had* taught her a few things. Sarah filed that away.

"If you come out," Asim called, "we will not hurt you!"

Silence.

"Lower your weapons," Asim whispered.

Rachael said, "They killed my family."

"And mine might be in the van," Sarah said, pointing her pistol at the sky.

"As might mine," Asim said.

Sarah stared at him. He hadn't mentioned anyone other than his dead wife. But now wasn't the time to explore that.

"We're coming out," someone inside the van said.

The van's right rear door opened.

Sarah could make out only darkness inside.

"Don't shoot!" A pimply teen with dark, greasy hair poked his head out.

"Hands up," Sarah said.

"I'm just opening the door," he replied.

"Do it with your body," Sarah shot back.

The teen's hands emerged, raised in supplication. He squeezed through the door.

"How many are you?" Asim asked.

"Any children?" Sarah added.

"Four," the teen said. "No kids."

Sarah's heart sank.

"The rest of you," Ed called. "Out."

Another teen emerged—dark-skinned, handsome. Next, a young woman, red hair, bangs, and full-figured. Last, a thin woman with stick-straight dark hair and slender eyes. They stood in a line behind the van, hands in the air.

"They're all unrecovered," Asim said.

"Where were you going?" Sarah demanded.

"Why were you chasing us?" the thin woman countered.

"We're the ones with the *guns*," Sarah said. "We'll be asking the questions."

"Fuck you, lady," the pimply teen said, then spat on the ground.

Koontz gave a loud bark.

A gunshot cracked the air.

The four unrecovered ducked down.

It took Sarah a moment to realize she'd been the one who fired.

"It would be better if you didn't antagonize us," Asim said. "You understand."

"Anthony," the redhead said through clenched teeth. "Shit."

The pimply one, Anthony, apparently, sank to his knees.

"On your feet!" Sarah shouted.

"He's carsick, assholes," this from the other male.

Sarah and Asim exchanged glances through the open cab.

Anthony reeled as if punched. "I can feel it coming...."

"Get back!" Asim shouted.

Anthony gagged, then sprayed the other guy with black bile.

"Fuck!" the stocky, dark-skinned guy said, shaking his goo-splattered hands.

Sarah ducked down behind the glass.

Asim did the same.

The spatter landed on the redhead.

Both the stocky guy and the redhead sank to their knees, limbs trembling.

"The hell?" Rachael whispered.

The affected teens' eyes rolled back in their heads. The trembling grew worse for a second, then stilled.

The soiled boy grabbed the redhead's arm, the change in his demeanor almost tangible. "You want this dick, don't you? Oh, we are gonna fuck all day!"

"Oh, I'm going to rip it off and wear it around my neck," she choked. She kneed him in the balls. "Tell me I'm powerful!"

Koontz alternated between barks and growls.

Anthony coughed up another quantity of dark foulness.

"Asian woman," Asim called. "Get away from them!"

"I'm from Cincinnati, asshole," the thin woman called.

"Get away!" Rachael shouted.

Ed shouted something, too. Sarah didn't catch it. Her gun was trained on the two fighting teens.

"Tell me I'm thin!" Redhead said, kicking her dazed aggressor again. "Tell me you like me for me!" She raised her foot again, but the wounded teen managed to catch the kick before it landed, sending the redhead sprawling.

"I'm going to fuck you until there's nothing left—"

A rifle cracked.

A spray of gore painted the white van red.

The aggressive guy fell back, slamming into the vehicle, then crumpled on the pavement.

"What the fuck is happening!?" the thin woman cried, backing away.

Koontz kept baying out the alarm.

Anthony heaved again. Strings of black fluid clung to his lips, inching their way toward the buckled blacktop.

The redhead got onto her hands and knees. "Tell me I'm beautiful!" she shouted, crawling toward the slender woman. "I neeeeeed it! Tell me! Tell me or I'll rip your fucking tongue out!"

"Y-you're beautiful," the other woman stammered, still backing away.

"Yeeeesssss!" the redhead said. "Oh, fuck yes!" She grinned a wide savage grin. "It feels so fucking good! Say it again!" She got to her feet and moved to follow the other woman, who was backing toward the trees. "Tell me!"

"Stop where you are," Asim called. "I will shoot you!"

"Please." The dark-haired woman kept moving, putting her hands in front of her. "You're gorgeous."

"Oh fuck, yeah! Yes!"

The rifle barked again. The bullet tore a gouge in the pavement at the redhead's feet. "On your life," Asim called. "Stop!"

The redhead appeared not to hear him.

"What do I do?" Rachael asked, her voice an octave higher than usual.

"Stay cool," Sarah warned. The last thing she needed was Rachael going off half-cocked into stage two bullshit. "Let Asim handle this one."

The redhead lunged at the dark-hair. "Tell me I'm popular!"

Another rifle shot.

The redhead dropped, blood pouring from a wound in her calf. She kept on, crawling toward the dark-haired woman. "Tell me I'm cool! Say it!"

"Y-you're cool..." The slender woman had reached the place where the pavement met an embankment. With nowhere to go, she turned toward Asim.

"Stay out of my line of fire, woman," Asim said.

Sarah risked a glance at Asim. Each time she sighted down her pistol at the infected redhead, she saw Penny. There was no resemblance, of course, but this was someone's baby. Someone's little girl. "There's no cure?"

He'd said as much, but she needed to hear it again. Needed to be sure.

"None," Asim said. Then he fired his rifle.

Chapter 21

Mike

Mike's ass hurt. They'd bumped along in the old school bus all day, crisscrossing two-lane blacktops, logging roads, and occasionally traversing fields and backyards, all pre-cleared of obstacles. In some places, Mike saw above-ground pools and children's play sets bulldozed out of the way, the tread prints fresh in the frosty January soil.

"Are you seeing this?" he whispered to Dr. Parks.

"This took an incredible amount of planning," Carl whispered back. "More than Dale could pull off alone. Not from the unrecovered campus near New Hope. This thing is big."

A sense of dread hit Mike like a wall of water, knocking him back in his seat. "Something's happening...."

A few seats ahead, one of the Knights coughed, then sprayed vomit onto the unrecovered next to him, and in front of him, and behind him.

Mike watched the black spatter tumbling through the air, almost in slow motion. He cursed his old eyes, unable to track every drop. "Move!" he shouted to the doctor, hemming in the seat.

Carl moved forward.

"Away from it, Carl." Mike said, grabbing the man's collar and hauling him back.

"But—" Dr. Parks started.

Mike did his best to push Carl into the aisle and toward the back. "Move, or you're going to end up like the jerkoff guy, but worse!" That seemed to get the doctor's attention.

"Okay, okay. It's just... I took an oath. I'm supposed to help," Carl said.

A Knight, tall and lanky with silver stubble, blocked their path. "Sit the fuck down. It's just a little puke—"

He didn't get the chance to finish before Carl kneed him in the crotch.

"Get out of the way," Carl said.

To Mike's amazement, the Knight complied, flopping into a seat, holding his balls.

The bus slowed to a stop.

Mike turned to face the sound of growing pandemonium behind them.

A woman, chubby and beautiful, with black goo on her face, stood bare to the chest, slashing at her skin with a hunting knife, over and over, shouting, "Oh yes! Oh, fucking yes! Cut! Cut! Cut! My blood! My control!"

The seats obscured Mike's view of the man in front of her, but his pistoning arm told the story. He stared wide-eyed at her bloody, swaying breasts.

"Jesus," Mike whispered.

"What—" Carl started.

"It's the same," Mike said.

"What's the same?" Carl asked.

"The same thing that happened to me. I threw up on that guy and then...."

"Yeah, but she's cutting herself," Carl insisted.

"It's the same thing."

"No," Dr. Parks insisted, "it isn't. Completely different pathology. Self harm—"

"Help!" a woman across from the mayhem screamed. "He's biting me!"

Again, the green Naugahyde seats blocked Mike's view, but there was no mistaking her struggles. A Knight reached down and hauled a man with a blood-soaked mouth out of the seat. "You're steak tartare, motherfucker," the biter said, and sank his teeth into the Knight's arm.

Other unrecovered in the area were following Mike and Carl's example, getting out of their seats and forming a knot of people in the back of the bus.

Gunshots boomed in the small space. Three, four, five.

Mike's ears rang.

The jungle came back, surrounding him.

He ducked down.

Head on a swivel, soldier...

He grabbed for his rifle and found only empty air.

The legs of the people knotted around him were tree trunks. The green seats, fans of foliage...

Head on a swivel, soldier...

Screams.

The sharp tang of cordite on his tongue.

He couldn't see the threat.

Head on a swivel, soldier...

"Mike!" Carl's voice...

Medic! an old voice called, far away...

"MIKE!"

Strong hands hauled him to his feet.

The world snapped. He stood with Carl's arms under his, nose to nose with the doctor.

"Are you—"

Mike pushed him away. "I'm fine."

Carl grabbed his shoulders and spun him around. Behind him, the bus was empty. A Knight stood on the ground, hand reaching in through the open emergency door, beckoning Mike.

"Go," Carl said.

As Mike approached the opening, he hesitated. The ground was a long way down.

A second pair of hands appeared on the other side.

"Hurry up, old man," a gruff voice belonging to the second set of hands growled.

Mike grunted, but disoriented and shaken, he didn't have it in him to combat the rudeness. Instead, he propelled his body through the opening, trusting the men outside to ease his fall.

He landed on his feet. Pain flared in his popping knees as he hobbled away.

Carl followed.

They'd only gone a few steps when Jonathan appeared like a wall of denim in front of them. "Boss wants to see you."

"Of course he does," Carl said.

Jonathan led them a little way down the track to a copse of pines.

Dale stood, pacing back and forth, breath steaming into the gathering shadows. He turned at Jonathan's approach, shoved the massive Knight aside, and wagged a finger at Mike. "You! You..." His face twisted into a snarl. His mouth opened and closed soundlessly. And then, "What the actual *fuck!*"

Mike shrugged. "What?"

"All this craziness started with you! You puked on Kyle and now he's cuckoo for boner puffs!" He pressed his lips together, nostrils flaring, and nodded to Jonathan. "Search them!"

Jonathan patted Mike down and found nothing. But when he searched Carl, he came away with the doctor's brown zippered pouch.

Mike knew the pouch. Knew what it contained. The tau. Not good.

Jonathan handed the pouch to Dale, who unzipped it.

Dale held up the syringe. "And what is this?"

"Medication for Mike's lingering post-coma ailments. Steroids mostly," Carl said.

"Bullshit!" Dale said. "This has something to do with the black puke that turned Kyle into a happy ending machine. And now you've dosed someone else, and I've got two more nut jobs and four bodies. We're going to stand here until you tell me just exactly what the fuck is going on!"

"I honestly have no idea," Carl said.

He sounded convincing to Mike. Probably because it was the truth.

Dale waved the syringe. "You know something! Out with it!"

"I don't—"

Dale snapped his fingers at Jonathan. "Get the little girl."

Jonathan turned and strode away.

"One of you is going to tell me something. Something about all this. I know you know. And if you don't, that little girl is going to have a very bad night."

Jonathan returned, frowning, holding Mike's struggling, crying granddaughter.

"Shut up, kid!" Dale shouted. "Or I'll give you something to cry about!"

"Hey," Mike held up his hands.

Dale turned. "Last time we spoke, you said you didn't care. That she was nothing to you. I knew you'd change your tune. You're a liar. But now, dear old Mr. Sampson, you're going to tell me the truth."

"The truth," Mike said, "is that it just happened to me, okay? It just happened. We were in battle. My chest got tight. It was like Vietnam—"

"Don't give me that war hero bullshit—"

"Mr. Sampson suffers from PTSD," Carl offered. "Gunfire can trigger flashbacks."

Mike didn't know what the hell PTSD was, but wondered if it was the same as Post-Vietnam Syndrome, which he had heard of.

"I don't care if he suffers from psoriasis." Dale's small, dark eyes bored into Mike's. "You'd better start talking. Your granddaughter is counting on you."

Mike glanced over at the scared little girl. "You're going to let me start caring for her. Carl and me." He knew it wouldn't fly at first. But even as that thought crossed his mind, another followed it. A delicious, evil thought.

"You don't tell me—"

Mike leaned forward, making retching noises in his throat.

Dale jumped back.

Mike stopped and straightened, smiling.

Dale drew a pistol. He pointed it first at Mike, then at Penny.

"Hey!" Jonathan shouted, jumping out of the way.

Mike didn't let the smile fall. "Pull the trigger and you'll never know what's going on. Carl certainly has no idea. He can't. He's not unrecovered. And neither are you."

Dale slapped his forehead with the flat of the pistol hard enough to leave a red mark. "Fuck!" He looked at Jonathan. "Give him the girl."

Mike had never seen the big man move so fast. Before he knew it, his two-year-old granddaughter wept into his jacket.

"Fucking talk," Dale snarled.

"You've heard about the dark water in our minds?"

"None of you will fucking shut up about it." Dale tapped the pistol on his thigh and made 'go on' gestures.

"The vomit comes from there. From down under the surface. I sink down in all the confusion. The guns. Then I felt sick. Before I knew it, I was throwing up on that guy...."

"Kyle," Dale supplied.

"Whatever. The point is, I knew not to touch it. It's all the darkness, despair, hopelessness. Call it whatever you want. It's all the stuff that makes us unrecovered."

"What do you mean, the stuff that makes you unrecovered? You've got brain damage. *That's* what makes you unrecovered."

"Then why am I getting better?"

Dale frowned. "Better?"

Mike gave him a faint smile, then kissed his granddaughter on the head. "Better."

Dale waved the gun at him. "You're faking."

"Ever seen an unrecovered fake happiness?" Dr. Parks asked. "They don't even remember how."

"Well, if you're getting better, it's because of whatever that is," Dale said, pointing at the discarded syringe case.

"Maybe," Mike said. He rocked Penny gently, remembering what it was like to sway with Sarah in his arms. "But if I'm telling the truth, then the guy who puked on the bus is going to start feeling better, too."

Dale strode over and stood in front of Carl. "Is this going to happen to all the unrecovered?"

"Mike was right," Dr. Parks said. "I really have no idea."

"I should just shoot the three of you now. Stop the spread." He raised the pistol.

Chapter 22

Rachael

My stomach heaved. I held it in. There's no way I'm going to deliver the vengeance Dale's Knights desperately deserve if I barf every time there's gore and violence. No. Deep breath in, slow breath out. I tried to look at the bodies on the pavement like a mortician or a coroner or something. It helped a little.

"What the *FUCK* was that?" the thin woman screamed. She still stood at the edge of the road, between the van and us.

"I—" The lanky kid stood where he'd been sick. He spat and tried again. "I didn't mean to...."

"Of course you didn't," Asim said. "No one does."

"Jane...." The lanky kid's voice cracked. He stared at the redhead's body, then turned to the dead guy. "Steve...."

The thin woman was approaching the redhead's body.

"Stay where you are!" Sarah shouted.

She froze. "What the—!" she swallowed.

"The vomit," Asim said, "is highly contagious, you understand. If you touch it, the same will happen to you."

"You mean... I did that?" the guy asked.

"No," Sarah said. "The smiling flu did that."

"But the smiling flu is gone," the kid said. "We got the treatment."

"But not a cure," Asim said.

"So now what?" the woman asked.

"Strip," Asim said.

"It's freezing!" the woman shouted.

"And you could have highly infectious material on your clothes," Sarah said.

"Strip *naked*?" the guy asked.

"No one here cares what you look like under there," I said. Even the woman wasn't my type. And there was *nothing* sexy about this situation.

"To your underclothes will suffice," Asim said. "Then check for moisture, dark spots. Any chance the vomit got through. One touch...." He inclined his head toward the bodies.

"Son," Ed called, "you should move away from that spot."

The kid backed up. "What did I do? Will it happen again? W—what are you going to do with me? Why—"

"Settle down," Sarah said, "and strip."

The woman was already shedding her coat.

I felt bad for them. I was fucking cold, and I had on all the hunting gear we took from the house. And the entire operation took time. Especially since Sarah insisted they cut their shoelaces, so they didn't risk touching them.

The guy covered his junk, even though his baggy boxers revealed nothing. I've heard cold affects guys... Gross. Anyway, the woman named Mae bitched about going barefoot on the frozen pavement. I couldn't blame her.

It turned out they had some clothes in the van, but getting them out was tricky. In the end, Ed volunteered to climb a little way down the buckled bridge and open the side doors of the van. He said it looked stable enough. One at a time, the two human popsicles were allowed to go in and get their things.

It still sucked for them. Carrying a change of clothes is something you don't think about. Who travels with spare shoes? A spare parka? Add it to my list of shit no one tells you about the apocalypse.

And it sucked for me. I was hoping I'd get to waste a Knight or two. Just thinking about it sent me reaching for my pistol. And of course, Cassie's face flashed in my mind. God, I missed her.

"Now what?" Mae asked, standing near the back of our truck in layers of shirts, pants, and socks, still shivering.

"Now you tell us where you were going, and why."

"Can we do it somewhere warm?" the guy asked.

My sympathy drained away. I wanted payback for Cassie. And I didn't want these two puking on me. "Dead is warm," I said. I didn't realize my pistol was out again until it was raised in front of me.

"Rachael!" Sarah said. "Calm down."

Sarah scolding me like that pissed me off. "They need to tell us," I said. "Now!"

"Perhaps," Asim began, "a kinder approach will yield better results."

"Not in our truck," I said.

"You don't call the shots here, Rachael," Sarah said.

Heat rose in my face. "That's a good point. Maybe that should *change*."

Sarah just stared at me.

I stared back, holding her gaze. I wasn't backing down.

"We're wasting time," Jamie said. I'd forgotten she was even here. She limped forward from Ed's truck, arm cradling her taped-together ribs. "They have our children," Jamie directed her words to Mae. "Please...."

Mae turned to Jamie, stamping her feet and rubbing her arms. "Your children?"

"These people you're meeting," Asim said, "are not what they seem."

"I told you it was too good to be true," the guy said.

"Oh, shut up, Richard," Mae shot back. She frowned at Jamie. "They...took your kids? Are they unrecovered?"

"Mine is," Jamie said without a trace of emotion. She nodded to Sarah. "Hers isn't."

"Um," Richard said, "could someone *please* tell me what the fuck just happened?!"

"We did," Sarah said.

Richard's eyes bugged out. Veins stood out on his neck. His upturned hands formed claws, grasping at the air. "We're standing over the dead bodies of my friends! Who died because they touched my puke! And all anyone wants to talk about is our travel itinerary!?"

And this is why I don't like guys. Also, penises.

"If you don't give us some answers soon," I said, "you'll be joining them."

Jamie put a hand on my shoulder.

I looked up into her blackened, swollen eyes. Her bruised face showed no emotion. Her words came with a bit of a lisp from her fat lip. She said, "I want them all dead. I want Aella back in my arms. I want to feel her mind next to mine again on the dark waters. She is the only comfort this world has left for me. You'll get your pound of flesh. I swear by all that is holy, you'll get it. But for now, please, shut the fuck up."

I opened my mouth to speak. But what could I say? If anyone had a right to revenge, it was Jamie. Beaten half to death, kid stolen for God knows what kind of fucked up reason. Something in me wouldn't let it go. Wouldn't let her, Sarah, and Asim be right. Wouldn't let them have control of me. I needed to make my own choices. Be my own woman. Kill some Knights.

I made a wry face. "Well, Heil Hitler!" I snapped a Nazi salute and stomped off back down the road the way we'd come.

Well, fuck. That was *wayyyy* over the top, even for me.

"Rachael!" Sarah called.

I ignored her. They could all eat shit. I was warm enough. There were houses here and there. Maybe I could even get a car going, or something. Then I'd be the queen of my own destiny for once. Just for one time, since the entire world fell apart, I wanted to be in charge of *me*. No bosses. No Keeper Corps. No Sarah or Jamie. Just me. Who needed them?

I wasn't the same spoiled innocent girl that slept in a potato chip truck after DC fell. The same idiot who drank unfiltered lake water. The same...the same girl Cassie saved from the Confederate Army. The same woman Cassie took time to train. To teach. To love. And now, there was no one. No mom, no brother, and no Cassie.

As I walked, I realized how stupid I was being. Of course I needed people. No woman is an island. I couldn't remember the last time we passed a house on this snowy mountain road. Two sets of tire tracks pointed back the way we'd come, and those reflective markers along the guardrail. The boots I got from the house were a little too big. My toes started to get cold.

Not good. I didn't know much about mountain survival, but even a city girl like me knew about frostbite.

I checked my pockets. A knife and a headlamp. No matches. The gray sky left me without a shadow. The light started growing dimmer. Still no houses. I looked back. The others were far out of sight. I tried to figure out how long I'd been walking. An hour? More?

The longer I walked, the stupider I felt. My anger turned to shivers despite the winter gear. The cold crept in through the cracks between my wrists and gloves. And my face, where it stuck out of the hood, burned. And my toes. I couldn't feel them anymore. Bad sign.

I could turn back. My feet kept going forward. In my head, a battle raged. Part of me said I could do it. That I'd just keep walking until I came to a house. The other part wanted to know if I was so stubborn that I was willing to die for my pride. My numb feet seemed okay with that option.

The dusk was very quiet. Just the muted noise of my feet in the snow. The apocalypse was a quiet place. A cold place. A lonely place. Just my footfalls, my breathing, and the blood rushing in my ears.

And then, engines behind me. They'd turned around. Of course. They'd have to. The bridge was out. Something in my brain clamped down. When they got here and told me to get in the truck, I'd keep walking. Refuse. Make them beg for me to go with them. I wanted to show how strong I was. How determined. But none of that was real. It was playacting, and I knew it. All it would show was that I was a stupid, childish woman who would rather die than have someone else tell her what to do. I would rather freeze to death than let anyone besides Cassie care about me. And the truth was, I really, really wanted someone to care about me.

By the time the trucks got to me, I was crying.

Sarah rolled the truck alongside me as I walked.

Asim rolled down the window. "Get in, Rachael."

The battle inside me raged.

"Please," Asim said. "We know where they were going. We need your gun."

I looked up.

Behind the wheel, Sarah nodded. Her eyes held me in their stern embrace. Not judging. Not angry. But maybe just someone who'd stood in my shoes.

I scrubbed a hand over my face. "Well, why didn't you say so?"

Chapter 23

Sarah

Sarah couldn't be mad at Rachael. Not really. She'd been like that once: angry and volatile. Hell, she still was, sometimes. It occurred to Sarah, not for the first time, that she struggled to make room for other people to be imperfect, even if they shared the same flaws.

Though Rachael's emotions were spent, she let out a residual sob now and then, like a body twitching long after death. The only other noise was Dickens's tongue lapping the salt from her face.

Honestly, it was a blessing Rachael stormed off when she did. It took Sarah and Asim another twenty minutes to calm the situation and gain Mae and Richard's trust, and twenty more to hash out what the hell to do with them. In the end, the two survivors agreed to ride in the back of Ed and Jamie's truck as far as the rendezvous point, which they supplied.

"The problems, as I see them," Asim said, breaking the silence, "are twofold. First, the agreed meeting time is at dawn, and if we want to get any kind of situational awareness, we'd need to take a look around in the daylight. Chances are, whoever they're supposed to meet is already on watch."

Rachael mumbled something.

Asim held a hand to his ear. "Please?"

"Never mind," Rachael said. "What's the second problem?"

"We can't trust Richard and Mae. They've come a long way for this meet. They have expectations of happiness to come. We can't have them at our backs should it come to violence."

"Oh," Rachael let out a derisive snort. "It'll come to violence."

Sarah let out a breath.

"What?"

"Not now." She desperately wanted to talk to Rachael, but the young woman wasn't ready to hear what she had to say.

"Rachael," Asim started.

"Are you going to give me the 'revenge won't bring Cassie back' speech?'"

"As you say—"

"Or the 'we become monsters to fight monsters' speech?'"

"I had not thought of that. But I'm sure that's a good speech. It makes me think of the atrocities in Abu Ghraib. You've heard of Abu Ghraib?"

"Yes," Rachael said.

Sarah raised an eyebrow in the darkness. Rachael's tone, as she mouthed the simple affirmative, grew thoughtful and quiet. Was it possible Asim found a way to reach her?

"It means, 'Father of little crows,' in Arabic. Ironic, don't you think? The prison was named for the city that housed it, but the west could not have come up with a better name if it tried. Father, for the jailors, and little crows, for the inmates. Oh, the US did some terrible things to make those men crow. Do you have any idea how many young men became radical, violent haters of the West when word of the abuses there got out?"

"I..." Rachael trailed off.

"A lot," Asim said. "But here's the ultimate irony: The reason the US targeted the city of Abu Ghraib, was that your Colin Powell said it was a weapons production plant. He turned out to be right, but only after the fact. The plant was actually a baby formula factory. And that factory, after it was destroyed, produced more hungry, angry, young people than any weapons factory ever could."

"So," Rachael said, "the 'we become what we hate' speech."

"As you say," Asim replied. "How many radicals do you want to make? How many do you want to fight later?"

Rachael said nothing.

Sarah leaned back in her seat and unclenched her jaw. Goddamn. Asim had actually gotten to Rachael.

"You can kill Richard and Mae," Asim said, pressing his point. "And you can kill everyone in this place they are supposed to meet. And your Cassie will still be dead. But, when the truth comes out, and even in this empty world, it will come out, you will have created an untold number of people who seek revenge on you in an ever-descending spiral of violence."

"You just shot two people," Rachael said.

"Please," Asim waved a hand in the air. "I performed a service. I saved two lives. Had we not been there, or let the two stage two infected survive, Mae and Richard wouldn't be here."

Sarah gaped. She'd always just played into Rachael when the young woman got like this. Asim just shut her down, and without pausing for breath, made his point. Why hadn't she thought of that?

"Asim, back there," Rachael said after a long silence. "You said your family could be in that van."

Sarah glanced at the man out of the corner of her eye.

His face fell.

"In Atlanta, before the power failed, we were in touch with a few survivor colonies. They had my daughter's name on a list. Unrecovered, you understand. At a colony in South Carolina." Asim lapsed into silence.

"How old is she?" Rachael asked.

"Not much older than you," Asim said. "She was at university, following in my footsteps. Now, I'm following in hers, or, trying to."

With no GPS, and nothing but headlights and starlight, homing in on the meetup location proved difficult. And even in the before times, the Waffle House wouldn't have been Sarah's choice of venue. Although, the big yellow sign would be easy to spot.

Her headlights alighted on a sign declaring the edge of the town in which the Waffle House of Fate waited. Sarah didn't know how big the town in question was, but she doused her headlights and tried to navigate through the use of her parking lights alone. The going was slow. Not only did Sarah not want the light, but she didn't want the noise, so they coasted along at an idle. And even then, they almost ran into a few stalled cars and other abandoned items best not dwelt on.

Rachael pointed. "There."

Sarah squinted. "You can read that?"

"No, but only the Waffle House has signs shaped like that. It's like Scrabble tiles stuck together."

"Okay. We're on foot from here." Sarah pulled the truck onto the waist-high grass on the roadside.

"What about Mae and Richard?" Asim asked.

"We'll have to tie them up until we know what's what. I've got some of those cable ties in the back of the truck."

"They're not going to like it...." Rachael said.

"We'll have them covered," Sarah said. "They'll do it."

Once they parked, everyone circled up. Here in the low country, where the sun shone down all day, there were few patches of snow, which made the occasional footfall crunch. That was going to be a stealth problem. Not much she could do about it.

"Okay," Sarah said. "Mae and Richard, Rachael's got something for you."

Rachael moved forward and produced the cable ties, already circled, ready to cinch around their captives' wrists.

"Hey, what the fuck!" Richard took a step back, bumping into Ed.

"Can't have you at our backs," Sarah said. "Sorry."

He opened his mouth to scream, but Rachael was faster, punching him in the solar plexus, knocking the wind out of him, and sliding the heavy plastic tie around his wrists.

Sarah was on Mae before she could run. She started to yell, but Ed clamped a hand around her mouth.

"Don't suppose you thought of gags?" Ed grunted, struggling to keep Mae quiet and simultaneously keep his hand out of her biting mouth.

Koontz gave a deep growl from beside Sarah.

"Quiet, boy, you don't want to give us away, do you?" Sarah asked.

In the end, they had to hog-tie and gag the two struggling travelers. Rachael lamented the pair of wool socks she gave up for the cause, but quietly, and only for a moment.

"I'll stay behind," Asim said when they had their captives safely ensconced in the back of Ed's truck. "Keep watch on the trucks and the...cargo."

"Actually," Rachael said, "you'd be more useful with that rifle someplace high with a little cover."

Asim spun in place, squinting into the night.

The intersection featured only dormant grass flattened by a recent snow. The road was higher than the convenience store on the opposite corner, and the Waffle House itself. The only thing screening them from their target was a thin stand of pines growing just above the ditch. The trees ended only a dozen yards ahead, leaving the approach to the restaurant completely without cover, except for some defilade in the ditch itself. But even that was a long way from the eatery's front doors.

"What about that box truck?" Rachael asked.

Sarah turned and scrunched her eyes against the darkness. Just past the intersection, a small rental truck sat, roll-up door open.

"Those things are practically paper mâché," Ed said. "If they open up, he'd be a human pincushion."

"You are all assuming the worst. Choosing the way of violence," Asim said. "Why must it be so?"

"They took our children and killed Rachael's family," Ed said.

"Perhaps not these unrecovered," Asim said.

"But perhaps so," Rachael slid the magazine from her pistol, peered at it, then slammed it home.

"As you say," Asim said. "But that is a long walk with no cover. I will set up on the tree line there." He pointed to the last of the pines lining the parking lot.

"So," Rachael said, "Asim will cover us, Jamie will watch the captives, and Sarah, Ed, and I will skirt the tree line in that direction and come up on the kitchen side where there are no windows."

Sarah reared back as if slapped. This wasn't the dynamic they'd established at all. She was the leader. Except she could find no fault with Rachael's plan. In fact, Sarah figured they'd just walk right up. What if Penny was in there? Stupid. She couldn't let this turn into a power play or pissing contest. "May I suggest," Asim said. "That once you get in place, you watch for a while to see if there are any lights or movement inside?"

"Good idea," Sarah said. She didn't want to, though. She wanted to storm in and find Penny. Of course, the odds that her daughter was in there were fairly small.

Everything made noise. Dead leaves, crunching snow, frozen twigs in the dormant underbrush. Everything. Sarah cringed and winced her way along the edge of the wooded parking lot.

They waited.

No signs of life inside.

No sounds.

"They could have been lying to us," Ed whispered.

The thought had crossed Sarah's mind, too. But no. "The information was too specific. How would they know this place was here?"

"Maybe they're from here and just wanted to trick us into giving them a ride back?" Rachael said.

"Kinda thin," Ed said, "when you put it that way."

"I'm going." Rachael scooted forward, "before I freeze to death." She shot out of the trees and made a ducking run to the enclosure that housed the dumpster behind the restaurant.

"Goddam woman is going to get us all killed," Sarah muttered, following Rachael.

"Or save us all," Ed mumbled, following.

When they reached the garbage corral, Rachael shot out ahead, sidestepping along the brick-sided building. She reached the window, peeked in, and ducked back. Then, more boldly, leaned her head out and took a long look through the window. "Holy fuck," she whispered.

"What?" Sarah and Ed hissed back in unison. They'd followed Rachael's path along the wall, and now stood just behind her.

Rachael dug in her pocket, produced a flashlight, and moved to look again.

"NO!" Sarah made a grab for her but came up with empty air.

Rachael stood in full view of anyone inside, shining her light in, gape-mouthed.

Sarah took a furtive peek around the edge of the window. Then she joined Rachael, standing, mouth hanging open, stomach twisting. Bile rose in her throat. She turned and vomited onto the pavement. The sight inside would never leave Sarah, not as long as she lived. She'd see it when she closed her eyes. She'd see it... she'd see... the bodies....

Chapter 24

Mike

The hospital stank of death. The Knight gripped Mike's wrist like a vise, sending pins and needles into his hand. He and Carl were being frog-marched through the trash-strewn corridors toward the lab area. The swinging battery lantern clasped in the Knight's other hand cast crazy, macabre shadows along the hall.

"This is insane!" Carl protested as he struggled to free himself from the grasp of a second Knight marching him ahead of Mike. "I can't just walk into an abandoned lab and whip up a batch of tau protein."

"You can, and you will!" Dale's voice boomed from somewhere behind them.

"There's no power. No refrigeration of the biological agents I'd need, even if I had the knowledge to work the specific equipment in this lab."

"You tell me what you need, and I'll figure it out!" Dale shouted.

Mike kept quiet, racking his brain for a way out of this mess. After the last round of vomit and violence, Dale had clearly come unglued. They'd piled into the bus and driven straight to the nearest hospital. All the while, Dale insisted Carl's tau shot was to blame for this new manifestation of what he'd begun to call the vomit virus.

"Damn it," Carl insisted as they marched along the creepy corridor, "I'd need live yeast, the tau DNA coding sequence, which, you know, I haven't exactly committed to memory. I'd access to the database—"

"Shut up!" Dale shouted. "I'll fucking get you whatever you need. I told you that!"

At last, they came to a door marked Chemical Pathology.

"This one," Carl sighed.

The Knight in the lead pushed open the door. Then the Knights hauled Mike and Carl into the room.

"Jonathan," Dale pointed at the mountain of a man, "you stay here and keep an eye on them while we get power to the lab. Make sure Doctor Parks is working. He is to gather what he needs in readiness for when we get the electricity going. Understand?"

Jonathan nodded. "Yes, boss."

"Jake will be outside standing watch."

"It's the middle of the night!" Carl said. "I'm exhausted."

"Shut up and get to work... *Doctor*," Dale sneered. He turned on his heel and pushed through the door.

Carl surveyed the disheveled lab. Discarded exam gloves littered the floor. Tubes and vials sat askew at the workstations next to overturned microscopes. "Well... shit."

Mike honestly had no idea why Dale had directed him to stay with Carl. What use could he be in this situation? His knees burned from the forced march, and the returning blood flow to his hand stung.

Carl turned to Jonathan. "You know this is never going to work?"

"I don't know. I'm not a doctor. And, anyway, I don't know what you think I can do about it?"

"Ugh!" Carl threw his hands up.

"Want my advice?" Jonathan asked.

"No!" Carl snapped.

"Look busy," Jonathan said, ignoring Carl's outburst.

"This is insane!" Carl stared around the trashed lab.

Mike sat on a nearby stool and stared at the toppled stack of petri dishes. Something nagged at him. Something right in front of him he'd overlooked. He'd vomited on Kyle, and Kyle had gone sex-crazy. Something about him vomiting. Something about *him* vomiting. The stress. The flashbacks of Nam. He'd had to do something, anything. The desperation.... He'd submerged in the dark waters of his mind... and brought them out. He'd done this. On purpose, sort of...

"Carl?" he said, not taking his eyes off the petri dishes and the gray countertop.

"What?!" Dr. Parks snapped.

"I think.... No. What if I could do it again? Or maybe teach Jonathan?"

"What the hell are you talking about?" Carl asked.

"The black bile. You know? On the bus? Made that guy go crazy jerkin his gherkin?"

"What good would that do?" Carl asked.

"What if we saved it and used it as a weapon to get out of here? Also, it would give Johnathan his joy back," Mike said. "Isn't that enough?"

Carl didn't look up from sifting through the chemicals in the cabinets. "It's as disgusting as it is dangerous. No telling what the person you throw it on would do. What if they became homicidal?"

"You could give me my joy back?" Jonathan asked.

"It's what I didn't tell Dale," Mike said. "Ever since I got sick on Kyle, I'm getting better, recovering."

"Can we do the summer of love stuff later? Help me get this stuff organized so I can see what we have to work with," Carl said, lining up bottles on the opposite counter.

"Do you really think that will help?" Mike asked.

"No, but—"

"Then what's the harm in me helping Jonathan?"

"Because," Carl rounded on Mike, "even if you did that yourself. *Made* yourself get sick, and even if you can teach Jonathan to do it. He'll just be a weapon. And if Dale finds out we can somehow manufacture happiness, then no one will need the Prophet, and by extension, Dale. And that means we'll be a threat to this messed up little fiefdom he's building, and he'll kill us."

"If you can make it so I don't need the Prophet's touch to be happy, I'll help you escape," Jonathan said.

Carl's gaze went to the giant Knight, then back to Mike. "You really think you can?"

"We won't know until we try."

"What am I supposed to do in the meantime?"

Mike shrugged and gave him a half-grin. "Look busy?"

Jonathan stared. "It's true? You really are getting better?"

"Yes," Mike said.

"Teach me then."

The lights came on.

"I'll be a son of a bitch," Carl said. "You do that. I'll see if there's anything that might help us escape."

"Let's go over here," Mike said, getting off the stool and heading for the most remote corner of the lab. "If this works, I don't want that sickness anywhere near Carl."

"Seconded," Carl called.

They grabbed a couple of lab stools and sat facing each other with a waste basket between them.

"First," Mike said. "I was scared. Completely in fight-or-flight mode. What are you scared of?"

Jonathan shrugged. "Not much."

"Not helpful," Mike said.

"It's not a flex, man. It's just that not much gets to me. It's why I'm still here. I mean, I'm scared of going back to prison, but there isn't much chance of that now."

Mike heaved a sigh. He wasn't sure how much the stress played a part in what he'd done. But he couldn't afford to leave anything out. If he wanted to escape, to help Penny and Sarah and everyone, he was going to have to take some risks.

He punched Jonathan in the face.

"Ow, hey, what the fuck!"

Mike punched him again.

"Fuck you man!"

"You want to hit me?" Mike asked.

"You bet your ass."

"I can't wait to tell the other Knights I kicked your ass. An old man, barely able to stand, beat the shit out of big scary Jonathan!"

The giant stood and grabbed Mike by the collar.

"Good," Mike grunted. "Now feel the dark water in your mind. Reach for what's underneath...."

Jonathan's grip loosened. Mike kicked him in the knee and jumped back.

"Fucking fuck!" the Knight yelled.

The door to the lab opened, and a Knight stuck his head in. "Everything okay in here?"

"Fuck off Jake!" Jonathan yelled.

The door shut.

"Close your eyes," Mike said.

"Screw that. You're going to hit me again."

"No. Keep the pain. Keep the anger. Use it to swim down into the dark water."

"I don't want to."

"Are you scared?"

"Yes," Jonathan whispered.

"Good. Every bad thing that ever happened to you is under there. Every bad thought. Every time you hurt someone. Every time you lost control. It's all there. You have to find it. You have to face it. Face how awful you really are. You're a monster. And the thing that makes you a monster is there, waiting."

"I..." Jonathan trailed off. "Cold... terrible...."

"Yes," Mike said. "It's awful. Find the darkness. Go to it."

"No... I..."

"GO TO IT!" Mike shouted. "It is you. It's always been who you are!"

"No."

"Then grab it, and throw it out."

"I... oh, God. I'm horrible.... I can't..."

"Embrace who you are, loser," Mike goaded.

"I feel it," Jonathan said. "It's disgusting."

"You are disgusting," Mike kept on. "You are trash. Feel that black ball of trash that makes up your soul."

"I'm not. It isn't me..." tears crept from the corners of Jonathan's eyes and trickled into his beard.

"Then get it out of you!"

"I can't..."

"If that isn't the real you, Jonathan, then why are you keeping it? Why are you afraid of it? It's always been in your mind, even before you were unrecovered. You know it's always been there."

"I know," Jonathan's voice wavered.

"Then get it out!" Mike yelled.

"I feel disgusting." Spittle formed strings between the Knight's agonized lips.

"Then get it out!" Mike yelled.

Jonathan's chest heaved.

"Get it out—get it out, get it out, get it out, get it out, get it out," Mike chanted, keeping the pressure on.

The convulsion worked its way up from the center of the big man's abdomen.

Mike backed away.

Chapter 25

Rachael

I stood frozen, disgusted, and unable to turn away from the carnage inside the restaurant. The building was almost all windows, hiding not a single detail of the unimaginably gory scene. There was no way to tell how many mutilated bodies rotted inside. A dozen maybe? Closest to the window, a corpse lay in a booth, head back as if in sleep, but no one sleeps with their ribcage ripped open. Literally ripped, as if by hand. Her ribs were cracked open as if someone had bent and snapped them to get at what lay under her breasts. On the table in front of her, a man's hand and part of his forearm lay on a plate, still wearing a wedding ring. There were bite marks on it. Human bite marks. And that was just in the first booth.

Blood spattered the glass. A lot of blood. Strewn about the rest of the place were parts from, I don't know, a dozen more bodies. Before this, I couldn't imagine what the phrase 'torn limb from limb' meant. Now I knew.

"Holy shit," Ed gasped.

Ed's words broke the spell. The bile rose in my throat. Everything inside me rushed up, seeking escape. I turned in time not to hit Sarah and puked all over the painted blue symbol in the disabled parking space.

Sarah put a hand on my back.

I twisted my arm back and held up a finger, doing my best to let her know to just leave me alone for a minute. I puked again. Then spit, and spit, and spit, trying to clear the foul bile from my mouth.

Something thumped on the glass.

I wiped my mouth on my sleeve and turned.

A man in priest's clothes banged on the glass, smearing blood across the inside. "The body of Christ! The body of Christ! This do in remembrance of me!"

"Holy shit!" Ed shouted, jumping back.

Sarah had her gun and flashlight trained on the window, teeth clamped together, lips curled back in a grimace of disgust.

I brought my pistol up, holding it and my flashlight together like Cassie taught me.

My stomach turned. Blood pounded in my head so loudly I wondered if they could hear it.

"I sent them to heaven!" the priest shouted. "He who believes in me shall have everlasting life!"

No one said anything. My finger moved from the side of the gun onto the trigger.

"God is inside each of us!" the priest shouted. His dark eyes were as big as pie plates, wide and crazy. "To look inside yourself is to know God. Let me look inside you! Let me look for God inside you!"

"Shut up!" Ed shouted, drawing down on the man.

"Give me my communion!"

"Fuck me," was all I could manage. "What do we do?"

"We shoot him," Ed said.

"Fuck that." I adjusted my grip on the pistol. "I'm not taking a chance of breaking the window and getting spattered with crazy juice."

"She's right," Sarah said. "Besides, it's best not to make that much noise. We don't know if there's anyone else dangerous around."

I squared my shoulders and shook off the urge to puke again. "I'm pretty dangerous."

"I think we should get Richard and Mae," Sarah said, not taking her eyes off the priest. "Show them what they missed out on."

"The body of Christ!" the priest shouted. "Let me eat your bodies of Christ!"

Goosebumps prickled my skin. "Sarah, this guy's really freaking me out."

"Me too," Sarah said.

"Me three," Ed agreed.

"Ed, go back and get Asim, Richard, and Mae," Sarah said. "I want them to see this guy before we have to end him."

"Why me?"

"Just do it, okay?"

"Yeah, not your do-boy," Ed said, but started backing away just the same, never taking his eyes off the priest in the window. Poor Ed, he just couldn't compete with Sarah's big-dick energy.

"How long before he figures out he can just walk out of there and come after us?" I whispered.

The priest looked at the door.

"Oh," Sarah said, "any second now."

The priest slid out of the booth.

I checked the path behind me with a quick turn of my head, then started backing up, putting some distance and a better angle between me and the door.

Sarah did the same, adding some distance between me and her as well, so that we formed a rough triangle with distinct fields of fire.

"Holy communion!" the priest inside yelled.

I sidestepped again. I didn't need to. My firing position was perfect, but my body needed something to do. Seconds ticked off into the night, uncounted. Faint noises and hushed voices drifted through the cold air as Ed got the others.

Inside, the priest ducked. The trash can and tray counter, obstructing my view. "You got him?"

"Yup," Sarah said. "Oh—oh, God..."

"What?" I asked, taking a step to the side.

"Don't," Sarah said. "Better that you don't see."

"What?" Damn her, I wasn't a kid.

"Let's just say, he's taking communion again."

Puke rose in my throat. I swallowed, hard.

"Get off me," Richard's voice came from behind me. "I can walk on my own."

"Now it's a party," I said, trying to sound casual.

Shuffling feet on pavement broke the winter silence.

"What is the situation?" Asim asked, drawing up beside me. He trained his rifle on the door. Jamie stood at his side, silent, and stoic as a stone. Her usual.

"Stage two," I said.

"Merciful God," he said.

"I thought you weren't religious?" I asked.

"Like... before?" Mae massaged her wrists where her bonds had been cut.

"The same thing as at your van earlier," I agreed.

The priest popped up in the beams of our flashlights like a jack-in-the-box. He held aloft something red, stringy, and dripping. "This do in remembrance of me!"

Richard recoiled. "Je-sus!"

"I don't think that's what Jesus would do," Asim said.

The bumper sticker from my neighbor's car back in DC popped into my head: WWJD.

The priest teased the stringy stuff into his mouth like a long, fat spaghetti noodle.

"Is that...." Richard turned, startled.

"Entrails," Sarah supplied.

Richard turned away.

"What are you going to do?" Mae asked.

The rifle cracked.

I jumped, nearly squeezing my trigger.

The priest fell.

"That," Asim said, lowering his rifle.

In my flashlight beam, all that remained was a spider-webbed hole in the glass.

"I—" Sarah started, checked herself, then said, "thanks."

"Why didn't it shatter?" Richard asked.

"Because," Asim said. "I'm shooting a rifle, perpendicular at twenty-five yards. I'm not, as you say, throwing rocks."

"Oh," Richard said.

"Now what?" I asked. "Do we go in?"

Asim turned to me and tilted his head. "Did you not listen to what I told you before, about what happened at the CDC? What I told you about my wife? Burning my vehicle? Did you not see what happened this afternoon at the van? No. We don't go in. We never go in. We hope that no one else ever goes in. It is a highly infectious biohazard zone, you understand."

He could have just said no, and I said as much.

"I am sorry, Rachael. My wife's death... the circumstances... it comes boiling out."

Now *I* was the dick.

"Hey!" Ed called. "There was a map in there!" He stood next to a passenger van in the parking lot, waving an atlas.

"So?" Sarah called.

"So there's markings for here and another place on the other side of the state," Ed said. "That's what."

"We got lucky," I said.

"You call this lucky?" Sarah asked.

"We've all got the parts we came here with, and we didn't have to go inside," I said, holstering my pistol. "So, yeah." She could be such a buzzkill sometimes.

"I guess we drive," Ed said.

"What about us?" Richard asked.

"What about you?" Ed said. "You're not riding with us and turning us into some kind of vomit psycho cannibals."

"Take the van," I said.

"And who's going to go in and get the keys?" Mae asked.

She had me there.

"Walk," Ed said.

I shook my head. "You're such a dick."

"Let them ride with you then," Ed shot back.

Uh, no.

"There's a used car place." Jamie pointed up the street. I could just make out the pennants draped between the darkened lampposts fluttering in the moonlight.

"Worked for us once," Sarah said.

I was kind of dubious about sending Richard and Mae off in some clunker from a third-rate place in this hick town. And after the way we treated them, I definitely didn't want them at our backs.

Chapter 26

Sarah

The going during the night was way too slow. All she could think about was Penny getting further and further away from her. It didn't help that everyone argued about everything before they could even get going: which car to take, who would get the map, who would drive, whether they would take the interstate in the interest of speed, everything.

Mae and Richard decided on a Jeep, much to Sarah's consternation. She'd passed enough of them on the side of the road in Montana to know they should have taken the Toyota pickup. Whatever. She'd won the battle of the map. This served two purposes: one, she got to set the pace, and two, she wouldn't have to worry about Richard and Mae ditching them. Though she questioned their motives for wanting to continue on to find the unrecovered. It was possible she'd still have to fight them at some point, but like the saying said, 'keep your enemies closer.'

Now, as the day crept into the afternoon, Sarah drummed her fingers on the steering wheel, sewing machined the leg she wasn't using to drive, and fidgeted in her seat. Between stops to siphon gas, scrounging for food, and Mae's pea-sized bladder, they must have stopped ten times between the Awful House and now.

Her stomach gurgled, but not hungrily. She wasn't getting proper nutrition. At all. Refusing to stop, she'd had Rachael, who was napping in back with Koontz and King, pass her up a pack of ramen, which she ate by taking bites out of the raw brick. She wouldn't stop again, not with the possibility that Penny could be at the next rendezvous. But the thought that Penny could be killed at the hands of a vomit psycho, or have become one herself, sent the mix of ramen and canned food quaking toward its inevitable release.

The asphalt of the two-lane had an odd tan color, like it had been made of dirt, cracked, buckled, and weedy. At least this rural route was blessedly free of stalled cars and wrecks. Sarah's mood was as dark as the threatening January sky and the black cloth hanging from the occasional house they drove past, indicating bodies. Bodies that no one would ever clear. Not in her lifetime. What if the unrecovered she chased had stopped at one of these? What if Penny's body lay there? What if she never found her child? No. She had to stop thinking that. Instead, she needed to steel herself for what was to come. Plan for possibilities.

They were getting close now, thirty miles. Asim wasn't any help at the moment, dozing with his head jammed between the doorpost and the seat. "Rach?"

In the rearview mirror, Rachael's head appeared in the little cloth tunnel connecting the bed cap to the cab. "Yeah?"

"We're getting close."

"How close?"

"Depends on traffic." Sarah tried to smile. It didn't work.

"Hilarious," Rachael said without a trace of humor.

"Less than an hour."

In the mirror, Rachael made a wry face. "I'll put the coffee on."

"Yeah, that's not funny either." Sarah would kill for a decent cup of coffee.

Sarah drummed her fingers on the steering wheel again. "Would you come on up here? We need to come up with a plan for how we're going to handle this."

"Are you okay?" Rachael asked.

"Okay... was another lifetime. Why?"

"You're being nice."

Sarah gritted her teeth. "Just please come up here."

Rachael grunted as she squeezed through the windows between the cab and the back. "Good thing I'm not a big girl." She righted herself in the back seat and kissed Dickens's head. "Who's a good boy?" Then to Sarah, "What's the meeting place again?"

Sarah handed the map to Rachael and let out a long sigh. "Frank's Transmission under a billboard of Jesus holding a beer that reads, *King of Jews, King of beers*. God, I hate the South."

"As you say, but It is not the South you hate." Asim righted himself in the seat and adjusted his stingy-brim hat. "It is poverty, ignorance, and indoctrination that are the root of this, you understand. There are, or, were, kind, educated people in the Southern United States. And there were small-minded bigots in the North."

"Thanks for the social studies lesson, *professor*," Rachael said. "But your ancestors weren't lynched here. Enslaved here. It wasn't unsafe for you to travel here. Go into the wrong store, the wrong town, the wrong—"

"It has *always*—" Asim slapped his knee. "—been unsafe for me to travel in the American South, you understand. Afraid to wear a keffiyeh, a kaftan, afraid to open my mouth and speak for fear my accent will mark me as a terrorist and get me killed. It has always been unsafe."

As Sarah listened to the exchange, she realized how privileged she'd been before the world fell. How little she thought about these kinds of struggles. She'd run away from the South because of a different set of terrors, ones she didn't want to bring to mind. So, she changed the subject.

"We need to talk about what we're going to do when we get to Frank's Transmission," Sarah said.

"It is impossible to know what to do when we don't know the situation," Asim said.

"Then that's first," Sarah said. "Find out what the situation is."

"An advance team," Rachael said, "like last time."

"Hopefully, better than last time," Sarah said.

"Two, perhaps," Asim said. "And a pair of binoculars."

"What about Mae and Richard?" Rachael asked.

"As the advance team?" Sarah asked. "What if they just walk in and warn—"

"No." Rachael sighed. "You and I are going ahead. I thought that was a given. I mean, what are we going to do with Mae and Richard?"

"Good question," Sarah agreed. "I don't relish the thought of tying them up again."

"Perhaps they can be persuaded to wait with Ed, Jamie, and I," Asim said.

Rachael spotted it first—the billboard in the distance, partially obscured by a stand of trees, featuring Jesus holding a beer. "There." She pointed.

Sarah squinted into the twilight, then pulled the truck onto a dirt driveway behind some trees. The house belonging to the driveway was just visible in the distance, an eighth of a mile or so up the track. The field on her right, encased in a barbed-wire fence, featured dead, knee-high grass. Most likely, there's no one home. They'd have to chance it.

Ed's truck and Mae's Jeep pulled in behind Sarah.

In the back seat, Dickens spun in a circle, panting.

"Hey," Rachael grumbled, "watch the tail, buddy."

Sarah got out, quietly pulling her door to, instead of slamming it shut. She opened the door for Dickens, who jumped out, ran to the closest tree, and watered it. She'd pushed hard to get here and needed to water a tree of her own.

Richard got out of the Jeep and shut the door with a thump.

"Quietly!" Sarah hissed.

At her side, Koontz let out a soft "woof."

"You too," Sarah chided. To everyone else she said, "we leave in five minutes. Everyone shut up, focus, and put your game faces on."

"No one has a watch," Rachael said. "We all just used to use our phones. How will—"

Sarah let out a loud sigh and rubbed her temples.

"I have a watch," Asim said.

"Of course you do," Rachael waved a derisive hand.

"Shut. Up!" Sarah growled through gritted teeth.

"I've gotta pee," Rachael said, and started heading up the driveway.

Sarah needed to empty her bladder as well, and started walking in the opposite direction, along the place where the overgrown hedges met the field. Asim followed. Weird. She wondered idly, as she made her way along, if the social mores of toileting were different where he came from. When Sarah heard his footsteps stop, she went a bit further. Then she had to hiss at Dickens to back off, lest he get peed on.

Koontz woofed.

"I told you," Sarah said, "we have to be quiet."

And just as Sarah lamented not having TP, Asim hissed something.

It took a second to register, but when it clicked, he'd said, "get down." Sarah sidestepped her puddle and dropped. His barely audible voice drifted through the grass. "I think Rachael's in trouble. Can you see?"

Sarah tried to move closer to Asim, but the noise of just moving her hand in the grass rustled louder than Asim's words. From a crouch, Sarah could just make out some kind of moss monster or something marching Rachael down the road at gunpoint.

Koontz let out a low growl.

They were out of effective pistol range, and if Sarah tried to move closer, it would be noisy as hell. There was no way to help.

Sarah ground her teeth so loudly she was afraid the bad guy would hear it. Her pistol was in her hand. She didn't remember drawing it.

Again, Koontz growled his displeasure at being silenced and unable to do his job.

"Hush," Sarah whispered.

The voice of the gunman, then Sarah's friends' replies, drifted across the field, but the stalks rustling in the winter breeze swallowed their words.

Goddamn it! King was out there somewhere. Rachael knew his attack command. Why didn't she give it? But, Sarah knew King was a well-trained dog. She alone could compel the hundred-pound K-9 to attack. Rachael must know that too.

And then they were moving, marching off down the road in a wide line with Mossman behind them.

"Shit," Sarah cursed when they were lost to sight behind the trees that shielded the trucks from sight of the transmission shop.

Asim rose cautiously and swept the area, looking through the sight of his rifle. "There may be others, but I don't think so. If there were, they'd have known we were here."

"We've got to do something," Sarah said.

Dickens panted at her side. Koontz looked into the distance, ears pricked up.

"I think we must watch the building," Asim said. "It's not safe for just the two of us to approach. Not in daylight, you understand."

"Shit." First, they took Penny and the other kids. And now, Rachael, again. As if Rachael hadn't almost died escaping the first time. A deep chasm consumed Sarah's stomach. She couldn't protect anyone. Not Penny, not Rachael, or Jamie, or Ed.

"They are in grave danger," Asim said, cautiously making his way back to their trucks. "If any of those unrecovered go into stage two near them..."

Chapter 27

Mike

Jonathan vomited violently into the rubber wastebasket between them. As the big man bent over, Mike stepped back again, his eyes tracing the stray droplets of viscous black slime spattering the floor around Jonathan.

Again and again, Jonathan's chest heaved. Each time, more inky goo plopped into the brown, rubber, rectangular bin. Mike's eyes never left the floor, mapping each poisonous particle that marred the linoleum.

"Clean-up on aisle seven," he called to Carl.

Carl rounded the row of tables and cabinets with a beaker in his hand. "You really *are* feeling better."

"Huh?" Mike asked.

"You just made a joke." He stared at Jonathan, still bent over, spitting black, stringy mucus into the bin.

"I guess I am," Mike said. "We did it. We proved the unrecovered can do this voluntarily."

"You beat the shit out of me," Jonathan said between expectorations.

"Well," Mike admitted, "almost."

"And?" Carl asked.

"And it feels good," Mike said. "Feels like there's hope."

"How are you feeling, Jonathan?" Carl asked.

"I honestly don't know."

"I'll take it," Carl said. "All I can come up with in here is a sedative. Maybe we can dose some of the unrecovered?"

Mike's eyes fell on the trash can. "I've got a better idea."

"No," Carl said. "You'd be killing them. It's a death sentence."

"They're dead already," Jonathan said. "No hope. No joy. And no promise of anything better. All they have is the presence of each other's minds on the dark water of despair."

"You're like a damn poet," Mike said.

"I wrote a little in prison. Took a class. Point is, Mike's right. If there's any way out of this, it's over Dale's dead body... Hey... I feel something...."

"What?" Carl asked.

"It's like the mind water going down a little. Like a hint of sun behind the clouds."

"So," Carl said. "It wasn't the tau."

"Might still be," Mike said. "Remember, I was starting to feel a little better before the puking episode on the bus."

"Maybe," Carl admitted. "And maybe we'll never know."

"Well," Mike said. "We're going to need an action plan for when Dale comes back."

"Is there another way out of here?" Jonathan asked.

"I think," Carl said. "In the back, by the offices. I didn't explore too far. I was looking for chemicals, not paperclips."

"We'd better find out." Jonathan nodded toward the brown bucket of bile. "I want to hit

Dale and whoever is with him the second they open the door. And if this shit is as toxic as you say it is, we need to find another way out."

"It'll contaminate the entire area," Carl agreed.

A quick search yielded a locked door at the far end of three small offices, but the door had a small window.

"We can knock it out when the time comes," Mike said.

Jonathan shook his head. "Safety glass. See the wire mesh? Better to bash the whole door open."

"You're sure you can do that?" Carl asked.

The mountainous man frowned down at him.

"I'm asking because based on what we've seen, I think you have to be the one to douse Dale. Mike and I can't take the risk of coming in contact with it."

"So I'm just fucking extra?" Jonathan asked.

"It's not like that," Carl said. "It's yours, so it's less likely to affect you the way...."

The big man nodded. "I got you."

"So you have to throw it, then get past us to get the door open."

"Seems like I'm pretty important to this plan," Jonathan said.

Mike couldn't tell what the giant was getting at. "Sure," he drew the word out.

Jonathan looked at the backs of his large, scarred hands. "I never had kids...."

"I don't..." Mike started.

Jonathan waved a hand. "I kind of always thought I would, you know, before all this. Settle down, maybe get a bouncer gig, or well, I guess I'd never pass the background check for a security job, but... Yeah, even though I knew I was no good, I figured if I could just straighten out." He drew a deep breath. "I want to help you save those kids. Let's go fuck Dale over."

"Gloves, gowns, masks, and face shields," Carl said. "Full Level Three PPE."

"You might have mentioned that before I made Jonathan throw up," Mike said.

Carl looked him up and down. "You're fine, aren't you?"

Once they put on protective gear from head to toe, Jonathan rapped on the door.

A Knight outside cracked the door open.

"They've got something. Get Dale," Jonathan said.

The door closed.

"If we've got all this shit on," Jonathan said, "then it doesn't have to be me who throws the bucket, does it?"

"I guess not," Carl said.

"Then I'll stand by the back door with Mike. You throw the puke."

"Why Mike?"

"Cause he can't run fast, can he?"

"I'm right here," Mike said.

The door interrupted their conversation, banging open.

"So what is this cure you've con—"

Dale never had a chance to finish.

Jonathan grabbed the garbage can full of puke and hurled it.

Dale pushed the Knight into the room and slammed the door.

"Jesus," the Knight screamed. "What the fuck!"

"Shit!" Jonathan yelled.

"Go!" Mike screamed. Mike didn't wait around to see any more. He started moving for the door, white vinyl gown rustling.

Jonathan pushed past him in the narrow corridor, sending Mike bumping into the cubicle partitions on his left.

Carl had a hand on his back, steadying him.

"You get the fuck back here!" Dale's muffled voice came from the corridor.

A thunderous pounding came from the hallway.

Metal groaned.

"Gotta go," Carl urged.

"No shit," Mike gasped.

"Goddamn you!" Dale shouted.

Jonathan ran at the offending door, shoulder first. It banged open.

Shots whizzed down the hallway.

"What now?" Carl asked.

Jonathan ducked through the doorframe and sent a few shots down the hall. "He's getting more Knights, come on!" Jonathan led them down the hall, then ducked inside the first open door. He closed it carefully behind them and put a finger to his lips.

"I guess we never had a chance to flesh out this part of the plan," Carl said.

"Shut up," Jonathan hissed.

"Where are you fucks?!" Dale screamed.

Footsteps, running, fading.

"Come on out, and I won't harm you," Dale said.

"He's full of shit," Jonathan whispered.

"The other guy headed back toward the others," Carl said, his eyes wide with fear.

"So?" Jonathan asked. "He infects them and it clears the way."

"I need you to synthesize your cure," Dale called. "I can't kill you, see?"

"You idiot," Mike said. "The kids!"

"Shit," Jonathan said. He opened the door, leaned out into the hall, and fired.

Chapter 28

Rachael

Behind Frank's Transmission, a group of people stood silently at the side of a school bus, waiting to board.

"Found these sneakin' around behind the treeline," the gunman said.

A lanky middle-aged man dressed in army winter gear approached. He rubbed his large, triangular nose on his sleeve. "What for?" he asked Ed.

"What for, what?" Ed asked back.

"Don't jerk me around, son. Why were you hiding back there?"

"We were coming for the rendezvous," Richard supplied.

The gunman poked Richard in the back with the rifle. "Ain't no one asked you a damn thing, junior."

The army guy cocked his head at Ed. "You ain't unrecovered. I can't feel your mind."

"Neither is she." The gunman poked me in the back this time.

I could just strike out with my right leg, maybe catch him in the crotch with my heel, maybe. Or maybe get shot and never find Penny or get my revenge for Cassie.

The army guy sidestepped to stand in front of me. “What’s your business here?”

Sometimes, the truth seemed the best. “I’m looking for my friend’s daughter.”

The army guy nodded. “Well, we’ll get you sorted out, one way or another. Until then,” —he nodded to the gunman— “we’ll tie ‘em up. We’ll take ‘em with us. Don’t want to be late for the next stop.”

My muscles coiled in readiness. As soon as he approached, I’d end him with a throat punch.

The army guy produced a fistful of plastic handcuffs from his pocket.

I tensed, ready.

That bastard in the mossy suit stuck the muzzle of his gun at the base of my skull. Fuck. There went that idea.

The army guy held my eyes as he slid the plastic over my wrists. He smiled, lifting the corner of a purple, livid scar running diagonally from eye to chin, crossing his mouth. This guy had seen some shit, and maybe not the best to engage him lightly.

“Why not just plug ‘em and leave ‘em?” the gunman asked.

“Because, Frank, what if there’s more? What if this whole thing is blown? How did they know we were going to be here?”

“Why not ask ‘em right here?” Frank asked.

“Because I’m calling this thing,” the army guy said. “You’re the one who isn’t that useful anymore, so shut up.”

The gunman snapped his mouth shut so hard I heard his teeth click together.

“Don’t worry,” the army guy’s tone softened. “When we get to The Prophet, I’ll put you in the front of the line... behind me.”

They marched us onto the bus and shoved us to the back. I sat wedged next to Mae and Richard in one seat. Across from us, Jamie sat on the aisle, with Ed by the window.

In front of Ed, a scruffy-looking young man tipped back an enormous bottle of tequila... and swallowed noisily.

The bus lurched into motion. The tequila splashed.

Ed licked his lips.

Chapter 29

Sarah

The pale disk of the sun cast a wan light through the thin, seamless layer of gray clouds. The dormant trees looked on, naked, silent, angular witnesses to perhaps the last group of people ever to pass this way.

Asim passed the rifle to Sarah. She pressed the stock to her shoulder and peered through the scope. Branches blocked her view. She shifted her weight, careful not to move her feet and rustle the dead leaves cushioning her middle-aged knees. The scope revealed the back of the transmission shop. In an empty space surrounded by defunct cars, an idling school bus closed its doors.

Sarah searched for tiny figures and found none. “See any kids?”

“No,” Asim said, betraying no emotion.

“What about Rachael, Jamie, the others?”

“They got on first,” Asim said, “surrounded by men with assault rifles.”

“Shit. Any bright ideas?”

“Nothing except to follow.”

Sarah lowered the rifle and turned to Asim. "How? It's not like I can blend in with traffic."

Asim scratched at the silver whiskers on his jaw. "This many unrecovered I can sense in my mind. We can stay well back, for a time...."

Dickens snuffed at Sarah's ear. She pushed his snout aside gently. "What do you mean, 'for a time?'"

"Please," Asim said. "My old bones are stiffening up in this cold."

"Explain."

Asim grunted with the effort of getting to his feet behind the cover of a tree. "It's fading," he said, rubbing circulation back into his legs. "The mind water, feeling the minds of the other unrecovered. Whatever happens with the vomiting, expelling the inner darkness..." He trailed off.

Sarah needed more than that. "Asim?"

"I think... I must be healing. My brain. My spirit. What precious little joy there is in these dire circumstances, whatever tiny shred of hope, I can feel it now. And, as I do, the connection with the unrecovered fades."

Sarah's heart sank. She couldn't win. Couldn't catch a damn break. "Let's get to the truck. Be ready to roll. Dogs, come."

They didn't have to wait long. Within minutes, the bus rolled out of the dirt lot behind the transmission shop, heading west over the leaf-strewn blacktop.

Sarah waited until the bus disappeared from view, then pulled onto the road, following. It turned out she didn't need Asim's guidance. Not yet. The bus left a fresh trail of tire tracks in the otherwise undisturbed layer of brown leaves and weeds growing from the cracks in the disused asphalt. She wondered how long until roads like this disappeared completely? How long until enterprising trees and shrubs took root under the buckling roadbed? How long until the deer, wolves, and coyotes ruled where once people remade the world according to their designs? Hers could be the last vehicle ever to traverse this stretch of blacktop.

Asim detached the scope from the rifle and looked ahead each time they came to a place where the road crossed a stretch of open ground.

"It is fortunate they're traveling in a bright yellow vehicle, and not a camouflaged army truck," Asim said. "The way is clear."

Sarah passed a wide stretch of farmland. Overgrown brown stalks bent and bowed to patches of snow.

"You still feel them?" she asked.

Asim nodded. "I do. The best I can tell, they're still ahead. Still moving." He coughed, cleared his throat. "But it's not exact, you understand. It is... an impression."

Sarah's stomach knotted. "Terrific." She needed facts. Certainty. Data. Impressions could go fuck themselves. She needed Penny.

The sun dipped below the horizon. Sarah dared not turn on the headlights. The needle on her truck's tank flirted with "E." She did not want to stop to siphon gas. But just like traveling in the empty country of her Montana home, she knew, when there was an opportunity to get gas, by God, you had to stop and get gas, or else risk getting stranded on some lonely stretch of road.

When she spotted a likely vehicle resting on the roadside, she parked with the fuel door facing the one on the stalled Lincoln. Her hand-crank siphon made reassuring gurgling noises. She cursed every second it took to transfer the fuel.

The bus, with its giant tanks, likely wouldn't have to deal with this problem. And based on the level of coordination she'd seen so far, they might even have fuel waiting at their pre-scheduled stops.

By the time Sarah finished and got underway again, her frustration at having lost so much time made her foot heavy on the pedal.

"Perhaps we should slow down," Asim said, "for safety, you understand."

"Can you still feel the minds of the unrecovered ahead?"

"Sometimes," he admitted.

"Then I'm not slowing down."

Sarah swerved around a stalled car, almost completely hidden by the tall grass growing from the cracks in the road.

"Slow down," Asim urged.

Ahead, the red glow of taillights gave Sarah permission to ease her foot off the accelerator. The unrecovered on this particular bus weren't worried about stealth, apparently. Sarah's mind drifted to the radio tucked behind the back seat. Almighty. The promised airstrike.

Asim dozed off and on throughout the night, but the thought of Penny somewhere ahead kept Sarah's focus sharp. She fixated on the taillights, staying just on the edge of sight. Creeping around curves, never touching the brakes. The hours of darkness stretched out into an interminable cat-and-mouse game with the twin glowing orbs on the back of the bus.

In the deepest bitter watches of that moonless, overcast night, Sarah held well back as the bus made its careful way across an empty expanse, then onto a bridge with cars crushed out of the way. About halfway across, a small sign riveted to the rotten, rusty green girders proclaimed, "Missouri state line." So, somewhere out there in the impenetrable darkness lay the black, untamed waters of the Mississippi.

She chased the bus along a series of turns onto a tiny two-lane road. And, after heading north into the cold most of the night, their path turned west again.

As the world grew light, Asim said, "Slow down."

Sarah didn't want to hear that shit again. "I've got it under control," she said.

"No. Slow *down*," Asim asserted. "I feel them ahead. I feel their minds. Something is happening!"

No sooner had the words floated across the stuffy air of the pickup's cab than Sarah rounded a curve to see the bus.

"Shit!" She hit the brakes.

The bus swerved back and forth across the road.

At first, Sarah thought the driver was trying to prevent her from passing, but as the juking bus tipped and rocked on its fat wheels, it became clear some shit was going down inside.

"Stay back," Asim said. "I think I know what this is."

Chapter 30

Mike

"Argh!" Dale screamed.

Running footsteps.

"Winged him," Jonathan said. "Come on!"

Mike followed as fast as he could manage, wincing at the pain in his leg.

Mike lost sight of Carl and Jonathan around a corner. But there was no mistaking the growing shouts and bangs of mayhem echoing down the corridor.

He rounded the corner in time to see the infected Knight attacking a woman in the ER waiting room. Half a dozen people tried to pull him off and became infected themselves. More people tried to help—twenty in all.

"No!" Mike's shout didn't carry. There wasn't enough air left in his lungs. Too late anyway.

The result was almost instantaneous. Groping hands and mouths pulled at the guy.

Across the room, Dale held a hand to his blood-soaked shoulder. "Everyone stop! Get out!"

Sharp cries of joy, pain, frustration, and avarice rose from the writhing scrum of bodies on the floor. A ring of onlookers formed, careful to keep back from the frightening outpouring of intense emotion now all but foreign to the unrecovered.

Mike slipped in behind the crowd, eyes searching the room for Penny and the other children. He saw no sign.

"She's fucking biting me!" someone shouted.

"Give me your seed!" a male voice pleaded.

"Candy!!"

Mike's ears pricked up.

"Candy!" the voice was adult—no mistaking it.

Mike gave silent thanks, skirting an overturned plastic chair behind the crowd. He righted it and climbed up. On the other side, by the doors, he saw Carl's dark shape, also looking for the kids.

A hand clutched his shirt.

Mike started and turned.

"Everyone stop!" Dale shouted again.

"Easy," Jonathan said. He helped Mike down. "They're not here. Come on."

The giant plowed through the gathered onlookers, practically dragging Mike in his wake.

The cries and exclamations from the pandemonium in the center of the room made him turn. He caught the briefest image of struggling bodies, torn clothes, blood, a foot in someone's greedy, slobbering mouth. Mike gagged.

"Sampson! Stop!" Dale shouted.

"Gotta move," Jonathan said.

Jonathan practically burst the sliding doors off their tracks as he shoved them aside. The icy bite of the winter air suppressed Mike's nausea.

"They must be here somewhere!" Carl said behind him.

A Humvee idled in front of the ER entrance. Standing beside it, a bored-looking Knight stood with his rifle on a sling, in hand, but pointed at the ground. Mike did his best to keep up with the young giant, but Jonathan loped ahead.

Carl took his arm, helping him take the pressure off his bad leg.

"What's going on in there?" The Knight asked as Jonathan approached.

"Boss is losing it," Jonathan said. "Better get in there."

"Stop them!" Dale shouted from the door.

The Knight had just enough warning for his eyes to widen as Jonathan's melon-sized fist slammed into his nose.

In one deft motion, Jonathan grabbed the gun from the Knight as he fell, then turned the gun toward the door.

"No!" Mike shouted. He gasped for breath and could manage no more.

"We don't know where the kids are."

Two shots came from inside the hospital.

"Gotta go!" Jonathan said. He opened the Humvee door and flung the surprised driver to the pavement and delivered a savage kick to the man's midsection. "Get in!"

"Not..." Winded, Mike couldn't finish. He didn't want to leave without Penny. But Carl manhandled him into the back seat, then ran around to the passenger side.

The Humvee started rolling before Carl had his door closed.

As Mike heaved, gasping for air, he stared at the slumped figure in the seat across from him.

"Who's that?" Carl asked.

Mike reached across, but the large raised hump of the Humvee's middle was too wide for him to tug on the man's coat.

"Hey!" Carl shouted. "Who the hell is in the backseat?"

"Don't especially care now," Jonathan said as he piloted the truck out of the hospital parking lot.

"What if he's got a *gun*?" Carl asked.

"Then he'd have shot at us."

Breathing a little easier, Mike leaned across the space again, resting his belly on the hump. He grabbed the man's sleeve.

The hooded figure turned.

"Vic?" Carl asked.

Vic nodded, then his head lolled.

"Are you sick?" Carl yelled over the engine noise.

"Too many touches," Vic said.

"What?" Carl asked.

"Too many," Mike gasped for breath. "Touches."

Vic rested his hooded head back on the window glass.

"We have to go back for the kids," Mike managed. Penny was all that mattered to him now. Escaping was good. Freedom of action. And he couldn't help Penny as a captive.

"The fuck we do," Jonathan said. "We got company!" The Humvee swerved across the road.

Mike turned to see two pickup trucks following them, trying to get alongside. But stalled cars and the detritus of the apocalypse littered the road, leaving them little room to maneuver.

"Buckle up bitches," Jonathan said. "It's going to be a bumpy ride."

The statement surprised Mike. Not its content, but its tone. Jonathan said it with something akin to glee in his voice. He'd gone through stage two only minutes before. It took Mike much longer to regain that level of joy... hadn't it?

He reached for the seatbelt and struggled to make the connection. Thinking as he did, that perhaps he hadn't really had anything to feel good about. The big man's words about being a bad-guy echoed in his ears. Perhaps the speed of Jonathan's return to joy was situational. It seemed Jonathan was in his element behind the wheel, on the run.

A thump jolted Mike in his seat. He turned to see one truck right on their rear bumper.

"Can't this thing go any faster?" Carl asked.

"Nope," Jonathan said. "It's pretty gutless." He cranked the wheel, avoiding a stalled car. "Not meant for speed." He cranked the wheel again.

Mike's head knocked painfully against the window.

"But it's got other qualities," Jonathan said.

Mike could almost hear the giant grinning.

The truck thumped over a curb, throwing Mike into his restraint. This time Mike was ready, hands out, bracing himself.

A loud crunch sounded behind them.

The sharp maneuvering threw Vic around like a rag doll.

"One down!" Jonathan reported with glee.

Mike craned his neck to see one of the pick-up trucks crunched against a telephone pole, steam rising from the ruined hood.

"Vic," Mike called, "put your seatbelt on!"

The Prophet complied, reaching for the straps as if swimming through molasses.

They sped across the great, knee-high lawn of a college or some municipal building. Ambulances, tents, and the abandoned hulks of trucks and support vehicles littered the grounds.

"Why aren't they shooting at us?" Carl asked.

"The Prophet," Jonathan said. "Can't risk killing the golden calf."

"Can we just call him Vic?" Carl asked, clearly disgusted.

Between the front seats, the radio crackled to life. "This message is for Mike Sampson." Dale's voice. "Are you listening?"

No one spoke or moved to pick up the radio mic.

"Hope you are," Dale's tinny voice continued through the speaker. "You have stolen something very precious of mine. And I have something very precious of yours. You have a beautiful granddaughter. It would be a shame if anything happened to her. And you have stolen the happiness of a large group of angry people. I might find it difficult to keep her safe under those circumstances."

Mike's heart seized in his chest. Fear's icy fingers crept down his spine and squeezed. He'd failed Sarah by not being there for her. He'd failed his wife, Penny, when he didn't return from Vietnam. No way was he going to fail her namesake. No. Way. "We have to go back."

Chapter 31

Rachael

Fucking pissed. That's what I was. Pissed at myself. Pissed at the Knights. Pissed that Sarah and Asim hadn't shot that shitbag, Frank. Captured again. Again! Between the Sea Ridge Power Station and the jail back in New Hope, this was the third damn time I'd been kidnapped in the last year. The second time in a week. What the hell was it about me? Just bad luck.

I sat in that green vinyl seat like a coiled spring, waiting for my moment, like Cassie taught me. Just the thought of her made my anger rise another notch. My heart pounded.

Across from me, Jamie sat in the aisle seat, with Ed by the window. Her bruises had turned a sickly yellow. Her face betrayed no emotion at all. Ed looked out the window, but his reflection in the glass showed unmistakable glistening tears.

The gun weighed heavy on my ankle. I wanted it. My fingers itched to feel its weight. Its kick, as I fired supersonic slugs of lead into Cassie's killers. There were six of them,

Knights, I mean, on the bus with me. Two up front by the driver. Two in the middle, and Frank and some other asshole about three seats ahead of me. Too many to take out before I got shot myself.

But I had an edge this time. These guys were amateurs. Not that I'm an expert, but they didn't search me, and they cuffed me in front. Mae and Richard wore cuffs, too. Neither would meet my eye. Well, fuck them anyway. They were nothing to me. Nothing but trouble.

The bus swerved.

I stuck a foot into the aisle to brace myself.

A thump next to me made me turn.

Jamie's head knocked into Ed's, hard enough for me to actually feel it across the aisle. She turned, dazed. Her confused eyes looked past me. Her chest heaved.

I scooted hard up against Mae.

"Hey," she grumbled, "what the..."

Jamie turned her head too quickly, spraying the people on the seat in front of her with black goo. Ed took the brunt of it, too, snapping out of his window woolgathering and turning, shocked, to stare at his wife.

He stood, reached his bound hands over the swearing, puke-covered guy in front of him, and grabbed the bottle of tequila.

Tequila guy and the lady next to him got to their feet, too. He shouted at Ed; she shouted at everyone.

"LOVE ME!" the lady screamed, grabbing up the guy in the seat ahead of me and squeezing.

"Hey, what the fuck?" the guy next to Frank shouted. He grabbed the woman, but grimaced, pulling his bile-covered hand back and staring at it. Then, just that fast, his face changed. "OH, Daddy's gonna get some pussy!" He lurched away toward the front of the bus.

I got to my feet, backing away from all the crazy puke-psychos.

People were getting to their feet, shouting and screaming all kinds of crazy shit. Somewhere in front, a gun fired. Once. Twice. Then a burst of three shots.

The bus swerved crazily. Tires squealed on the asphalt. I threw myself into the back seat on top of a fat, dazed, middle-aged man to avoid colliding with someone infected by puke.

We screeched to a stop. I got out of the guy's lap before he could perv-out. My back bumped against the emergency exit. I already escaped this way once. Old tricks are the best tricks.

I slammed my hip into the emergency release and jumped down, knees bent. The pavement rushed up and slammed into my feet. My ass touched my heels. The momentum carried me forward, and I face-planted anyway, kissing the road. It wasn't so bad though; my poor legs took most of the impact. I rolled into it, coming up on my feet and duck-walking into the tall grass by the roadside. The coppery taste of blood filled my mouth, kicking my adrenaline up another notch. Crouching with my hands bound, I pulled up my pant leg and fumbled the Beretta into my other hand.

The plastic cuffs didn't do anything for my grip, but still allowed me some measure of bracing for the kickback. I aimed for the front door of the bus.

An angry, confused, unrecovered guy stumbled down the steps onto the road.

I thumbed the safety off.

Another unrecovered came out of the bus, a lady this time.

I lined up the front and rear sights of my pistol.

A guy covered in blood staggered out.

I moved my finger to the trigger.

The first unrecovered with a gun came down the bus steps.

I squeezed.

The pistol barked.

The gunman dropped with a hole in his chest.

"For Cassie," I whispered.

More unrecovered came out, some confused, some crazy with dopamine lust.

I didn't care.

Inside and outside the bus, people shouted all manner of shit. I don't know what they were saying. To me, it was only noise. Sonic clutter.

Someone tumbled out of the back of the bus.

I glanced. Not a Knight. I lined up on the door again.

Another gun.

Squeeze.

Crack.

Center mass, baby! Right in the chest. Two down, four to go. I had a taste for it now. The knack. The will. I was stronger. For once, I was the one in control. Literally calling the shots. It was my turn. Cassie's turn.

Tears threatened to ruin my aim. I put my tongue between my teeth and bit. Pain and anger pushed the sorrow down.

Movement at the back of the bus.

A Knight on the pavement.

I swung my arms around.

He saw me and raised his gun.

Sight. Squeeze. Crack.

He stared open-mouthed, gun half raised, then fell backward on the blacktop. Three down.

I turned my gun back to the front.

Fucking Frank. His fat, shaggy form leaped from the bus, rolling toward the grass. A strategic maneuver. That meant two things: he was thinking rationally—so not infected, and he knew I was there.

Squeeze, squeeze. They weren't perfect shots. But I was pretty sure I'd winged him.

Again, I trained my Beretta on the front door of the bus.

Another gunman.

Squeeze.

This time, all I got was a click.

Shit. Empty mag. I hadn't even noticed the slide was retracted.

The guy with the gun lined up on me.

My brain told my body to move in two directions at once. *Dive into the grass* and *go for the dead guy's gun.*

My body didn't answer.

Chapter 32

Sarah

"Who's shooting?" Sarah asked.

"Not me," Asim said, not taking his eyes from the scope, "but someone with some skill. A Knight, as you call them, was killed as soon as he got off the bus."

Again, a distant gun barked.

"And another."

"Rachael," Sarah said, breaking cover and running forward. She drew her pistol as her feet pounded the pavement.

"Out of my line of fire!" Asim called after her.

The gun, most likely Rachael's Baretta, cracked again. This time, a Knight who'd jumped from the back of the bus stared at his chest, then fell over backward.

No time to worry about Asim's rifle. She had to save Rachael from herself.

The same mossy bastard who'd captured Sarah's friends jumped from the bus and scampered for cover.

Rachael fired three times. That made six by Sarah's count. She'd be out of ammo. Sarah urged her legs to pump faster. Fit, but still fifty-one, her breath came in gasps as she closed the final feet to where she thought Rachael hid in the weeds.

The gray woodland camo of Rachael's coat stood out among the tan stalks, twenty feet away.

Another Knight got off the bus and raised his gun.

Sarah heard Rachael's pistol dry fire just as she dove on top of the young woman, knocking her to the ground.

The gunshot and hiss of the bullet past her ear were simultaneous.

Behind her, Asim's rifle cracked.

Tumbling in the weeds atop Rachael, Sarah couldn't see the result.

"Fuck," Rachael said, "get off me, you stupid cow."

Sarah didn't care. She'd saved Rachael, now she had only one consuming thought. "Penny?"

Rachael bucked her body, throwing Sarah off. "She's not there."

Sarah righted herself and brought her gun to bear on the scene by the bus. Muffled shouts and curses came from inside. Murky shapes moved and struggled behind the windows, which partially reflected the gray sky and brown weeds.

Sarah adjusted her grip on the gun. "What about Jamie and Ed?"

"Stage two," Rachael said, crawling up beside her, "all over Ed."

"Shit."

"Yeah. I think his thing is alcohol, thank God. He grabbed some guy's tequila and pounded most of the bottle."

"Mae and Richard?" Sarah asked. She didn't have much affection for either one, but their brief association made Sarah feel she should ask.

"They were okay when I bailed out, but Jamie nailed at least two other unrecovered with barf. It's gotta be a fucking freak show in there by now."

"How many Knights?"

"Six that I saw," Rachael said. "I dropped three, and at least winged that bastard in the fuzzy suit."

Rachael's boasting struck a sour note in Sarah's heart. Casual killing. She'd have to have a long talk with the young woman when this was over. If, that was, Rachael could still be reached. "Looks like Asim dropped the one who had you in his sights," Sarah said, focusing on the business at hand.

"That leaves Mossman in the weeds somewhere over there," Rachael pointed. "And one still on the bus."

The shrieks, shouts and moving shadows inside the bus made Sarah doubt anyone would be coming out in any condition to fight. Outside, about a dozen unrecovered crouched by the side of the road, some crying, others staring dazedly at the rocking yellow horror show.

"Dickens, no!" Rachael said, grabbing the panting lab by the scruff of his neck and preventing the wagging dog from launching out of the cover of the weeds to greet the distraught people by the roadside.

"Heel," Sarah said.

The dog sat.

Koontz growled. Then began barking an urgent alarm.

Something rustled in the reeds.

"The fuck?!" a man's voice right behind her.

She rolled onto her back in time to see King's massive jaws trying to bite through Mossman's thick woolly arm.

One-handed, Mossman raised the butt of the stock over King's head.

Sarah fired into the center of the man's chest.

The guy lurched forward, grunting an exhalation of air and nearly falling on King.

Sarah collapsed in the flattened weeds. She'd pulled something in her back tackling Rachael.

King kept biting. And the man kept struggling. Her bullet should have killed him. He must have been wearing armor under that suit.

The cement-colored sky spun overhead. Like so many times before, when she'd had to choose violence, her stomach churned.

The sounds of the struggle at her feet in the grass told a different story. It wasn't over. The fuzzy-suit guy was still at it. King was still at it. And now, a raging female growl told her Rachael was still at it.

Sarah winced as she pushed up onto her elbows.

Rachael tried to wrestle the machine gun away from her furry-suited attacker. King had the guy's other arm. And though Sarah's K-9 protector couldn't seem to sink his teeth into the thick suit, King was using his immense jaws and a hundred pounds of muscle to flail the guy's arm around like a toy.

Sarah did the only thing she could. She extended her leg hard and fast, driving the heel of her boot down on top of the guy's head. The jarring thump reverberated up her leg.

Rachael wrested the gun from him and hurled it into the grass.

She jumped on him.

Something cracked inside the man.

Rachael kneeled on his broad chest. She wrapped both hands around his throat.

For the rest of her life, Sarah never forgot the snarling grimace of pain, rage, and hatred on Rachael's face as she strangled that guy.

"This is for Cassie," she snarled.

"Cassie wouldn't want this," Sarah said, her voice woozy and unsteady.

Rachael only squeezed harder, the tendons in her neck standing out.

Without thinking, Sarah scooted forward, still on her back, and got close enough to deliver another kick, this one knocking Rachael off the man and into the grass beside King.

"You bitch!" Rachael screamed.

King stood in the grass, stoic, alert. He'd dropped the man's arm when the resistance ceased.

Sarah got to her knees, reached out to check the guy's pulse. "Come on...."

"What the fuck?" Rachael demanded. She reached out to knock Sarah away and finish the job.

"King...." Sarah stopped short of giving the attack command. She wouldn't. But she wanted Rachael to think she might.

Sarah let out a breath as the steady rhythm under her finger told her she hadn't been too late. And King, God love that dog, knew exactly what Sarah wanted, even without the command. He put his body between Rachael, Sarah, and the unconscious attacker, front paws on the guy's belly, staring at Rachael.

"King...." Rachael pleaded. She wasn't stupid enough to cross the pit bull, no matter how familiar she was with the dog. No matter how many naps she'd taken with the giant curled up at her feet. He belonged to Sarah. And, Sarah belonged to him. It was understood. Written in stone. Biblical.

Sarah drew her hand back. "He's still alive."

"And whose fucking fault is that?"

"You just don't get it, do you?" Sarah said, anger supplanting her nausea.

"Oh, get it. You can kill whoever the hell you want, no problem. Asim? Shit, he can treat the world like his personal shooting range, at Mae's van, the Waffle House... but me? No. Poor Rachael. She's innocent. She doesn't know what she's doing—"

"You *don't* know what you're doing. When you were strangling that guy, that wasn't even you. Your face was like a mirror of his. His hate."

"That was for Cassie!"

"Fuck that, Rachael. That was for *you*. That's not what Cassie would want. Not for you, and not for her."

Mossman groaned.

"You keep out of this," Sarah said, kicking him in the side.

"It was for Cassie...." The words petered out to a whisper. Rachael's lip quivered.

"You can never kill enough of them to take the pain away," Asim said.

Sarah craned her neck to see him standing on the line between blacktop and grass, pointing his rifle at the bus. "I'm going to put a bell on you."

"A bell?"

"Never mind," Sarah muttered.

"It was for Cassie...." Rachael turned away but didn't make a sound.

Sarah tried to get up but felt as if someone had stabbed her in the back. She dropped and rolled over instead. That hurt too, but not as bad.

Asim, who'd been pointing the rifle at the bus almost casually, took a knee, set the stock against his shoulder, and peered down the scope.

Sarah's eyes followed an imaginary line from the weapon's muzzle to a new target.

Jamie staggered off the bus covered in black goo... and blood.

Chapter 33

Mike

"We have to go back!" Mike yelled again.

"No fucking way," Jonathan said.

Carl picked up the radio and keyed the mic. "If you want your precious Prophet back, call off your hounds!"

"And let you escape?" Dale crackled back. "I thought you were smarter than that, Doctor."

"The Prophet for the kids!" Mike yelled, unable to contain himself. He cast a furtive glance at Vic, whose head lolled with the motion of the Humvee.

Vic raised his head. "Hey!"

"The Prophet for the kids," Carl echoed into the microphone.

"I'm interested," Dale said.

"Call off your pursuit!" Carl demanded again.

"We'll start there," Dale said. "Jerry, Hal, back off. Follow, but don't engage."

"Call them off completely," Carl demanded.

"Return to the hospital, and we'll make the exchange," Dale countered.

Jonathan grabbed the mic. "That's the same as calling us stupid!"

"If the shoe fits, Jonathan," Dale's sneer was audible through the speaker.

"Fuck you," Jonathan spat.

"Tsk, tsk, Jonathan, think of the children." The leader of the Knights purred, unable to keep the glee of derision from his voice.

Mike tapped Jonathan on the shoulder and held his hand out. "Give me the mic."

Mike leaned in so the curly cord could reach. He clutched the hard plastic to his lips. "Now you listen to me, you piece of shit. You're going to hand over the children unharmed, or your followers will never be happy again."

"Oh, but they will. Thanks to your vomit sickness, more and more are getting happy all the time. And since the doctor left without providing the antidote, and you stole my Prophet, the others won't be so willing to part with the kids who are destined to replace him."

Dale's circular argument didn't make any sense. He had no way of transferring Vic's powers to the children. They both knew it. But you couldn't talk down crazy. "Two, then," Mike said. "Penny and Aella."

"That's ghastly," Carl said.

"Now you want me to give up my celebrity? Patient zero?" Dale said between bursts of static.

"The Prophet for the two girls," Mike said.

"Even *I* think that's fucked up," Jonathan said. "What about the other kids?"

"I feel bad about that," Mike said. "But not bad enough to give up on my granddaughter. And my daughter cares about the Hargrave family. So Aella comes too."

"You're doing this to get your daughter's love?" Carl asked. "And you're willing to let the other kids twist to get it?"

Mike knew he should feel worse about making that choice, but he didn't.

"I'm a reasonable man," Dale's voice drifted from the speakers after a time. "I accept your offer. We meet in one hour at the place of my choosing."

"Two hours at the place of *our* choosing," Mike countered.

"On either side of a bridge," Dale said.

"You've been watching too many movies," Mike said. "Done. But no Knights."

"No!" Jonathan shouted.

"There are three of you," Dale said. "So I get two of mine."

"He's full of shit," Jonathan said.

"No shit, Sherlock," Mike said. "But maybe we can keep them contained on one side of a bridge." He keyed the radio. "Fine. Give us some time to find a map."

"Oh, okay," Dale sounded surprised. "Three hours then. TTFN."

"Why was he surprised?" Carl asked.

"Because there's a copy of the route in here somewhere," Jonathan explained. "Maps and all. I guess Dale figured once we got close enough, it was safe to distribute them."

Carl started rooting around in the front seat. "Ah, got it."

"Find us a river," Mike said. "I've watched too many movies, too."

"When?" Carl asked.

"In the hospital," Mike said. "I had a lot to catch up on."

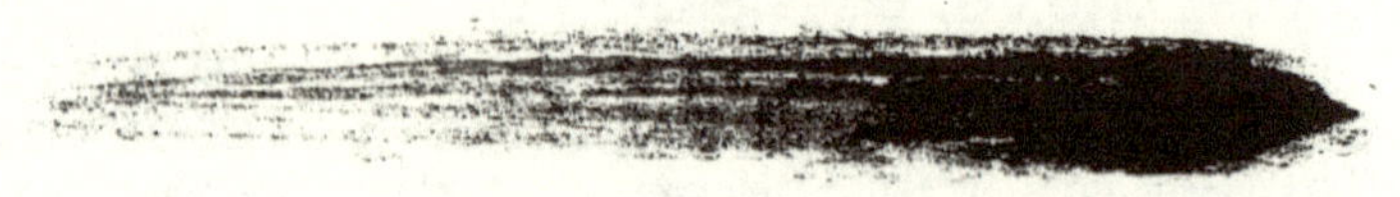

The river Carl found rushed under a rusting green steel bridge. Lines of orange rust ran from the legion of rivets festooning the girders. Below, a wide river rushed fast enough to ward off winter ice. Its black waters churned among submerged rocks with white-water fury.

"Well, here you go," Carl said. "Here's your river bridge. What now?"

"Cross," Mike said.

"What's your plan?" Jonathan asked.

Mike fell back on his tactical training. At least Mike could pull something useful from the tornado of destruction the army had made of his life. "Stop here," Mike said.

Jonathan rolled the Humvee to a stop just past where the grating of the bridge deck met the pavement on the far side.

Vic, who'd been silent through this exchange, unbuckled his seatbelt with speed Mike hadn't expected, and opened his door. He was out of the truck before Mike could react.

"Hey!" Carl yelled.

"Shit!" Jonathan undid his seatbelt and leaped after Vic.

Mike exited the Humvee as fast as he could, his joints popping and crackling in protest.

Not far away, the big man had tackled Vic.

"Get off me!" Vic shouted. "I'd rather die than go back!"

"Works for me," Jonathan said. He had his knee in the center of Vic's back. He grabbed for the Prophet's wrists. "We need to tie him up."

"With what?" Carl asked.

"Paracord wrapped around the steering wheel. There's a knife in my pocket."

Carl strode forward. "Which?"

"Front left," Jonathan answered.

"I usually make a guy buy me dinner first," Jonathan quipped as Carl reached into his pocket.

"That's not what your Grindr profile said," Carl shot back.

"My what?"

Carl pulled his hand from the big man's pocket, clutching a buck knife. "Never mind."

While his companions worked on securing Vic, Mike transformed. Mike Sampson, the elderly survivor of a nearly fifty-year smiling flu coma, receded into the background. In his place, Sergeant Mike Sampson, grizzled veteran of dozens of brutal battles in the jungles of Vietnam, surveyed his surroundings. On their side of the bridge, the western side, sparse, leafless trees wreathed in snow, clung to a hillside sloping up and away from the bridge. Not a lot of cover and concealment, but enough, maybe. On the other side, the ground was flatter and sloped down to the river under a blanket of snow. Slippery going. They'd have the high ground. It would do.

"All right," Mike said, as Jonathan carried Vic, whom he'd bound at the wrists, elbows, and ankles, back to the Humvee. "I know what we're going to do."

Chapter 34

Rachael

"Rach," Sarah said. Her voice held an urgent note.

"Fuck off."

"Could you be pissed at me later? We're still in the shit here."

I turned and held out my still-cuffed hands.

Sarah, still lying on the ground, pulled out a pocket knife and cut me loose. She turned back to stare at something I couldn't see through the tall weeds. I stepped on Frank's unconscious form so I could see. It was Jamie, covered in blood and black shit. "Shit. What do we do?"

"Jamie," Sarah called. "You okay?"

"No!"

I wouldn't be either.

"I mean...." Sarah trailed off.

"I went into stage two," Jamie said. "It's... I..."

"Ed?" I called.

"He's still alive," Jamie said. "I think..."

I wanted to get up and go to her, but felt naked. I held out my hand to Sarah. "Give me your gun."

Sarah rolled onto her side and stared up at me. "Are you nuts?"

"Mine's empty, Asim is covering me, and someone needs to go get this shit under—" a sob hit me. One of those stuttering breaths that happens sometimes after an ugly cry. "—control."

"Get *yourself* under control," Sarah said.

"I'm—" I took a breath, "—fine." Goddammit.

Sarah snorted. "Yeah, you're great."

Something... Why was she still lying there like that while I stood over her? Why had she scooted across the ground on her back to kick me off Frank instead of pushing me? Sarah tried to sit up, and winced. Hmmm. New tactic. "Okay," I said. "You go, get it all sorted. I'll wait here with Asim until it's safe."

Sarah gave me a distrusting look.

I shrugged and folded my arms. "Don't you think someone should be helping Jamie right now? Go on."

"Shit," Sarah whispered, handing me the gun.

I ran toward Jamie.

"What are we supposed to do?" one of the unrecovered crouched beside the road wailed.

"What the fuck was that?" another asked.

And then, not far from me, a third unrecovered started convulsing.

I swerved, trying to keep out of barfing distance.

The woman, a chubby housewife type with hair in a frazzled bun, hurled on the asphalt. Beside her, the woman who'd asked what that was also started gagging.

"Fuck me," I whispered, backing out of there.

"Jamie," I called. "Go around where it's safe. Get out of there!"

A third unrecovered started coughing and choking. Then another.

By the time I'd backed up to where Sarah and Asim were crouched in the grass, the entire busload of unrecovered were puking their guts out all over the road.

"Asim?" Sarah asked.

"We should go," he replied, getting to his feet then helping Sarah up.

The three of us stood there in a line in the breakdown lane, far enough away not to get hit with the hurl.

Jamie made her way around the other side of the bus and stood some way off from all of us. "This is what it was like inside. I managed to get far enough away from everyone else to not touch their... stuff. But by the time I got out, everyone left was in stage two." She went to put a hand to her face, then looked at it in disgust. A racking whimper burst from her. "Oh, my poor Ed...."

"Is he still alive?" Sarah asked.

"Does it matter?" Jamie asked through her tears. "He's infected."

"But you're okay?" Sarah prodded.

Jamie held up her hands, dripping with a combined coating of blood and black bile.

"I mean—" Sarah swallowed. "You're not... you know..."

"You're not a puke psycho?" I cut in. For a tough bitch, Sarah sure could dance around stuff sometimes.

"I..." Jamie looked down at herself. "No. I guess I'm okay."

"We should get far away from here, Asim said. "Quickly."

"I'm with him," I said. "Any second now, someone is going to touch someone else's barf. And then anther, and then another."

"Jamie can't go with us," Asim said.

"Not like that," I agreed. "Come on, let's get you cleaned up so we can get out of here." I didn't wait for Sarah or Asim. I just turned and headed for the pickup truck.

"It doesn't wash off," Asim called after me.

I turned my head but kept walking.

"Rachael..." Sarah called.

Fuck them. If they wanted to talk, they could get off their asses and follow. I heard Jamie's footsteps behind me, so I knew at least she was on board.

"We've got to get you out of those clothes," I said as Jamie and I got around to the back of the truck.

Jamie was way ahead of me. She was already pulling off her shirt, standing a good distance from both me and the truck.

I opened the back to see what Sarah had that we could use to disinfect Jamie.

"It doesn't easily wash off, you understand," Asim said, huffing a little as he arrived at the truck.

"We need to talk," Sarah said. Her voice sounded strained.

"What disinfectants do you have back here?" I asked, rooting through the sleeping bags and food.

"There is nothing Sarah has that the CDC hasn't tried," Asim said. "As I said, the CDC closed off the rooms where stage two vomiting occurred. They weren't able to clean the areas. Not alcohol, not ammonia, not iodine, or any of the other chemicals they had were effective. Only, perhaps, time."

I slumped. "Well, fuck." I turned to Jamie, who was rapidly becoming naked. "We have to do something. We can't leave her here."

"How about keeping me from freezing to death?" Jamie asked, sliding her panties down her legs.

"Rachael..." Sarah started.

I held up a finger. "If you're going to get touchy feely with me, can we do it later?" I rolled my eyes—and that's when I saw it. The siphon, strapped to the roof of the truck's cap. "Hey, we have one thing the CDC didn't."

Sarah and Asim followed my gaze.

"No way," Sarah said.

"It could work," Asim said. "There's no way to know. But gasoline is what we've got."

Shouts and screams drifted through the air from the bus.

"Whatever we do," Jamie said, "let's hurry. If you're going to hose me down with gas, let's get it done."

"It'll burn her skin," Sarah said.

"Better burned than turned to a psycho," Jamie said. She let out a wail. "I... Oh God...." A fit of ugly crying overtook her.

"If it's going to burn her, then we wash her with something else after," I said.

"Such as?" Asim asked.

Sarah frowned. "I once used windshield washer fluid to disinfect my hands."

"It might be effective," Asim said. "Might, you understand."

Something Cassie said to me when we were doing tactical training came to mind. "A good plan right now is better than a perfect plan—"

Running footsteps interrupted me.

Both Sarah and Asim turned, raising their guns.

I reached for the siphon.

Asim fired.

"Let's hurry," Sarah said.

I put one of Sarah's T-shirts over the end of the siphon hose and got it soaked. Jamie wiped herself down. Her crying jags were interrupted by coughing and gagging. The stink of gas was so strong my eyes watered, and I was several feet away. When Jamie was done, Sarah called her to the front of the truck. She'd bent the windshield washer nozzle to spray out to the side. Jamie took a pair of Sarah's panties and wiped herself with the spraying washer fluid while Sarah worked the switch in the cab.

All I could do was stand and watch while Jamie wiped.

"Cupcakes!" a teen boy shouted, running at our position. "Candy!"

I pulled Sarah's gun from my waistband and brought it to bear.

"Turn around!" Asim shouted. "I *will* shoot you!"

The guy kept running at us. "You have candy?"

"No!" I screamed.

"I'm gonna get your goodies!" the kid shouted.

Asim's rifle cracked.

The guy's guts exploded out of his back in a spray of blood. He fell, hitting the pavement with a sickening smack.

I saw the guy at the door of the bus go down. Again. And again. The guy I shot. And then, the guy at the back I shot. Blood sprayed. Someone screamed.

I fell to my knees.

The hole in Cassie's chest.

"Rachael?"

My hands on Mossman's neck. His loose, stubbly flesh squishing under my fingers.

My guts left my body through my mouth.

"Rachael!"

Blood spurted onto the door of the bus behind the guy I shot.

He fell again. And again.

I fired.

I fired.

I fired.

Hands on mine, pushing the gun down.

I struggled.

"Rachael!"

Sarah stood over me. She eased the empty gun from my hands.

I let her.

"It's okay," she said. "I've got you."

"I'm fine," I said, getting to my feet. I wasn't, though. I knew I'd had some kind of episode. I hadn't been there for a minute.

"I know," Sarah said. "You're a tough bitch, just like me."

I fell into her arms.

She stroked my hair.

"They're coming," Asim said. "We need to go!"

Chapter 35

Sarah

Rachael clung to Sarah, the young woman's bony fingers practically hooking into her back. And even with a swarm of psychotic unrecovered approaching from the direction of the bus, a small blossoming flame of hope flickered inside Sarah. Rachael could still be vulnerable, reachable, teachable.

Asim's rifle barked.

One of the approaching unrecovered fell on the pavement. The other five kept moving, shouting for food, or sex, or... Sarah wished she could plug her ears. "Rachael," she whispered, "we need to go."

"Yeah, yeah." Rachael snuffed, pulled back, and wiped her face.

Jamie had finished wiping herself down and was struggling into a pair of Sarah's sweats from the back of the truck.

"We must move!" Asim said.

"Let's go," Sarah said. She winced with every motion.

"There's no guarantee the decontamination worked, you understand," Asim said.

"I'll get in back," Jamie said.

"Dogs, come," Sarah called.

All three dogs leaped into the truck.

Asim held the rifle trained on the approaching unrecovered until the last moment, then climbed in and closed the door.

Sarah hit the gas, swerving to avoid the half-dozen dopamine freaks heading for them.

She swung onto the shoulder to go around the bus but couldn't help casting a glance up at the windows, looking for signs of life. It wasn't until the bus diminished, then disappeared behind them, that Sarah let out a huff, and a sob. Her back, somehow forgotten in the chaos of their escape, arched as if someone had hooked jumper cables to her spine.

"Have you got nine by nineteen para up here?" Rachael asked.

It took Sarah a moment to realize Rach was asking for ammo. And another second or two to connect that kind of professional talk to the young woman's training with Cassie. Sarah didn't really want Rachael to reload. Not until she'd talked to and debriefed the woman. To talk about what happened with the fuzzy-suited guy. About Rachael's rage-fueled revenge frenzy. And then there was Rachael's flashback, or PTSD episode, or whatever she was supposed to call it.

"Sarah?" Rachael prodded.

In this fucked-up world though, the young woman needed a loaded gun. Sarah sighed. It hurt. "Yeah, uh, should be some in the center compartment." Sarah lifted her elbow while Rachael fished for the box of cartridges.

Her back ached with the effort.

The sound of weeping filtered in through the heavy tarpaulin tunnel connecting the cab to the pickup bed. Jamie.

Seriously, screw this world.

She needed to find Penny, and find her now, before the unrecovered around her entered stage two—if they hadn't already. A chasm opened in her gut. She needed to empty her bowels.

The soft clicks of Rachael loading her gun overlaid the sobbing from the back.

Fuck this world.

Sarah turned onto a dirt road leading away from the weedy blacktop and cracked her window against the stink of gasoline and wiper fluid wafting off Jamie's skin.

"Where are we going?" Asim asked.

"We need a few minutes to regroup," Sarah said. *And to shit.*

The road widened back out into four lanes as they rolled into a little Missouri town.

"Look!" Rachael called.

"Where?" Sarah asked. But as soon as the words left her mouth, her eyes alighted on something out of the ordinary. A school bus sat in a heavy equipment rental yard. That wasn't right. Not even a little.

"Diesel," Asim said in answer to the unasked question. "They'll have a fuel truck."

Sarah let the pickup roll to a stop.

Asim opened the door and stepped out, bringing the rifle to bear. He stood looking through the scope for a long moment. "No movement."

"Maybe they're inside," Rachael said.

"I can't feel any unrecovered close by," Asim said.

"Neither can I," Jamie added.

"Let's be careful," Sarah said. She opened her door. As soon as her brain told her body to get out, her back answered, 'nope.'

"Anything to get out of this truck," Rachael said. She opened her door and slipped out quietly, followed by the dogs.

Sarah agreed. The stink of Jamie's gasoline bath wasn't getting any easier to take. They needed to do something else for the poor woman. Even though they'd washed her off with wiper fluid after, that couldn't be good for a person either.

Dickens came around, put his front paws on the running board beside Sarah, and whined.

She patted his head, careful to keep her back still.

"Sarah?" Rachael whispered.

"I need to keep watch," she said. Her insides gurgled. She needed to shit, is what she needed. Her back was having none of it.

Rachael racked the slide of her pistol. "Let Asim. He's good at it."

Dickens whined again.

Asim's eyes met hers. He suspected something, but kept it to himself. He nodded. One elder to another. Was she that old?

Jamie came around the side of the truck. Tear tracks cut the bluish hue left behind by the wiper fluid. She looked dead. "I'll go with them. Air out."

When Jamie's eyes fell on Sarah, a chill stole up her spine. Like a zombie was sizing her up.

Jamie held out a hand. "I'll need a gun."

Sarah wasn't giving up the pistol she'd reclaimed from Rachael. And besides Rachael's Beretta, and the rifle Asim had taken possession of and wielded like a third hand, there wasn't anything else.

"Yeah," Rachael said. She turned to Sarah. "Why don't we have more guns? You didn't grab them from the other trucks when we were captured?"

"I was more worried about following after and saving your ass," Sarah snapped. It came out harsher than she'd meant it to.

Rachael seemed to shrug off the scolding, for once. "Fair."

"Jamie, why don't you wait here with me?" Sarah said. In truth, she wanted Jamie to help her out of the truck, maybe scrounge the roll of TP out of the back. The thought of leaning into the truck's bed sent a pang through her back.

Dickens nuzzled the hand resting in her lap. Koontz and King looked on from the roadside, heads tilted. They knew.

Rachael opened her mouth to protest, but closed it and nodded.

Thank God. Maybe the day's events had forced her to grow up a bit. Shitty way to do it.

As soon as Rachael and Asim went silently stalking toward the equipment rental yard, Sarah said, "Dig through the back. Find me any kind of pain killer, and a roll of toilet paper."

"What...?" Jamie finished the question with her eyes.

"My back," Sarah said. "And my bowels."

Jamie nodded. "I could use a little help in that regard myself. My skin is burning."

"We'll hole up somewhere after this," Sarah said. "I can't remember the last time I slept." And with those words, the weight of the last two days settled on her.

She closed her eyes.

"Here."

The word woke Sarah from a light doze. She snapped upright, sending a bolt of lightning through her back. "Shit." She squinted, scanning the area around the school bus, but couldn't spot Rachael and Asim. "I should have sent the dogs with them."

"They'll be fine," Jamie said. "You're the one who needs looking after."

"I'm fine," Sarah said.

"Sure." Jamie gave a weak little half-smile. "So, do you still want these?" She rattled a little pill bottle in one hand and a roll of toilet paper in the other.

"I see your sense of humor is coming back," Sarah said. Why was she being such a bitch?

"A little," Jamie said. "Hard to, with Aella out there...with them."

Sarah's heart sank. Penny. Always Penny.

The hydrocodone kicked in blessedly quickly on Sarah's empty stomach. By the time she'd found an appropriately secluded tree to rest her back against and void her bowels, the pain was at about half what it had been.

Jamie's reminder that their children were out there with a bunch of stage two unrecovered ticking time-bombs made her promise to hole up null and void. But, both she and Jamie needed an hour of self-care and a shitload of hot water, and they needed it soon.

All these thoughts and a hundred like them went flying out of her head when Rachael and Asim returned, ashen-faced.

Rachael waved an atlas. "We know where they're going."

Chapter 36

Mike

Mike sat in the idling Humvee, its heater barely adequate to keep the interior of the machine warm. It was facing the wrong way to watch the bridge, but the right way to make an escape. Beside him, Carl knelt on the seat, looking out the back, keeping watch for Dale and the kids. Carl kept readjusting his grip on the pistol Jonathan gave him.

"Put that thing away," Mike said. "It's just for show. If shit goes down, I don't want you trying to shoot your way to glory and hitting the kids."

"I'll do what I have to to protect the children."

Mike sighed. "How's your weapons' training?" Carl didn't have any, of course. Mike knew that. "Your marksmanship? How did you do the last time you went to the firing range?" It was a harsh rebuke, but Mike needed the good doctor to understand—this wasn't the movies. "You have only one job if shit goes down. Drive."

Carl met Mike's eyes, frowning.

Mike stared Carl down, unwavering in his conviction.

Carl put the gun away. "I hate waiting."

Mike rubbed his hands together to chase away the cold. "You wouldn't have lasted five minutes in the army."

"That's one thing we agree on," Carl said.

In the front passenger seat, Vic struggled and tried to talk through his gag.

"I'm sorry it went down like this, Vic." He wasn't. They both knew it. Not at all, but he felt like he should say something.

Somewhere on the hillside, Jonathan lay in the snow, his gun barrel pointed at the bridge. Mike tried to make out the big man's position, and couldn't. Good. It meant this had a chance of working. Mike only hoped Jonathan wouldn't be shivering so hard he'd miss his shot and hit the kids.

Chapter 37

Rachael

I stared out the back window of the pickup, absently stroking Dickens's soft black fur. Light faded from the world. Images flashed across my mind of the things I'd seen in the rental yard. Sarah hadn't asked. I think she knew by the look on my face. After all, the unrecovered had Sarah's daughter, Jamie's, and maybe Asim's. And judging by the condition of the black goo-covered bodies in the rental yard, the chances of anyone surviving close contact with the unrecovered were dwindling fast.

The truck still stank like gas and wiper fluid, and Jamie still rode in the back. Something was up with Sarah, too. She kept grunting every time she turned the wheel to go around some obstacle.

I didn't have time to dwell on any of that too long before we pulled into the parking lot of some creepy backwoods motel. The kind run by an overall-wearing woman with a hyphenated name, smoking a filterless cigarette.

Except, from the looks of the place, Bobby-Jo was long dead.

We stayed about two hours. Asim had to get the propane water heater going, the water had to heat up, and we all desperately needed to use it.

Everyone ate but me. I couldn't. Not after what I'd seen. Didn't seem to affect Asim's appetite at all.

Jamie went first in the shower; we all insisted. Her red, cracked skin oozed in places, making her look like a demon woman from a horror movie.

After we were clean, we sat around the tiny table in the motel keeper's kitchen.

"I don't get why we're going to Destination, Idaho. Are the unrecovered being ironic? Did they choose it for the name?" I asked.

"It's where it all started," Sarah said.

"The smiling flu?" Now that she mentioned it, the name sounded familiar.

"Ground zero," Jamie confirmed. "My farm, mine and Ed's." When Jamie said her husband's name, she looked away, as if he might be standing in the corner.

"Well," I said, "let's hop on the interstate. We can beat them there, maybe."

Sarah shook her head. "We follow the route. They've got their refueling stops circled. Maybe we'll catch the group with Penny and Aella. Maybe we can end this without going all the way.

"Besides," Jamie said, her voice small and quiet, as if she formed the words in some faraway place, "what if..." She didn't finish.

She didn't need to. We all knew what Jamie was thinking, because we were all thinking it too. What if the unrecovered around the kids went into stage two?

The room was silent for a minute.

Sarah's head fell forward. She caught herself.

When was the last time she'd slept?

Come to think of it, when was the last time any of them slept?

"I'll drive," Asim said.

"The fuck you will," Sarah said. She could be so damn stubborn sometimes.

"How's that codeine working?" Jamie asked.

Sarah stared daggers across the table at Jamie. "Judas."

"Let Asim drive," Jamie said. "You need some rest."

Rest. My eyes got droopy.

"Everyone needs some rest," Sarah said. "But we can't stop." She stood. "The kids are in danger."

"I got some sleep last night while you drove," Asim said. "I'll drive."

After some arguing, Sarah and I bunked down in the back of the truck. We tossed the gasoline-stinking blankets and replaced them with ones from the hotel.

I woke up with Sarah's arm around me. Somehow I'd ended up as her little spoon. It felt weird, but good. Dickens was *my* little spoon. I buried my face in the soft fur of his neck. At our feet, Koontz stirred and put his head on my ankles. I went back to sleep.

The unrecovered were coming out of the bus again. The Knight with the gun. I fired. The Knight went down in slow motion. Blood drops hung in the air. But somehow, as he went down, he started telling me about his mother. His family. His children. He was talking about how he always felt inferior, how he just wanted to be cool. How he'd never get to be cool now. And then he dropped.

Then the next guy, the one I shot coming out of the back of the bus. Somehow I was up close, right in front of him, when the bullet parted his clothes in slow motion. It burrowed into his skin, then his muscle, finding its way between his ribs to his heart. As the lump of lead entered, his heart spoke to me. It told me he had loved a man once. It told me he always felt small and alone. That his parents never paid any attention to him. That he always wanted to work with animals, not pipes and toilets. That he really didn't like football, but pretended to, so he'd have something to talk about.

I woke in the morning light to the sound of my own weeping.

Sarah's hand stroked my hair.

"It's okay," she whispered. "It's all gonna be okay."

Did she.... Did she just kiss the top of my head?

"I'm fine," I whispered. "Just a bad dream."

"It's okay not to be fine," she said. "It's okay to be a little fucked up. We're all a little fucked up right now."

"I'm fine," I repeated. My body betrayed me with a sob.

"Okay." She squeezed my shoulder. "Just know that you don't always have to be tough. Sometimes, being vulnerable is a flex. It means you are so tough you don't give a shit how people see you."

Was *she* seriously saying that to *me*? The iron bitch?

"I'm so scared, Rachael—" her voice caught in her throat.

Holy shit.

"If something happens to Penny... I'm not sure if the dogs can save me."

That was silly. Koontz and King were an ass-kicking team. I knew for a fact they'd saved her life countless times. "I'm sure they—"

"No," she protested. "I mean, if I lose Penny, I'm scared I'll lose myself. They killed Nate, and I'd come to love him like a brother. He was... he was my Cassie."

That one hit hard. Another sharp breath left my body. The tears were so close to the surface, but I kept quiet. Sarah needed this.

"And Penny, she's more than a foundling I adopted. More than a daughter. She taught me I could love a person, not just animals. I didn't have that my whole life until her, not since my mother died when I was young. And now, if I lose Penny...." She sobbed. "Shit...."

I wanted to say something. Like, 'we'll find her,' or 'she'll be okay,' but I also didn't want to lie. We'd both know it was bullshit. Instead, I said, "I'll be with you, no matter what."

She buried her face between my shoulder blades and wept quietly for a little while.

I wanted to turn and hold her the way she held me, but I didn't think that's what she needed. Maybe it was what I needed.

After a while she said, "Thank you. I'm sorry I've been so hard on you. I just, well, I really like you. And, I've started to think of you as family, like Nate. I've been so scared you'd lose yourself in some revenge-fueled... I don't know. But, now I know you haven't. I know you won't."

I waited until I was sure she was done talking. Then I took a breath and said, "You're my family, too."

She put her arm around me again. "I need you here with me. I need your help finding Penny."

I got this big lump in my throat, but managed to say, "I'm going to help you find my little sister. No matter what."

"Little sister?" Sarah whispered.

The lump in my throat wouldn't let me answer.

"We're coming up on the next stop marked on the map," Jamie called.

"How's your back?" I asked.

Sarah stretched, then gave a little wince. "Better today. Believe it or not, just stretching it out and getting some sleep did me a world of good. Still a little sore. How are you doing? You ready for this?"

I cleared my throat. "Locked and loaded."

Chapter 38

Sarah

Sarah's heart pounded. She ran forward from behind a stalled car to rest her back against the side of the Kansas Highway Department building. Her breath steamed into the frigid morning air. Five minutes of observation had yielded no movement. Honestly, that's all Sarah could take. The thought that Penny could be here, or on the way here, or just have left here, made it impossible to sit and watch any longer.

Rachael left the position Sarah had just abandoned and made a crouching run to the building.

Sarah ducked, moved, and stood on the other side of the door. Careful to keep her arm below the door's small window, she grasped the knob.

Rachael held her pistol barrel up. She flicked the safety with her thumb, then nodded at Sarah.

Sarah turned the handle, then pulled the door toward her.

Rachael peeked and pulled back. Peeked again, then swung her body into the opening, leading with her gun.

Sarah followed.

There were a lot of little corners to check. A lot of equipment to hide behind. Rachael worked the right side of the building; Sarah, the left.

Empty cartons that had once contained water bottles, small propane bottles, and ramen noodles surrounded a table near the front. Sarah noted them and moved on.

"Clear," Rachael called from the back of the building.

Sarah wasn't far behind her. After checking behind the big pile of sand at the back, Sarah answered, "Clear."

"Looks like they've been here," Rachael said.

"Could have been anyone, at any time," Sarah said.

"The propane says maybe more recently?" Rachael raised an eyebrow.

"Well," Sarah said. "It's not like we're going to wait around here for them to show up if they're behind us."

"Chances are they're ahead," Rachael agreed. "Or maybe that bus in Missouri was the only one coming by this route."

"Maybe," Sarah shrugged. "There's nothing here. Let's go."

There was something there though—gas. They fueled up the truck from the big tank in back and hit the road.

Sarah took a turn driving, stopping only to pee and siphon gas. Her back pain had receded to a dull ache.

Asim slept in the truck bed. Jamie dozed in the back seat with Dickens, not wanting to lie down with Asim. Even though the man had proved trustworthy, Sarah got it. Men were men.

The sun sank low on the horizon as they crossed into Colorado. Fatigue took Sarah again. Her eyes drooped.

"Sarah, watch out!"

Rachael's voice snapped her alert just in time to avoid a snarl of cars stretching across the road.

A whimper from the back told Sarah that Dickens hadn't escaped the panic stop unscathed.

"Sorry everyone," she said.

"Trouble," Asim said.

"What?" As soon as the word left her mouth, she saw the soldiers rising from behind the cars. Behind her, two army trucks she'd missed on the way past drove up from the roadside and blocked the road behind her.

"Everyone out," one of the camo-clad soldiers shouted. Two approached the truck. A few more pointed rifles at them from behind the barricade of stalled cars.

"Safeties off," Sarah said.

"Diplomacy," Asim countered. "We will not be able to out-shoot these."

"Are they unrecovered?" Sarah asked.

"The ability for me to tell is fading quickly now. I think perhaps?"

Sarah opened her door. The cold hit her like an ice pick. "What do you want?"

"I'll ask the questions," the soldier said.

"Terrific," Rachael grumbled. "We've been stopped by the nineties cop movie fan club."

"Quiet," Sarah hissed.

"Where are you going?" the soldier asked.

"Montana," Sarah said. "Home."

"What the hell for?" the soldier asked. "Too damn cold. You'll freeze to death."

"Not any faster than sitting in the middle of the road in Colorado," she countered.

"Got any unrecovered with you?" the soldier asked. His breath steamed out of the mouth hole in his balaclava.

"Not anymore," Sarah said.

"They die? Run off?" He raised his rifle a notch. "You didn't kill them, did you?"

"They *recovered*," Asim said.

Sarah gaped at him.

"Bull-*shit*," the soldier said. "We don't recover. Ever. That's why we're called that. We ain't called, the Recovered."

"Search out my mind," Asim said. "You will feel the difference."

The soldier went silent. Then he said, "You had the pukes, din-cha?"

Asim nodded. "I have passed through stage two."

"You're to come with me," the soldier said. "Any more like you?"

"As you say. There is a woman in the back," Asim said. "She has been feeling sick all day, but has not yet entered stage two."

The soldier exchanged a look with his partner, the one in front of Sarah.

What the hell was Asim playing at? They might have passed this obstacle unmolested if he hadn't opened his fat mouth.

"I don't feel good," Rachael said.

Asim jumped out of the way.

"You should just let us pass," Sarah said.

"I can't do that," the soldier said. But his eyes were wide with fear.

"You know what happens if the sickness touches you," Asim said. "I can see it in your eyes."

"You seen any other people lately? Buses?"

"Are there some missing?" Asim asked.

Again, the soldiers exchanged glances.

"Fuck this, Archie," someone called from behind the barricade. "I'm a loyal red-blooded American, but I ain't signed up for this shit."

"You shut up, Stan."

Rachael gagged and took a step forward.

"One more step and I'll waste all of you," the soldier said.

His partner started backing away.

"Jimmy!" the soldier who'd been doing all the talking said.

"Screw this. You people get in your truck and get the fuck out of here."

"No!" the first soldier shouted.

Rachael got into the truck.

"I said no, damn it!"

"If she gets sick here, you'll all be stuck," Asim said. "Everything for one hundred yards will be contaminated. The virus will be airborne and preserved by the cold," Asim said.

"Shit," the soldier said. "Go! Go!"

Sarah jumped into the truck. She had the machine rolling before Asim's door closed all the way.

No one spoke as Sarah drove down the side of the sloping ditch, giving the roadblock a wide berth.

"What the hell was that all about?" Sarah asked.

"They know their plan is crumbling," Asim said.

Chapter 39

Mike

"They're here," Carl said.

The doctor's voice roused Mike from a doze. Curse his old bones. He should be amped up on adrenaline, leg sewing machine stitching the air. Instead, he'd been napping like a geriatric retiree, dozing in front of the TV in a nursing home. And now, instead of facing this stand-off alert, Mike had to fight off cotton-headed post-nap confusion. He turned in his seat, craning his neck to look behind.

At the edge of the bridge, another Humvee idled, its headlights hurting Mike's eyes. The clouds shielded the sun from the proceedings like a cement sarcophagus lid. No advantage or disadvantage for anyone having the sun at their back.

A figure emerged from the truck and stood behind the open door.

"Stay put," Mike said, reaching for the door latch. He reeled when the cold air punched him in the face. Then regained his momentum, swung the door open, and stood. Because their

Humvee faced away from the bridge, Mike had to maneuver around the open door to use it as cover.

"Where's the Prophet?" the man yelled across the bridge.

It wasn't Dale. Mike let the disappointment drain through his shoes. Penny was all that mattered now. "Where are the kids?"

The man nodded to someone in the truck. The back door on the opposite side opened. A girl about Aella's size stood holding an infant. At this distance, and with Mike's aged eyes, he couldn't tell if the figures were Aella and Penny or not. A feeling spreading out from the base of Mike's skull said maybe not. He'd have to risk it. Mike crossed in front of his Humvee, shielded by the rumbling machine's bulk, and opened Vic's door.

Careful to keep the Prophet in front of him, Mike drew his pistol and tugged on Vic's arm.

The Prophet placed his tied feet on the snowy ground and stood carefully. He shouted through his gag.

Mike elbowed Vic in the ribs. "Shut up." He squinted at the kids on the far side. The supposed Penny was too bundled up in coats and blankets to identify. The one who held her certainly looked like Aella.

"Start yours walking!" the man on the other side of the bridge shouted.

"Start yours," Mike countered.

"I don't like this," Carl said through the open door.

"What's to *like*?" Mike spat. He tapped Vic's shoulder with his gun. "I'm going to cut your feet loose. Don't do anything stupid." Might as well ask the sun not to shine. He stood behind Vic, laid his gun in the snow, and opened his pocketknife. The shoelaces binding Vic's ankles fell away. As Mike folded the knife to put it back in his pocket, Vic turned.

"Fucking—" was all Mike managed before Vic's foot caught him in the sternum.

Mike gasped for air. He could only watch, lungs clawing for oxygen, as Vic kicked his gun away into the snow and ran away.

A rifle shot cracked through the air.

Mike heaved a breath and crawled after the gun.

Another rifle shot.

The world spun around him.

Across the bridge, the children screamed and kept screaming.

Jonathan returned fire from the hillside.

Muzzle flashes made orange firework reflections on the snow.

The smell of cordite.

Head on a swivel, soldier...

The crack of return fire sounded from the other side of the bridge.

Mike thrust his hands through the snow, searching for the pistol. He found it and turned in time to see the figures of the children shoved back into the car.

Mike tried to get up. "Cease fire, cease fire!"

Head on a swivel, soldier...

Another gunshot, this one further away.

The sound of a ricochet on metal.

"Cease fire!" Mike shouted again.

Romeo Papa one-three, we can't get in there. We're taking heavy ground fire...

Mike looked to the sky. Instead of palms, smoke, and choppers, he saw threatening clouds.

"Get in the fucking Humvee!"

Romeo Papa one-three Pop your smoke, and I'll open up...

Footsteps in the snow marked Vic's trail. Mike stumbled to his feet. A bullet went by close enough to hiss in Mike's ear. Vic's trail led to the hill beside the bridge that sloped down to the water. There, the tracks became a long slide. No way Mike could do that and keep his feet. And, if he somehow managed it, no way he'd be able to get back up without a rope and winch.

Gone.

Vic had screwed them. Screwed Mike out of saving his granddaughter. Screwed Mike out of redeeming himself to Sarah. Anger rose in a massive crescendo inside Mike's chest. Fucked out of having a family life by Dr. Anthony Silva and his ruinous experiment. Fucked out of watching Sarah grow up by the smiling flu. And now, fucked again by the self-serving asshole Vic.

Mike screamed at the slate-gray sky, all the rage boiling out of him.

"Get in the damn truck!" Carl yelled.

More gunshots. Some from the hill where Jonathan lay, some from the other side of the bridge.

Beaten and broken, Mike stumbled toward the Humvee. An impact bit his shoulder, hard. A hail of bullets churned the snow around his feet.

Something that didn't quite sound like the ocean roared in Mike's ears. He stumbled forward. His shins hit the passenger doorjamb. His face hit the radio.

The world lurched into motion, dragging Mike's feet through the snow.

"The kids!" Mike yelled, spraying Carl with blood.

"Get the fuck in!" Carl yelled.

Mike scrambled to get his legs inside.

Romeo Papa three, how you doing?

The Humvee rolled forward.

Bullets pinged against steel.

Head on a swivel, soldier...

Mike reached for the helmet mic to move it closer to his mouth. It wasn't there. He closed his eyes and tried to ground himself in the here and now: the engine noise, the cold. Still, his past seeped in...

Cold, shivering, in the wet, winter jungle night. Cries of the anguished wounded. Urgent whispers.

Mike managed to right himself in the seat. His arm burned with white-hot agony. The door banged beside him and bounced open again.

The Humvee climbed the hill with agonizing slowness. The snow-covered road was visible only as a hole in the trees.

Carl stopped on the hillside.

"Yes," Mike gasped. "Go back for the kids."

"We can't help them," Carl managed between heaving breaths, "if we're dead."

That sixty is getting too close...

Jonathan loped toward them through the bare gray tree trunks. Covered in snow, the big man looked like a heavily armed Sasquatch. He fired his rifle in the general direction of the bridge. He fell before Mike heard the shot.

"Fuck!" Mike gasped. This whole thing had turned to worms. No kids. No Vic. Now, no Jonathan.

Carl gave the Humvee a little gas, no longer waiting for Jonathan. The tires spun.

"The back is too light," Carl said.

Mike wasn't sure that was true. These things were pretty heavy, and this one had some kind of armor package on it.

The back door opened.

Jonathan threw himself in. "Drive!"

"I'm trying," Carl said.

"Gas and brake at the same time," Jonathan gasped.

"Huh?" Carl asked.

"Do it!" Jonathan yelled.

The truck seemed to find its footing. The tires whined, and the engine screamed.

"Work both pedals," Jonathan said. "It's some kind of weird traction control with these things."

Carl ground his teeth. "You drive then!"

The Humvee crested the hill, started down the other side, and stopped.

"Why are we stopping?" Jonathan asked. He stared down at his leg and snarled.

"The kids," Carl said. "Give me the rifle."

"You aren't—" Jonathan started.

"The scope," Carl said, holding a hand out.

Jonathan gave it to him.

Carl took it and trudged back toward the hilltop.

Mike wanted to follow, but he couldn't catch his breath. He held his hand to the spot where the white stuffing of his coat puffed out, crimson.

"Where are you shot?" Jonathan asked.

"Arm." Mike grabbed the radio handset. "Sierra one-seven, this is Romeo Papa three. Broken arrow! I say again, broken arrow!" Mike gasped. He drew a breath. They would come. Every chopper. Every firebase would point their artillery. Every fighter-bomber in Vietnam would come....

"What the hell was that?"

This wasn't a field radio. He wasn't in Vietnam.

Carl came back to the truck, thrust the rifle at Mike, then got in.

"Are they—" pain choked off the rest of Mike's sentence.

"Stopped at this side of the bridge," Carl said. "Going after Vic, maybe."

That tracked.

"What do we do?" Carl asked.

"We go back and rain holy hell down on them," Jonathan said.

"The kids," Mike said, repeating his new mantra.

"We need to go," Carl said. "We lost. And if I don't stop your bleeding...."

No kids. No Vic. No redemption. "Dying is fine with me," Mike said.

Chapter 40

Rachael

We hauled ass, stopping only for gas and toilet breaks. Sometimes the roads were so covered in snow that we slowed to a crawl for hours. Sometimes we even had to back up and go around, taking us away from the routes marked on the map. At those times, I didn't speak, kept to myself. Sarah got real tense and bitchy, and I could see why. What if Penny was out there? Stranded with the other unrecovered in some snowed-in Midwest hellhole, freezing to death. I didn't like to think about it either.

We all stank. Sarah kept the truck kind of chilly, I think, to keep the smell down. Day turned to night, and then day again. On the clearer roads, in the light of day, I even drove, letting Sarah and Asim sleep. Jamie hardly said a word, and what was there to say, really?

I hadn't really traveled much outside the beltway before the smiling flu. And what I'd seen of the country between DC and South Carolina after, I saw on foot. Corpses and stalled cars. That's what the world was made of for me. And silence. And trees. Being a city girl, I was, you know, aware of forests and stuff, but it wasn't until I'd started south on foot that I realized how much of the country was actually made of them. My point is, driving through Kansas and Colorado, I was sort of stunned how much of the US was made of grass, and before, I guess, crops.

Okay, that's not my point. My point is—boring. Mind-numbingly boring. Nothing but flat, dead fields on either side for hours and hours and hours. Flat, snow-covered prairie where the only sign there was a road at all were the telephone poles and barbed wire fences on the side. That's what kept me awake, honestly, trying to figure out where the road was, and keep the truck on it. No stalled cars, few houses, no people, just some busted-up barbed wire, and a line of telephone poles vanishing into the distance.

Denver made me so tense I thought I was getting sick. My head ached so bad. That's when I realized I'd been clenching my jaw, hard. Here's why: On the open roads, in Kansas, the Colorado plains, you could almost forget you were following a route laid out by a massive (in post-smiling flu terms) conspiracy, probably laid out by the Confederate Army. But once we got to a big city like Denver in the 'for real' snow belt, there was no mistaking that this was all laid out. And that whoever set this up probably wasn't far off. The roads were plowed, and any stalled cars blocking the route were bashed out of the way. It was fucking creepy.

Asim clutched his rifle as we drove across the plowed and cleared I-70. Up and down offramps, driving on the highway the wrong way, just spooky shit, but there was no mistaking the way to go. And there wasn't any other sign of living humanity.

"I need to pee," Jamie said.

"Can you hold it until we're not in the city?" Sarah asked.

"How long will that be?"

Asim unfolded a map and checked it against the one we got from the unrecovered. "This could take a while," he said. "We're going all the way across the sprawl to the west, you understand."

She understood alright. I saw her face. And as freaked out as this dead city made me, I wanted to do something for her. "I have to pee too," I said.

"Oh, for fuck's sake. Here?" Sarah asked.

She seemed grumpier than usual, and that was pretty grumpy. I wanted to ask, but didn't think she'd tell me what was eating her. Still, she'd opened up to me in the back of the truck the other night, after...after I got rescued.

She pulled over under the shelter of an overpass.

"Make it quick," Sarah said.

"It's ass chapping cold out there," I couldn't help myself. Even as I opened my mouth, I knew I shouldn't. "Do you think we're going to hang around checking real estate prices with icicles on our coochies?"

"Just go, okay?"

Jamie and I squatted behind the truck, out of sight of the mirrors, but close enough to the tailpipe to get little puffs of heat.

"Why do you do that?" Jamie asked.

"Do what?"

"Antagonize Sarah." She pulled a tissue from her pocket and handed it to me.

"Thanks." I wiped. "I don't know." I pulled my pants up. "It just comes out."

Jamie nodded. "I guess that's just how families are."

I got a lump in my throat. She called us a family.

I heard the front door of the truck open.

Dickens trotted past.

When I went up to the front again, Sarah stood looking at the bridge above us.

"That's I-25," she said.

I almost said, 'so,' but held my tongue. Something about her face, about the way she looked at it....

"Something happened... on I-25. Something terrible, and, I guess, something wonderful." She turned to me. "Vengeance is a burden you carry, just like the crime that made you vengeful." She looked down. "I killed a man on that road. He deserved it. I know in my heart that man deserved to die. But did it break me? Did it kill something inside me, too? Sometimes it feels like it."

"I... don't know," I said.

She looked at me, her blue eyes drilling into mine, the crow's feet at their edges lending gravitas to her gaze. "That's all I was trying to do, Rachael. I was trying to protect you from the gravity of that. The weight."

I didn't know what to say.

Sarah turned her eyes to the road above. "Nate was here with me. Less than a year ago, we passed this way. He... held me, after it happened. He was so patient, so kind. God, his smile, his stupid jokes...."

"Aw, come on," I said. "He was funny. He had his own thing going on."

Sarah gave a faint smile. "Yeah, I guess...."

"He loved you." The words were out of my mouth before I could stop myself. Goddamn, when was I going to learn to shut the hell up?

Sarah's eyes dropped. Dickens came up and nuzzled her leg. She rubbed his head with a gloved hand. "He deserved better than me."

"He needed *you*," I said, "not anyone else. You."

"Maybe. Come on, let's go. It's fucking cold out here." Sarah turned, reached for the door handle, then turned back and threw an arm around my neck before I could even flinch. "You're alright, Rachael. I'm glad you're with me."

I was still trying to formulate a response when Dickens jumped up on me, paws on my chest, and licked my face.

"Guess he thinks so too," Sarah said, and climbed into the truck.

The dogs jumped in through my door, getting snowy paw prints all over the seat. I grumbled and wiped them off before sitting down.

We climbed out of the plains toward the roof of America. The snow drifted high on the sides of the road. How many feet, I had no idea. I could only see treetops and sky.

"I don't like this," Jamie said. She'd been getting more animated and friendly since her... since she... since stage two.

"What's to like?" Asim asked. "No way to maneuver. No help anywhere, and relying on our enemy to clear the way for us. Just one checkpoint, and we're finished, you understand."

"Well, aren't you two cheery," Sarah said. "What have you got, Rach?"

I swallowed. I wanted to be there for Sarah this time, and not the other way around.

"No one's going to put a checkpoint up here. Wastes too much fuel and resources. And, we haven't seen a living soul since..." I almost stepped in it. "...for days. Plus, our families are in front of us somewhere, and I bet there's nothing to like there either. Let's go get them."

"See," Sarah said, "that right there is what I'm talking about."

Sarah drove all night again. I dozed on and off, my fuzzy hood pressed against the cold glass. Most of the night we went up, and up, and up. Nothing to see but snowbanks on either side. When I straightened and looked over Sarah's shoulder at the road ahead, snowflakes curved in from above, in streaking white arcs ending in immolation on our windshield. Then, sometime before dawn, we nosed down, hitting the curves and switchbacks at an agonizingly slow speed.

"Want me to drive?" Jamie asked.

"Or me?" I asked.

"No," Jamie, Asim, and Sarah said at once.

"Oh, come on," I said. "I'm doing great."

"Not for your first time on snowy mountain switchbacks," Sarah said. "No way. Anyhow, I'm good for another hour or so. Just keep your eyes open. These clear roads and no people... the whole thing gives me the willies."

"Is that like elderly speak for the creeps?" I asked. This time I did it deliberately. Sarah was acting a bit punchy. If I could irritate her into wakefulness, well, that was alright with me. My words had the desired effect.

"*Elderly?!*"

I chuckled, letting her know I was kidding.

"One of these days, Rachael...."

"One of these days what?" I smiled. It felt good to be useful, helping keep Sarah alert. Plus, I wanted to know what she'd say.

"One of these days, you're going to wake up and find you've gotten old too."

"Let's hope so," Jamie muttered.

Ahead, two Humvees sat on either side of the road, looking like they'd been smashed out of the way by a dinosaur. Badly mutilated bodies painted the snow a gruesome red.

Chapter 41

Sarah

Sarah's heart sank as she piloted the truck through the erstwhile roadblock. The frozen corpses curdled her blood. The number of bodies she'd seen since the smiling flu destroyed humanity was beyond measure, but seeing these men frozen in clearly recent death ratcheted her ache for Penny to something almost unbearable. "Can anyone see their insignia?"

"These guys are regular army. The good guys," Rachael said.

So, the army wasn't just leaving them out here to twist. That intelligence should have made Sarah feel better. It didn't. If the army couldn't muster up enough resources to stop Dale and the Knights, what chance did she have?

"I have to get Penny," Sarah said, then slammed her fist painfully on the steering wheel. She goosed the gas, causing the truck to fishtail on the road's hard-packed snow.

"We will," Asim said. "Whoever did this isn't that far ahead."

"But what if...." Rachael let her words trail away.

There were too many what-ifs. What if the unrecovered with Penny went into the second stage? What if they got into an accident? What if the plan changed, and they didn't want or need the kids anymore? What if a thousand horrible things.

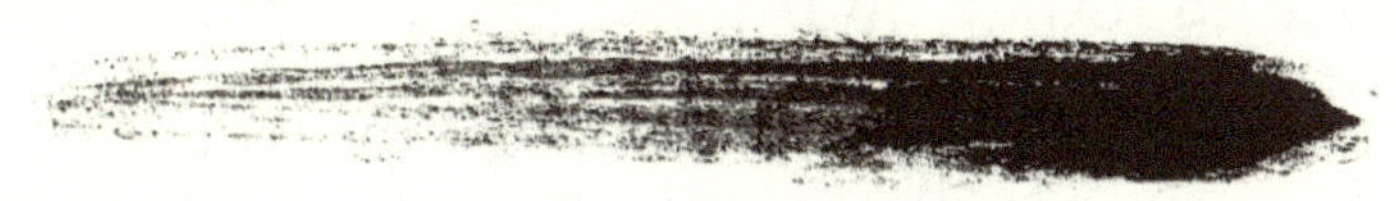

Sarah's anxiety didn't ease for two days, and then it got much worse. The drive to Destination yielded no new clues. Each time they stopped at a waypoint marked on their map, they found lots of tracks, empty food and water packaging, and sometimes, an unrecovered with the black stuff around their mouth and a bullet hole in their forehead. There were three such bodies between Denver and Destination. The roads stayed clear, and as they plowed deeper into the high desert west of the Rockies, the snow all but vanished, and the snarls of cars were bashed out of the roadway.

Two days of high alert hadn't done anything for Sarah's nerves. Neither did all the instant coffee and the insistence of the others that she sleep, eat, or share the driving. Truth was, she couldn't share the driving. Her need to find Penny was, literally, a *driving* need. She was simply incapable of riding shotgun. No, she had to be active, had to be in command, in control. Penny was all that mattered now.

Still, Sarah moved ahead with caution, watching for ambushes, unseen obstacles in the post-apocalyptic roadway, and signs of the unrecovered, hoping against hope to find Penny before the unrecovered reached Destination and enacted whatever nefarious plan they had for her daughter. This, coupled with the circuitous route, meant they didn't reach the area around Destination, Idaho until thirty-six hours after leaving the morbid roadblock at the foot of the Rockies.

Two pairs of headlights marked their entry into the land of the unrecovered. They stood close together, four pinpricks of light across the road. Another roadblock.

"Shit." Sarah jammed on the brakes.

Beside Sarah, Jamie woke from a doze. "Where are we?"

Sarah pointed at the map.

"I've got a bad feeling about this," Rachael said.

"When was the last time you felt good about anything?" Sarah asked, annoyed.

"Fair," Rachael replied.

"We can go around, here," Jamie pressed a chipped nail to the worn paper. She looked at the lights, then at Sarah. "Let me drive."

Sarah wasn't going to cede control now. "No way."

"I've driven these roads for thirteen years. I can get us around this," Jamie said.

"Tell me where to go," Sarah said.

"Perhaps we should move now and argue later," Asim put in from the back seat.

Sarah turned the truck around and headed away.

"You don't think they'll come after us?" Rachael asked. "That was just a tiny bit sus."

"Sus?" Sarah asked.

"God, you're old. *Suspicious.*"

"Little shit," Sarah muttered.

"Vulgarity, the last resort of a—"

"Will both of you shut up and let me drive?" Jamie snapped, throwing the map on the center console.

Sarah took her eyes off the road to stare at Jamie. The outburst was so out of character for the usually stoic woman that it caught her completely off guard. "Yeah, yeah, okay." There was no denying it made sense to let Jamie drive now that they were within a few miles of her home. Sarah only hoped she wouldn't combust from sitting in the passenger seat with nothing to do but worry. With the headlights behind out of sight, Sarah pulled off the road into the predawn murk next to the dead corn stalks lining the road.

After they'd traded seats, Dickens made his awkward way up from the back, stepping on Rachael and knocking the map to the floor to squeeze himself half into her lap and half in the footwell of the big truck's passenger seat. "Damn it, dog." She kissed the top of his head. "I need to be able to move. Go lie down." She pointed at the back.

Dickens gave a soft whine and did the same hog-on-ice scramble back the way he'd come, smacking Asim in the face with his tail and stepping on Rachael's hand. Of course, the dogs could sense the fear, tension, and anxiety wafting through the truck.

Jamie steered back out onto the road and, in less than a minute, turned onto a dirt track leading through the dead crops. "We'll cut through Gabe's place and try approaching from fifty-one on the west side," she said.

The truck rattled something awful on the frozen ruts. The ruined brown stems grew as high as the truck, obscuring everything. The corn seemed to close in on the road ahead, coming to a point in the distance where the dirt road seemed to die off between them.

"How far?" Sarah asked.

"About two miles," Jamie replied.

There were no telephone poles, no landmarks, nothing to distinguish one second from the next. Just dead corn squatting in the frozen mud under the indifferent gaze of a round, pallid moon. Each second fell like a domino glued to a ruined tabletop, refusing to trigger the next in line. It occurred to Sarah that perhaps they were already dead, killed at the roadblock. And their bodies were traveling down an eternal road. Purgatory. Awaiting final judgement. Well, this last part was true, anyway.

Sarah drew her pistol and held it in her lap, reassured by the weight and the cold metal promise of death and retribution. If anything had happened to Penny....

When she felt she could take it no longer, a wall of brown stalks barred the way. The end drew closer and closer. Sarah touched the floorboard, her foot unconsciously seeking a brake pedal that wasn't there.

Jamie slowed and killed the headlights.

The truck crept forward in the moonlight, finally stopping at the edge of a buckled, dirt-covered blacktop running perpendicular to their path.

Jamie stabbed the truck into park and held out her hand. "Asim, the rifle."

"What—" Sarah started, but Jamie only shook her head, lips drawn. "My turf."

Normally Sarah wouldn't put up with that from anyone, but the change in Jamie's nature was so sudden, so extreme, that rolling with it seemed the natural option. And, if she were honest with herself, relinquishing the mantle of leadership, at least temporarily, came as something of a much-needed respite.

"Outside," Asim said, opening his door.

They all piled out.

Sarah started for the edge of the corn, hoping to catch a glimpse of what lay down the road in either direction, but stopped when she saw Rachael. The woman had a small fire extinguisher in her hands.

"What?"

"Brake lights," Rachael replied. She circled around to the back of the truck and smashed the metal cylinder into the plastic. "Every time we stop, even if the lights are off, we flash big red warning lamps to anyone who's looking." She brought the fire extinguisher to bear on the other side. "No sense announcing ourselves."

Smart. Sarah nodded, then joined Jamie at the edge of the corn.

"They're there," Jamie said. "Their lights are off, but it's the same thing. Two trucks parked in a V-shape across the road.

"Now what?" Rachael asked.

"That's Ted's farm. Across the road, somewhere, the corn will stop at a burned area. The day this all started, there was a forest fire. We burned our crops to make a firebreak where our land met the forest. And...."

Jamie trailed off. Her face changed. "Oh, my God."

"What?" Rachael asked.

"I don't think that was a forest fire that burned Fort Johnson. This whole time all of us, the whole world, were operating under the assumption that the forest fire burned a base they were going to close anyway, so why bother putting it out?"

"You think they burned the base on purpose?" Sarah asked. "Why would they do that?"

"Perhaps to erase a mistake," Asim offered. "But the eraser still wasn't big enough."

"What mistake?" Rachael asked. "The smiling flu? Nice job. That got out anyway."

"Maybe," Jamie said. "Maybe something else."

"So, what are we going to do?" Rachael asked.

"Either way," Jamie said. "We've got to get in there to save our families. My farm borders the woods that surrounded the base. It's all burned, but there are farm roads along there." She pointed. "I think we have to sneak across the road and cut trail for a bit. Then hook up with a farm road and get to the edge of the woods."

"That's going to make a lot of noise," Asim said.

The macabre moonlight made Jamie's sneer positively evil. "Yeah, but good luck finding us, let alone following."

"Let's go," Sarah said.

Chapter 42

Mike

After sliding down the far side of the hill and weaving among the back roads, Carl parked the Humvee outside a drugstore with caved-in doors.

Mike's world alternated between light and darkness, between snowy suburb and jungle, between past and present.

"Did you see their armbands?" Jonathan asked from somewhere far away.

"President's guys, some of them," Carl said. "At least now we know who's been clearing the roads."

"For sure Dale couldn't pull that shit off by himself," Jonathan replied.

The blue sky filled with smoke. The cloudy sky didn't.

"Come on, Mike." Carl pulled him from the truck. Pain lanced up his arm, bringing him to coherence.

"The kids..." Mike murmured.

"They're okay," Carl said.

Carl couldn't be sure. Mike knew that.

The doctor guided him through the store's ravaged aisles. Snow drifted against the front counter.

"Here," Carl said, and helped Mike into a sitting position, leaning against a half-empty shelf of foot creams. "I'm going back to get Jonathan."

Last mag....

Mike reached for the pouch on his waist.

"Hey," Jonathan said, sliding to the floor beside him. "How you doing, old man?"

Romeo Papa three, how you doing?

"Last mag...."

Pain stung his face.

"Hey. Mike. Snap out of it," Jonathan said.

"Can you cut the sleeve off of his coat while I do the same for your leg?" Carl asked.

"Give me the scissors," Mike whispered.

"I think our friend Mike has gone to the zoo," Jonathan said.

"He's in shock," Carl answered from somewhere far away. "You both are. Can you cut his sleeve?"

Pressure on his arm. Pain.

The world darkened.

Light came again.

Treetops raced by overhead.

The engine roared.

Back in the Humvee.

Mike's arm throbbed. He chased the pain with his eyes. The right sleeve of his coat ended in a ragged cut. Below that, a red and black checked scarf wound around his limb and formed a sling around his neck.

"He's awake," Jonathan said from the back.

"How are you feeling, Mike?" Carl asked.

"Half-dead."

"How's the pain?"

"Not too bad." It wasn't, but his head felt thick. "Can't think...."

"You hit your head on the radio. Minor concussion. Also, I found some painkillers. Carl said. "We got lucky. That place wasn't picked over too badly."

"My arm..." Mike started, struggling to find the words he wanted.

"Just a graze," Carl said. "Missed the important stuff. A few stitches and a few days, and you'll be good as new."

Mike's chuckle turned into a fit of coughing.

Carl shied away, slowing the truck.

"It's not that," Mike managed. When he'd caught his breath, he asked, "Jonathan?"

"Same as you, just a bad graze," the big man said, answering his unspoken question.

Mike slumped back into the black.

When he woke again, it was night. The truck idled, still.

"Where?" he asked.

"Potty break," Carl said.

The back door opened. Jonathan climbed gingerly into the seat.

"Your turn, old friend," Carl said. He opened his door.

"I can piss on my own," Mike said.

"Sure," Carl said, but got out anyway.

Mike did need help, though. His legs were stiff. The ground was slick.

"Need help undoing your pants? Injuries in that spot—"

"You trying to get in my pants?" Mike asked, then coughed.

"You're not my type," Carl said. "Besides, I've been your doctor since you got out of the coma. Do you think this would be the first time I've been *in* your pants?"

"Pervert," Mike said.

"The drugs seem to agree with your sense of humor."

"Back off doctor feel-good, or I'll water your shoes for you."

After Mike relieved himself, they got back into the truck.

Soon, the pale dawn revealed a barren winter landscape free of snow. The detritus of dead leaves and branches littered the country road. The brown remains of summer weeds stood stubbornly upright in the cracked pavement.

"Where are we going?" Mike asked.

"Destination, Idaho," Carl said.

"How do we know where to—"

"Map book," Jonathan put in. "They put them in all the vehicles when we were in that highway building."

"That's where they're taking the kids?" Mike asked. His granddaughter Penny's tiny face flashed behind Mike's eyes. And then, the face of his late wife, Penny.

"It's where they're taking everyone, we think," Carl said.

We *think*. Fuck.

They drove in silence.

They ate garbage. Prepackaged donuts. Soda. Snack mix. Everything people left behind in the stores in favor of protein.

Mike slept again.

This time when he woke, Jonathan was behind the wheel, driving with his left foot.

"How far now?"

"A day," the giant said. "Feeling better?"

Mike found that he did, as a whole. "Sore," Mike said.

"Yeah," Jonathan said. "My leg too."

"Carl?"

"Sacked out," Jonathan said. "He did a twenty-four-hour shift."

When Jonathan started to nod, Mike took over. The Humvee was tough to handle one-handed, even with power steering. He'd been at the wheel for a few hours when the roadblock appeared. Two more Humvees parked across the road in a vee.

Fear squeezed Mike's insides. He had no idea what to expect from these men. Had Dale radioed ahead to have them arrested? Shot? His only ace in the hole was Vic.

One of the uniformed soldiers approached with a clipboard, rifle slung casually on his back. He motioned for Mike to roll down the window. It hadn't come up yet, and he found himself fumbling with the mechanism before learning the trick and pulling the knob.

"Group number?"

"I'm not sure—"

The soldier adjusted his stance impatiently. "It's on the cover of your map book."

Carl fumbled with the map book. "Sixteen."

"Sixteen," Mike repeated.

The private looked at his paper. "Says there's supposed to be a bus and another Humvee in this group."

"Oh, they're coming soon," Mike said, hoping he sounded believable. He wasn't a good liar. It was one of the reasons his wife always trusted him.

"Feel free to back off about a hundred yards and wait."

Jonathan opened his door.

"Remain in the vehicle!" a soldier shouted. Mike couldn't see where the voice came from.

Jonathan ignored the order. Hopping awkwardly on the asphalt.

"This guy is being polite with you," Jonathan said. "Because of who he is. You need to let him through. It's been a tough trip for the old guy."

"I don't care—" the private started.

"You do," Jonathan cut him off. "You just don't know it yet. This is Mike. Fucking. Sampson. Patient zero. Centerpiece of this whole thing."

The soldier squinted at Mike like an insect under a microscope.

"The man was in a coma for fifty years," Jonathan steamrolled ahead. "Don't you think the least you can do is let him through so he can get a cup of hot coffee?"

Mike tensed. They had no idea what lay on the other side of the roadblock. Jonathan was taking a risk making that assumption.

"Well..." the private looked at his clipboard again, as if some new information would magically appear.

"Can't you just get someone on the radio?" Jonathan asked, shifting his weight.

"Wait," the private took a step back. "Radio silence man. That was rule one from the start. Who are you saying you are again?"

Shit.

Jonathan grabbed Clipboard's rifle and yanked it off the man's shoulder before the surprised private had a chance to stop him.

He pointed the weapon at the soldier, keeping most of his weight on one leg. "Don't let me see that clipboard or pen hit the pavement," Jonathan said. "In fact, hand it to my friend Mike there."

The young man did, passing the writing implements through the window.

"Take ten steps back."

The private did.

The other soldier at the roadblock brought his gun up.

"Drop it or I'll drill you," Jonathan said.

To Mike's surprise, the guy did.

"Now," Jonathan barked, "Cuff yourself. Slow."

"How do—" the soldier started.

"Use your teeth, asshole."

Mike watched, dazed, as the quaking soldier placed a loop of plastic around his wrists and drew it tight with his teeth.

"Good. Now start walking away from the trucks. So much as turn around and I'll turn you into a spaghetti strainer."

The guy started walking.

Jonathan swung his gun back to Clipboard. "You." He motioned with his gun. "Same thing with the cuffs as your friend."

And when the soldier had tightened the cuffs around his wrists, Jonathan said, "Get in."

"What are you doing?" Mike asked.

"We're going to take our friend here for a little ride."

What the hell was Jonathan up to? Whatever it was, Mike didn't like it. "I'm too old to make new friends," Mike said.

"How bout friends who know might know where your granddaughter is?"

Something snapped inside Mike. Any trace of the softening old man disappeared behind *Sergeant* Mike Sampson. "Get in."

When he was seated in back, Mike asked, "What's your name, kid?"

"PFC, Dawson."

"Alright, Dawson. No sudden moves, no bull-shit. Answer my questions and you'll be back drinking coffee with your buddies telling a wild story by dinnertime. Do you copy me?"

"I got it," Dawson spat.

"How many people are here already?" Mike asked.

"Like in my camp, or in Destination?"

"Hmmm," Jonathan said. "This might take a while. Best we get out of here, Mike."

Mike couldn't agree more. "How far up is the next checkpoint, camp, whatever?" Mike asked.

"I guess that would be HQ in about three clicks," Dawson said.

"If we see anyone between here and there," Jonathan growled, "I'm going to shoot you."

Mike had to reach across with his left hand to put the Humvee in gear, then maneuvered around the trucks in the road, moving forward at a crawl.

"Now," Jonathan said, "you were about to tell me how many people are in town."

"I don't know. I turn in the numbers from my checkpoint at the end of my shift."

"Yeah, but you guys talk? Right?" Mike said. "Having a beer with your buddies, you know. About how many do you think?" He tried to keep his tone cool and conversational. By the way the kid was stammering and sweating, if he'd been in the service before the pandemic, it was as a guardsman. A weekend warrior.

"I-I have no idea." Dawson said.

"Okay," Mike said. "Let's try something else."

A dirt road appeared off to the left between the tall brown stalks. Mike took it, and a hundred feet on, veered to the left into the corn.

"Ow! What the fuck?" Jonathan yelled as the Humvee bumped across the furrows.

"We're gonna need privacy for what comes next," Mike said with as much menace as he could muster while driving a bucking bronco. Pain flared in his arm with every bump. He drove another hundred yards, then turned the wheel and piloted the machine into a small spiral, creating a clearing of flattened cornstalks.

"Seriously, Mike," Jonathan said. "My leg ain't what it used to be."

Mike shifted into park. "Let's get some air," he said. Every joint cracked as Mike extricated himself from the seat. With the adrenaline from the last ten minutes, Mike had forgotten how long they'd been on the road before the roadblock. The cold air made his fingers ache and his bladder contract.

"Get out," Jonathan ordered.

"Carl, get him on his knees," Mike said.

"I'm a doctor," Carl said. "I'm supposed to *help* people."

"Help him to his knees!" Mike shouted. He was using the pain, channeling it into anger and malice. For the kids. All in service of the kids.

Carl laid a hand on the man's shoulders and pushed him down.

"Wha—what are you doing?" Dawson asked.

"I forbid you from killing this man," Carl barked.

"Wouldn't dream of it, Doctor." He turned his attention back to the kneeling man. "You ever hear of Panther force?"

"Please..." Dawson whined.

"Panther force was the army's answer to the Marines Force Recon units." It was total bullshit. All made up. A mishmash of stories he'd heard, but he wanted to scare the shit out of this guy. "Long range reconnaissance patrols, deep into enemy territory in Nam. Every once in a while, we'd get lucky and snag some poor sonofabitch like you. And to survive, we'd have to get him to tell us where the bad guys were. Got pretty good at it." He bent down so that he was eye to eye with Dawson.

"P-please," Dawson said again. "I-I'll tell you w-whatever you want."

"Good." Mike said. He grabbed the open Humvee door with his good arm, slammed it, then opened it again. "Put his fingers in the door."

"No," Dawson said. "You're crazy. I-I already said I'd tell you."

Jonathan gave a snort. "You're more fucked up than me, Mike."

"Call me Sarg," Mike said, getting into the role now. To Dawson he said, "this is what's called getting yourself in a jam. See what I did there?" He gave Dawson a sardonic smile. "If I don't think you're telling us everything, you'll leave this clearing left-handed. Copy?"

"C-copy."

"Good," Mike said. "Now, where's my granddaughter?"

"I don't...who?" the private stammered.

Mike swung the car door back and forth, coming within inches of Dawson's fingers.

"Farmhouse! Farmhouse!" Dawson shouted.

Mike let go of the door. "Go on..."

"About five clicks to the northeast. They've got a bunch of kids there. That's all I know. I swear."

"Kids they kidnapped from New Hope?" Inside, Mike raged. He wanted to hurt this man. He wanted to hurt everyone who'd had a hand in taking innocent children from their families.

"I don't know. I just know there's a bunch of kids there."

Mike squatted down and grabbed the young man's chin. "Do you know who you're working for? Do you know what they've done?"

"I'm serving my country!"

The kid believed it, too. Mike let go and stood. This guy didn't have anything to do with Penny's kidnapping. He wasn't malicious. Like all of them, Dawson was just doing what he thought was right.

The anger inside Mike ebbed. "I'm sure you think you are. But whoever is running this operation sure as hell isn't. They kidnapped dozens of children to do medical experiments on. My granddaughter..." And as the words left Mike's mouth, he faltered.

"Let's go get the kids."

Chapter 43

Rachael

I grabbed the back of the driver's seat as Jamie plunged the truck into the corn. At first, the ride was like a bucking bronco, then Jamie turned, driving us parallel with the dead corn. The stems pounded the truck like a deafening hailstorm. Do not like. Would not recommend.

"How far?" Sarah projected over the noise.

"Not sure exactly. It's been a while since I was out this way. Another minute or so?"

Seriously, fuck this. It was like a horror movie. I couldn't breathe. The walls of the truck cab started closing in on me. Just as I started gasping, we broke through.

Jamie edged the truck onto a dirt track perpendicular to the way we'd been driving. To our left, blackened fields stretched out at the foot of a looming shadow on the horizon.

"I never drove out to see it," Jamie whispered. "Ed plowed the fields under for a firebreak, and the next day I got sick and drove off the road." She stopped the truck and peered into the darkness. "It's out there somewhere.

The burned-out shell of Fort Johnson. Home of the smiling flu."

Jamie's house was the real home of the smiling flu, if you asked me. I mean, patients one and two came from there. Of course, I didn't say that.

Jamie goosed the truck into motion.

The burn glistened with frost in the moonlight.

A road flashed by on our right.

"We're officially on my farm now," Jamie said.

I heard the catch in her voice and caught myself wondering how I'd do going by my brother's apartment in DC after all this.

"The house will be somewhere to the northeast of here," Jamie said. "About a mile."

"But we're not going there, right?" I asked. "I mean, if that was their target, there might be uninvited guests, right?" It occurred to me that after all this time on the road, we didn't really have a plan. And when I say 'really,' I mean, no plan at all.

"Shut up and look for lights," Sarah said.

"You ever see Ghostbusters?" I asked. "I watched the DVD at Cassie's. They're facing a ghost, and one says he has a plan, and when the ghost shows up the guy yells, 'Get 'em Ray!'"

Sarah turned to face me. "So?"

"So I'm asking if that's your plan. Is your plan, get 'em Ray?"

Sarah turned to look for the house again. "I...no...."

Jamie slowed the truck. "It kind of is, as far as I know."

"Let's just see if there are lights, signs of life," Asim said. "We will go to there, you understand."

"*From* there," I whispered, "go *from* there."

"Ah," Asim nodded. "As you say."

Lights twinkled on the horizon, but not from the northeast. These strobed faintly in the west behind the blackened trees sticking out of the ground like rotten teeth. Jamie stopped and rolled down her window. "Let me see the rifle."

Asim handed it to her, and Jamie peered through the scope.

"I don't believe it," Jamie said. "Fort Johnson."

I squinted into the glare. "I thought you said it burned?"

"It did." Jamie handed the rifle back, then dropped the truck into gear. "I want to go home."

"Who doesn't." I agreed.

After a few minutes of staring at the lights to the west, Jamie turned the truck away, and we crept along the burned corn.

"There," Jamie said, and pointed to a spot on the horizon only she could see.

I couldn't see shit. And since I was a generation younger than everyone else in the truck, my eyes were the best. Well, probably. It's not like we go for annual eye exams in the apocalypse.

A few minutes later, Jamie eased the truck north. We bumped across the furrows and drove back into the frozen stalks. Every minute or two, Jamie would stop, open the door, and stand on the running board looking into the distance.

No one spoke. My heart pounded in my chest. My fingers were literally white-knuckled on the oh-shit handle.

Jamie stopped again, checked, and said, "looks clear. Let's go."

She didn't give any of us time to ask questions or talk about tactics. She just drew her gun and disappeared into the frozen corn.

"Fuck sake," Sarah muttered, getting out and going after her.

"We should—" Asim started.

"Yeah, yeah," I said. Climbing into the cold and following the trampled path.

King walked ahead of me, and it wasn't like I was going to pass him, so I followed the pace the giant pit bull set.

It wasn't far, maybe twenty feet or so, before the corn ended in a frosted grass yard. A rusted swing set sat silent and still in the moonlight. My heart caught in my throat. This was where Jamie's daughter, Aella, had played a thousand times in another lifetime. Another universe. The universe of *before*.

Asim came out of the corn and stood beside me. "Let's sweep the perimeter," he said.

I nodded. "I'll go left." I clutched the Beretta through my thin gloves, crouch-running up to the house and resting my back against the cold clapboards.

The side yard held nothing but a bunch of muddy tire tracks and footprints. And I mean a lot. It looked like there had been an army here. Other than that, the yard was just a thirty-foot space between the house and the corn.

I came to the corner and took a quick peek around front, then ducked back, cursing my steaming breath, clearly visible in the moonlight. If there were bad guys out there... but there weren't. Just a sea of muddy imprints from trucks, people, trailers, all kinds of shit, all so muddled I couldn't really tell what was what.

I crept around to the porch. A shattered coffee mug lay on the weathered wood next to a rocking chair. A faint noise came from inside the house. Whispers. Creaking. Most likely, Sarah and Jamie.

When Dickens clicked onto the porch through the open front door, I nearly shit myself. And where the hell was Asim? A glance in the other direction showed the front of a barn. I should go help him clear that.

I crouched, approaching the barn by stealth. Dickens, on the other hand, just walked along beside me, crunching the thin crust of ice in the tire tracks and panting like we were heading for a playdate at the dog park.

"Could you keep a lower profile?" I hissed.

Dickens closed his mouth and tilted his head at me.

"Better." I leaned against the side of the barn, just past the edge of the big open doors.

Dickens started panting again.

"Gonna get me shot," I muttered.

"The dog is not what will get you shot."

I froze, nearly peeing my pants.

"I could hear you halfway across the yard," Asim said.

I let out a long breath. "That was Dickens."

"As you say," Asim said. "The barn is clear."

We made our way to the porch. As we got there, Jamie came out of the house, sniffling and holding something to her chest. Sarah followed her out.

"What now?" I asked. The cold seeped into my bones. And even though getting to Destination increased the urgency for finding the kids, I wanted a warm place to hole up and formulate a plan better than 'get 'em Ray.'

Jamie sniffed, swallowed, and said, "storm cellar."

We followed her back into the barn. Inside, the murk swallowed her silhouette almost completely. I reached for my flashlight.

As if reading my mind, Sarah said, "No lights. Just because we didn't see anyone doesn't mean no one's watching."

I put a hand on Sarah's coat. Asim took a handful of mine, and together we made a stumbling, blind, human centipede. In the back corner, we entered an old horse stall. I could just make out Jamie crouching on the ground.

Metal clanked. Wood creaked. Jamie lifted a trapdoor in the floor. It fell open with a bang.

My heart leaped into my throat.

The barn burst into the searing blue-white light of approaching headlights.

"Go! Go! Go!"

Chapter 44

Sarah

Jamie shooed Sarah and the others down creaky wooden stairs into a dark hole. Sarah saw spots of light, night-blind from the approaching headlights. Jamie closed the lid behind her. Their bodies bumped together in the dark. The scent of each of Sarah's truck mates distinguished them: Asim's leathery breath. The sharp, vibrant, and slightly sour scent of Rachael's pits. The loamy smell of Jamie's hair, in desperate need of a wash and brush. Sarah wondered how she smelled to them.

Light flared above her. They were still on the stairs. Jamie and Rachael ducked a bit.

Jamie grabbed a two-by-four leaning against the stairs and barred the door.

"May I?" Asim asked, gesturing to an oval door in front of them.

"Yeah," Jamie whispered. "Go."

And when the lights came on inside...well...

Sarah sat sipping coffee on a somewhat rickety surplus Boy Scout bunk bed. Instead of the dusty, dirty storm cellar she'd been expecting, this was a bunker, made from a buried sea container. And not just any bunker, but a bunker complete with batteries continuously topped off from solar cells on top of the barn. It had a small curtained-off area with a chemical toilet, a tiny sink that pumped water from a five-gallon pail, a propane heater, and, praise God and pass the mashed potatoes, a little 12-volt coffee maker.

And honestly, not a moment too soon. Sarah could feel the end of the rope she slid down. The bitter end. Without a few hours' sleep and a cup of coffee, she didn't know how she'd keep it together to find Penny.

No one spoke. Jamie sat silently weeping over a picture in a frame she'd taken from the house. A house the CDC had pretty much destroyed from the inside out, looking for the bug. The virus. The smiling flu.

But where were the trailers Jamie described on the ride here? The CDC trucks and mobile operations centers?

Either way, it didn't make much difference now. Right now, all that mattered was whose headlights were outside. Sarah needed to know. They all did. "The headlights...." Sarah said. It could be Penny out there, or Aella, or Asim's daughter, Ghada.

"Yeah." Jamie put the photograph on the pilled woolen army blanket. "There's a kind of periscope. It's just a couple of mirrors inside a pipe. Mostly so we'd know if the storm had passed."

"Won't someone see?" Rachael asked.

"It just looks like a pipe sticking out of the ground on the side of the barn," Jamie said. She slid aside a small steel plate on the ceiling. Fitted a pipe into the hole the plate revealed, then snapped a latch into place and peered through.

Minutes passed.

"Well?" Sarah asked finally.

"Can't see anything. Driveway's clear," Jamie said.

"I think we should get some sleep," Asim said.

"I'll take first watch," Sarah said.

"I will," Jamie countered. "I couldn't sleep right now. Now that I'm home...." She pulled away from the periscope and surveyed the bunker. "...sort of."

Sarah lay on the bunk, facing the wall. All three of the dogs crammed onto the bunk with her. Opposite her, Asim did the same. Above, the lump of Rachael's form sagged the top bunk's springs. There was no way Sarah could sleep now. Not so close to where Penny might be. Not this near getting her daughter back...

Except the proof was in the drool on her hand, and the grittiness of old instant coffee mixed with sleep in her mouth.

Sarah raised up on her elbows to find not Jamie, but Asim staring into the pipe poking down from the ceiling. "What time is it?"

Dickens licked her ear.

"Dawn," Asim whispered.

"Anything?"

"Come look," Asim's voice was grave.

Sarah launched off the bed and did her best not to trip over her rousing dogs in the cramped space. The metal made a cold ring of flesh around her eye. Outside, the night gave way to a pale stripe of gray on the tan cornstalk horizon. Shadows moved and then resolved themselves into people. A lot of people. Each as gray and hopeless as the dawn. Cars and buses dotted the driveway and the yard. And people walked silently into the corn.

"What the hell, Asim?" Sarah asked. "Why didn't you wake us?"

"To what end?" he asked. "No one was in a condition to do anything."

"What's going on?" Rachael rasped from the top bunk.

"People," Sarah said. "Unrecovered from the looks of them. A lot of unrecovered."

"Can you feel them?" Sarah asked, looking pointedly at the older man.

"No," Asim said. "My mind no longer feels the unrecovered. I cannot find the dark water, or the other minds on it." He tilted his head. "Do you suppose that means it's over? I'm cured?"

"What if there's a stage three?" Rachael asked. "Or four? Five? Will we ever know?"

Sometimes, Sarah wanted to put tape over Rachael's mouth. The young woman was a repository of truths best left unspoken. Questions best left unasked.

Asim's eyes fell. "As you say."

Jamie roused. She sat up and rubbed the sleep from her face.

"Have you been listening?" Sarah asked.

Jamie nodded. "We need a plan."

"Get 'em Ray," Rachael mumbled.

"Will you stop that?" Sarah snapped. "Do you have a plan?"

Rachael made a wry face. "I guess we go out there and look for the kids."

"We must keep three meters from the unrecovered," Asim said. "With this many, if one goes into stage two...."

Sarah didn't like to think of the chaos and carnage a mass stage two vomiting event might cause.

"A super spreader event," Rachael said.

"There's no plan," Sarah said, finally taking her eye from the primitive periscope. "Not without knowing where the kids are. If they're here."

"They're here," Jamie said. "They have to be. Otherwise, what's the point?"

"We go out," Sarah said, refusing to despair or get sidetracked, "we find the kids, and we get them the hell..." Sarah swallowed, "...out of there."

"We can cover more ground if we split up," Rachael said.

"How will we know if someone else finds the kids?" Sarah asked. She saw the utility of splitting up, but didn't like it. She needed to know the second someone found Penny... if it wasn't her.

Jamie brightened. "Wait!" She shuffled around food and water totes and canisters until she found a red rubber tote in the back of the shelter. From it, she pulled a blister pack of two small radios and a pistol. "Ed went on a doomsday prepper spree a couple of years back. I almost forgot about this stuff."

Thank God for Ed. The thought took Sarah by surprise. Guilt crept over her. They'd treated Ed pretty badly. Everyone had. Sarah, because she'd read Erica's journal and blamed Ed for the reporter's death. Rachael, because Ed was an older, straight, white man, and Rachael was incredibly...not. And Jamie, because of years of marital bad blood. But Jamie was also the closest to forgiving Ed. When she spoke of him, the fondness in her voice still lingered. Maybe for what he once was, or could have been again, if not for Jamie stage-two-ing all over her erstwhile husband.

"Two teams then," Rachael said. "I'll take Sarah."

Sarah opened her mouth to protest. People didn't pick *her*. *She* picked other people. She was in charge... but what did it matter? It felt good to be picked. To be wanted. And Rachael was family now, by mutual decree and consent.

So, of course, Rachael wanted to go with Sarah to get Penny. The word "okay," slipped from her mouth.

They ate a meager breakfast in near silence, slurping their coffee and nibbling absently at breakfast bars just this side of expired. The dogs ate crumbled ramen. Sarah's mind drifted into the fields, trying to reconcile the miles of nothingness they'd passed for a destination that drew the unrecovered. What was out there that brought all these desperate people to a dead Idaho cornfield in freezing January temperatures? It made no sense.

As they ate, they took turns looking through the pipe at the dooryard between the house and the barn. When Sarah took a second turn, groups of unrecovered—twos, threes, and even one group of about a dozen—wandered past, heading west, then vanishing in the dead brown cornstalks. They were all shapes and sizes. Dressed in finery and rags. All adults, and all silent as the grave.

The whole scene creeped Sarah out. She set down her lackluster protein bar, chugged her coffee, and stood. She was done waiting, preparing, worrying. "Let's go. The truck is the Alamo."

Rachael gave her a blank look.

"I don't know this reference," Asim said.

Sarah sighed. "The fallback position. I'll leave the key under the back driver's side tire. Radio is behind the seat. Once the kids are here," Sarah swallowed, "and not until all the kids are here, we call in the airstrike. The code is: Almighty."

"May I have the pistol you found with the radios?" Asim asked Jamie. "The rifle will be too conspicuous. I haven't seen any of the unrecovered carrying firearms except the soldiers."

Jamie looked at Sarah, which gratified her. She nodded.

"Let's leave the rifle at the truck, too," Rachael said. "Might have to provide cover for someone coming back with the kids."

"Good luck," Jamie said at the bunker's upper door.

"Never say that," Rachael said. "Say—"

"Good hunting," Asim finished.

Rachael nodded.

"Good hunting," Sarah said.

She did her best to look like an unrecovered as she crossed the dooryard with Rachael and Koontz at her side. She made her eyes dead, like the corn, like the farmhouse, like this world. They didn't hurry, though Sarah wanted to run screaming, 'Penny?!' She hoped Dickens didn't make them too conspicuous, bounding ahead, snuffing at the patches of snow.

When Sarah paused to leave the key under the tire, Rachael hopped into the truck bed and slowly rose from a crouch.

"Rachael!" Sarah hissed.

"Gotta see what we're walking into. You wanna distance yourself from me, do it. You're the mama bear. Do what you think is best." There was no anger in Rachael's voice. No sarcasm. Just maturity, understanding, and the cold, cold calculation of a huntress out for blood.

Days before, hours, minutes even, Sarah might have been concerned. Given Rachael another speech about revenge, or becoming what she hated. But now, as long as Rachael's bloodlust served the goal of getting Penny home alive, Sarah welcomed it.

Sarah stood by the side of the truck as Rachael stood in back, surveying the scene.

"There's a big crowd gathering in the burned area of the fields on the edge of the forest."

"Hey!" a voice shouted from the house. "You in the truck!"

Rachael jumped down. "Time to go!"

"No shit," Sarah huffed, running after her. Frozen, fibrous leaves slapped her face. Some breaking, others scratching along her cheek. She couldn't see where she was running. Just corn, and now and then glimpses of Rachael's woodland camo jacket running in the corn beside her.

Someone was laughing. Running and laughing.

Sarah burst into the burned area.

Rachael laughed beside her.

A soldier emerged from the corn.

Rachael put up her hands.

Sarah drew up short.

"Go," she whispered. "This time, I was trying to get captured."

"What the fu—" Sarah started.

"Walk away, stupid," Rachael grinned. She turned to the soldier. "Hey, asshole!" Rachael sidestepped away from Sarah.

"Freeze, bitch!" The soldier held up his gun.

"Last chance," Rachael whispered, "walk away like you don't know me." She winked, then turned once again to the soldier. "That camo makes your dick look tiny. Are you like a Ken doll under there?"

"You fuckin..." the soldier sighted down his pistol. "Don't move!"

Sarah started walking away. She hated herself. Koontz looked from Sarah to Rachael, a low growl rising in his throat. "Not now, boy," she whispered. Casting her eyes toward Jamie's house in the distance, she realized the military must have taken up a post there during the night. She cursed her stupidity. It only made sense. That was the only structure for what seemed like miles...except the base.

"You gonna hide behind that gun, baby wiener?" Rachael goaded.

"I said stop fu—"

Something behind Sarah thumped. She wanted so much to look back.

Penny was all that mattered now. Just Penny. Rachael had taken herself off the board with some half-assed plan she hadn't told Sarah. That pissed her off royally. She needed the help. They all needed each other. There was a lot of ground to cover here.

Footsteps raced up to her side. Two sets. It took all Sarah's energy not to look. Rachael fell in step with her. Then, so did Jamie.

"Seriously," Sarah said. "What. The. fuck. Was that?"

"Last minute change of plan," Rachael said. "Can't have the house full of army guys if we're going to escape back there with the kids."

"So how—"

"Asim and Jamie were right behind us. And we needed that soldier's radio."

"Where's Asim?" Sarah asked.

"Back at the edge of the dooryard, covering the house," Jamie said. "He's got the dead soldier's radio, and the little radio from the storm cellar."

"That's...." Sarah was a little pissed she hadn't been quick enough to figure all that out. And she was pissed the others had to clue her in.

"Don't be grumpy," Rachael said.

"You're kind of a pain in the ass," Jamie said.

"She's old," Rachael said, sticking up for Sarah. It would have been cute if she hadn't called Sarah old.

"I was talking about you," Jamie said.

Sarah turned to her.

Jamie smiled. A real, genuine smile. So, the second stage had done its work. Jamie had some of her joy back.

"Let's go get our girls," Sarah said.

"We have to keep a lookout for Ghada," Rachael said. "I promised Asim."

"What does she look like?" Sarah asked.

Rachael handed Sarah a small photograph. Creased, as if it came from her father's wallet. The young woman bore a strong resemblance to Asim. Strong, dark-complexioned, and more handsome than traditionally beautiful. Boyish, almost. Her long hair was pulled into a ponytail over one shoulder of her business suit. On the other breast, a pin of horizontal bars, oranges, whites, pinks. "That pin," Sarah said, "is that...?"

"She's one of us," Rachael grinned.

"I'm not a lesbian," Sarah protested. She didn't want to have this conversation right now. Instead, she scanned the horizon. Others were walking up from who knew where. Black dots growing closer, walking out of the corn.

"Queer," Rachael said. "She's queer."

"I'm not queer," Sarah said.

"You're ace. Hate to tell you...."

"Can we do this later?" Jamie asked.

"Thank God," Sarah said. "What do you think this crowd is about?"

"Looks like some kind of stage up there," Jamie said.

Rachael squinted into the distance. "It's a flatbed truck with a podium on it."

"Unrecovered!" a voice boomed. "Welcome to your Destination."

Chapter 45

Mike

The farmhouse squatted on the frozen ground. No sign of life escaped its dark interior. Only a curl of smoke, gray against the stars, betrayed any life within.

"We should slip into the corn and watch the place," Jonathan said.

Mike frowned.

"I don't see any lights," Carl said. "No reason for them not to have it lit up if they're there. We're well inside the security zone."

"You're both right," Mike said. "But, as shitty and cold as it is, I agree with Jonathan."

They got out, bundled their clothes tighter around themselves, and slipped as quietly as they could into the rows of dead, dried stalks.

Dawn arrived mercifully swiftly, and with it, cars, soldiers, and a bus. The damn thing blocked Mike's view of the front porch. He heard kids, though. Some crying, others asking questions his old ears couldn't quite make out.

"Now what?" Jonathan asked.

"Let's see if we can get a better view of what's going on," Mike said. He rose, pushing off the ground with his good arm. His head ached. His stiff, frozen joints protesting, letting him know this was a young man's work. Fuck that. And fuck young men. And fuck the unrecovered. He wanted his granddaughter back.

The others followed Mike's lead, moving with excruciating slowness. Jonathan made way too much noise, limping along. They circled around, trying not to disturb the corn. An inch a minute, or that's how it felt. Like the jungle. When each minute might be your last, you try to savor it. Now, here in Idaho, in January, it was just too cold for that shit. Still, getting a better view would serve them.

It wasn't the sound Mike worried about. The commotion of soldiers, voices, and vehicles masked their steps, but not the telltale swaying of the plants they disturbed. Finally, they found a position on the opposite side of the house from the barn. From this vantage point, Mike could see some of the front porch and the door. Also, the backyard. This became important as they were circling around because people had come down the road on foot, bypassing the house and walking into the cornfields on the other side. Whatever was going on, the house wasn't the focus of it.

Shouts erupted. Someone yelled from a window. The back door banged open. Mike wasn't in position to see it.

More shouting from the corn in back. Several people running. Then, as quickly as the commotion started, there was nothing again.

The tromping of scattered unrecovered through the dead, frozen stalks made Mike's skin crawl. There was something vaguely predatory and insectile about the sound. As if a swarm of locusts were gathering for the feast. Emotional locusts, the unrecovered were.

That thought stopped him for a moment. He now felt himself as something other. He was unrecovered, that couldn't be denied. But he was transcendent. Stage two had lifted him out of the barely survivable depression and existential malaise. And now he was looking down on these poor creatures. Seeing them as less than human. It was a trick, he realized, Uncle Sam had played on him to get him to kill Vietnamese communists. Dehumanizing them. Making it feel okay to kill. It wasn't, though. Not for its own sake. Only in defense of his buddies. His comrades. His brothers in arms. And now, his kin.

Mike shook himself and focused on the house. The back door opened. Armed Knights trooped down the small set of crooked wooden steps onto the brown grass. Behind them, children marched out. Ten... fifteen... He recognized Aella, and in her arms, Penny.

Damn it. There were too many soldiers, too many kids. No action plan Mike cycled through in his head could save all the kids and kill all the soldiers. No plan could keep Penny safe.

The loud chattering of a big diesel caught his ear coming up the road. It grew louder and louder until a giant green six-wheeled army truck drove between the house and the barn and stopped in the backyard.

The soldiers started loading the kids onto the back. The youngest, chattering and crying. The stone-faced soldiers offered no comfort, only rough hands up into the back of the open truck.

"The fuck do we do now?" Jonathan whispered.

The soldiers got in. The truck started moving.

"Back to the Humvee," Mike said.

"You sure you're still in?" Mike asked Jonathan. "You don't have any skin in this game, and the odds just got pretty long."

"If I don't do this, help with this, then, who am I?" Jonathan asked. "If the kids die, or you do, then you might as well have left me with Dale. I probably would either be his servant for life, or have died getting puked on by someone in stage two."

They reached the Humvee, pulled to the side of the dirt driveway among a bunch of other cars and trucks tucked into the corn.

"I'm going," Jonathan said. "If this is the one good thing I do before I die...."

"Redemption," Mike nodded. "I want that too." He turned to Carl. "You stay here, Doc."

"And do what?" Carl asked, incredulous.

"And live to help the kids once we get them back," Mike said. "You're the only doctor we've got, and let's face it, you're not great in a fight."

"I..." Carl paused. "Yeah okay."

"Hide in the corn," Mike said. "We'll be right back."

Carl closed the door and trudged into the cornstalks.

"How are we going to stop that truck?" Jonathan asked as Mike fired the Humvee's engine to life.

"Don't think we can," Mike said. "We're just going to have to follow and see what that brings."

Mike steered the Humvee onto the driveway, around the house, then followed the trampled path left in the deuce's wake. Several hundred yards later, Mike stopped where the corn did. Ahead, the fields were burned to the soil. Nothing but a furrowed black, ashy plain. People walked here and there, moving west, heads bent into the effort, watching their footing.

"My eyes aren't what they used to be," Mike said. "Can you make anything out in the distance?"

"Crowd at the far end of the fields. I think that's where the truck went."

"Where?"

"Two o'clock," Jonathan said.

Mike goosed the lumbering machine forward, bumping over the furrows until he could turn and roll with them toward the crowd. Some of the unrecovered looked up as he passed them, squinting at him through the truck's dirty windows. Sometimes he forgot about his dubious celebrity and wondered how he could use it to get Penny back.

"This would be easier if we had uniforms," Jonathan said.

"You, maybe," Mike replied. He parked the Humvee a hundred yards behind the now empty deuce-and-a-half. "I'm seventy. No one would believe that shit."

Mike checked his pistol, then tucked it into his jacket pocket. His arm still hurt, but he figured even injured, he had serviceable aim. He picked his way carefully through the frozen mud. Breaking an ankle now would fuck up any chance he had of getting Penny out of here. He approached the deuce-and-a-half and stopped.

Jonathan stood at his side. "What?"

"That truck is the only chance we have of getting those kids out of here."

A cloud of cigarette smoke rolled out of the driver's window.

Mike smiled to himself. "There's your uniform."

Ahead, in Mike's somewhat blurry long-distance vision, a fuzzy pink face stood behind a podium. "Unrecovered," the voice boomed. "Welcome to your Destination."

Mike climbed up on the driver's side of the truck and knocked on the window.

"Fuck off," the driver said.

"I just want to bum a smoke," Mike said.

"I *said*—" the door opened.

Mike stepped off the running board.

There was a crack inside the truck.

The driver started to fall out, then was yanked back inside by an unseen force.

"Come on," Jonathan hissed.

Mike got in.

The giant winced and cast a pained glance at his leg. "This guy's tiny," Jonathan said, surveying the unconscious soldier between them on the bench seat. "His pants will be like shorts on me."

The soldier wasn't that small, actually. But the giant Jonathan was right; the uniform wouldn't fit him.

"You put it on," Jonathan said. "Wait here. Be the driver."

"No way," Mike said. "I didn't come all this way—"

"To what?" Jonathan asked. "Fall and break a hip in this frozen hell? What good are you going to do the kids out there? And what good will it be if someone comes in here and takes this?" He slapped the metal dashboard for emphasis. "I'll free the kids. You be ready to come get them in the truck."

Something caught in Mike's throat. "Yuh," he managed. "Shit. Okay."

Jonathan limped away toward the stage.

Mike sat in the driver's seat wearing the soldier's coat, while the unfortunate man's body cooled on the passenger floorboards.

Ahead, while the man at the podium bellowed greetings and bullshit, the kids marched onto the stage in a long, shivering line.

Chapter 46

Rachael

The ass clown at the podium was some kind of politician. I recognized the bullshit claptrap pouring out of his food hole. My eyes moved back and forth from the stage to my feet. I couldn't afford to trip and twist an ankle, but I also didn't want to miss a moment of what was happening up there, and the crowd's reaction.

A hand on my shoulder stopped me.

"Not too close," Sarah said. "No telling who's gone into stage two."

"Shit," I said. It was always at the back of my mind these days. Sarah was right. Crowds were a deathtrap if someone started puking.

"And now, the future saviors of all the unrecovered," the guy on the podium was saying, "led by Doctor Sasha Fewkes, Doctor Silva's most trusted collaborator."

"Never heard of that guy," I said.

"Me either," Sarah whispered.

"What the fuck is going on?" I mumbled. New collaborators with the dead and gone Silva?

That name was never in the news, back when there was news. And saviors....

"Look!" Jamie jumped and pointed violently.

Onstage, a gray-haired man in a white lab coat led a group of frightened-looking children across the stage.

"That's...." Sarah started moving. "That's Penny!"

I grasped her shoulder.

She shook me off.

I grabbed it again, stumbling to keep up with her. "What's your plan, mama bear? You gonna go up there and take her away from all of them just like that?"

"Fuckin' A," Sarah spat.

What did that even mean? "Stop. Sarah, we need a plan. Penny needs you to have a plan." That got her. And not a second too soon. We were on the edge of the crowd.

I tried to pull her back, but she just stared at the stage, literally digging in her heels.

I got up on tiptoes to whisper in her ear. "Let's go around to the side. See how many guns are around them?"

"Penny...." Sarah's hands reached out. Paused, then reached for her pistol. Stopped. Started reaching out again.

I don't know where I got the balls, but I slapped her.

Some faces in the crowd turned toward us. I didn't care.

Sarah stared at me, murder in her eyes.

"That's better. You wanna be pissed at me? Fine. But you don't get to fall apart. Not now. Not when this is all over. Never. You're a parent. Now smarten up. We've come all this way. You've held all of us up, all of us together. And all I'm asking you to do is walk around to the side of the stage with me—" I lowered my voice to a whisper, "—and *count* the *guns*. Can you fucking *handle* that?"

Tears chased their way down Sarah's pale cheeks. It brought out her wrinkles. God, she looked old.

Sarah nodded.

"Good." I took her elbow. "Fuck me. If *I'm* the one acting like the adult, you *know* we're screwed. I need you to snap back in."

Jamie fell in step with us as we skirted the crowd heading for the north side of the stage, where the children came up the steps.

Sarah kept turning her head, searching for a glimpse of Penny. I kept her arm tucked in mine. Let her look for the moment. I'd be the mama bear for a minute. Let her look at her kid.

"Thank you," the President said. "This is a great day for all of us. A tremendous day. An amazing day. I have gathered the greatest team of scientists, researchers, and smart people from all over the globe. Except, of course, that no one has smarter scientists than America, so really, I didn't have to go anywhere else. And who'd want to? Criminals to the south—"

A gunshot erupted from behind the stage. The President didn't even flinch at the gunshot. He just kept spouting his usual bullshit. But the whole thing did seem to snap Sarah back to reality.

"We've got to get the kids out of there," Sarah said, eyes scanning the backstage area for the shooting.

"Aaaaannndd, she's back," I muttered.

A commotion broke out in the front of the crowd near the stage. Shouts erupted.

"Look at this disgusting guy," the President said. "Get him out of here!"

I turned. It was like when people slow down for a car crash. I couldn't look away.

"How can one guy puke so much?" the President asked.

The noise grew across the shivering unrecovered. It rippled across the crowd, gathering in waves. And when the wave broke on the edge of the crowd nearest us, I knew we had to get the fuck out of there, now. They were gagging.

"Oh," the President shouted, "Rick!"

I turned away.

Sarah and Jamie quickened their steps.

Someone on stage started gagging and puking into the microphone.

That sound went off like a shot in the crowd. People started puking everywhere. I didn't look. Didn't need to. The sound of two thousand people puking at once is something I never need to hear again. I won't describe it. I don't even like remembering it. But something else came to my ears in that moment. Loud and mechanical.

A giant army truck revved its engine.

"That's it!" Sarah pointed. "That's our way to save the kids."

She started running.

I ran after her. It was easy to think of Sarah as old. She certainly had the 'get out of my yard' vibe nailed. But it was also easy to forget all her karate shit or Wushu, or whatever she called it. Man, when I tell you Sarah was fast for an old chick, I mean to tell you, Sarah was fast for anyone. She left me in the dust, and I'd trained with my army sister at five AM every day.

It looked like she was going to fall for a second, but then she jumped onto the gas tank of the thing.

Chapter 47

Sarah

She tripped. Despair filled her before she could hit the ground. But Sarah didn't hit the ground. Instead, her momentum launched her forward at the same time the truck swerved into her path. Sarah's fingers closed around metal. She hauled herself upright on the bucking machine.

The dogs kept pace, Dickens and Koontz barking out an alarm.

The face behind the glass, indistinct at first behind the reflected concrete-gray sky, was familiar. So much like her own that despite the bumps and the fear and the vomit and the President, Sarah's heart skipped a beat. "Dad?"

The man looked at her. He steered one-handed, cradling the other. "You've got to get in back! Get ready to get Penny!" he shouted.

Sarah nodded. It was more of a plan than she had a second ago.

The truck slowed to a stop.

Sarah jumped down and headed for the back. There, Jamie and Rachael caught up with her and climbed on. The dogs followed, leaping onto the tall tailgate. "Go!" Sarah slammed her fist on the hard metal behind her father's head.

The truck lurched back into motion.

Sarah gripped the splintered wooden rail and knelt on the bench, surveying the scene. It was a tragedy almost unbelievable in scope. The crowd, about two thousand by Sarah's estimation, were either vomiting up stage two bile, or were embarking on a death spiral of overindulging their basest instincts. Already, less than two minutes into this super spreader event, clothes were flying, and Sarah could see nude people of both sexes in the crowd. The sex freaks Sarah could handle, could fight off, or kill without guilt. But the other behaviors emerging in the crowd. Shit.

A kid, about twenty, ran at the truck with a bloody knife screaming, "Fresh blood! Fresh blood!"

"Don't do it, kid," she whispered.

The truck hit a bump.

The crack of a pistol came from behind her.

"I'm gonna cum all over you!" a male voice screamed.

Another pistol shot.

Koontz and Dickens barked fiercely at something behind Sarah.

She glanced back to see Rachael pointing her pistol at the tailgate, and a pale, half-dressed male body fell on the black, ashen ground receding behind them.

"Fresh blood!" the chant came again, this time much closer.

Sarah slammed her pistol butt down on fingers gripping the wooden rail.

The fingers fell away.

The man's scream was cut short by the driver's side of the truck rising and falling with a pronounced thud.

Sarah turned back to look for Penny. Still there. Thank God. Huddled in with some bigger girls at the end of the flatbed stage closest to the cab. A couple of men in suits stood shielding the kids, arms akimbo, guns out.

At least there was that.

"I'm the supreme commander of the world!" the President shouted, banging his hands on the podium. Black bile stained the right side of his blue suit. "I'm the smartest man in the United States, and you should all kneel before me! You should be kneeling!" He reached for his belt. "Look at this symbol of my manhood!"

The way ahead was becoming increasingly blocked by members of the crowd, either uninfected and running away, or infected by stage two bile and heading out to indulge their secret desires.

Banging on her right made her turn. A guy the size of a refrigerator stood on the running board next to her father's window.

Sarah brought the gun to bear.

The truck bumped and moved so much, she couldn't chance the round going wild and puncturing the metal cab and killing her dad. Sarah scooted closer.

The guy got the door open, forcing him to lean out.

Sarah shot him once, twice, and a third time before he fell.

Shit. How many shots had she fired so far?

A woman, naked to the waist, sat on the ground, covered in bloody two-inch horizontal cuts. She looked up from slicing her forearm as the truck passed. Her wounded eyes begged to be seen. For connection and absolution.

Sarah had none to give.

The mayhem grew louder. Shouts and exaltations floated like a malevolent ozone layer above the crowd.

The truck clanked and churned the scorched earth as it drew closer to the back side of the stage. In front, a crowd of maniacs closed in. They waved shirts and sticks.

The President presented his penis to the crowd. Or, that's what it seemed like. Sarah doubted anyone past the first row was getting any kind of show at all.

The world was fucked.

One of the guys in suits protecting the kids shot a man climbing up on the stage.

They passed a man licking the feet of another man who no longer had hands... or a head.

Sarah's stomach turned.

Some people in the crowd had started fucking, rutting like pigs in the churned-up ash.

Others fought.

There were more than a few corpses already.

One man carved strange symbols into the corpse of another with a massive hunting knife while he fucked a hole in its side.

Sarah puked, spraying her shoes and the floor of the truck. It wasn't black. She wiped the sleeve of her coat across her face with her pistol hand. The other gripped the wooden rail.

They passed the cab of the truck that pulled the stage into place.

Her father steered them toward the back corner where the kids were.

Something bumped under the tires.

Sarah didn't look.

The clusters of people behind the stage fell into three categories: puking, fucking, or fighting.

People thumped, banged, and screamed off the truck. As soon as they were close enough,

Sarah climbed over the side and leaped onto the stage.

One of the guys blocking the kids from the chaos a few feet away rounded on her.

"I'm her mom!" Sarah shouted.

Koontz barked savagely. King bared his teeth at the man.

Sarah bulldozed her way through the knot of children, seized the crying Penny by the jacket, and held the child to her. "Oh, Penny! Mommy's here! Mommy loves you!" She broke down. All the terror and despair in her body left through sharp, wracking sobs and tears.

"Mommy...." Penny managed, then continued crying.

Dickens lapped at their tears.

"Aella!" Jamie shouted. She turned frantically from one direction to another, yelling.

Sarah sniffed the top of Penny's head, completing some primal maternal verification. It was Penny.

"Okay, kids," Rachael said, scooping a wild-eyed young boy up and depositing him not all that gently into the military truck.

"You can't do that!" one of the suits guarding the kids said. "They're for the medical—"

Koontz barked at the man, his vicious German Shepherd canines fierce and prominent.

Rachael had her pistol in the guy's face. "Medical experiments. Say it. But if you do, I'm just going to shoot you."

"We have to go!" Sarah shouted. She didn't know what to do. Aella was nowhere in sight, so how could Jamie leave? The other kids whose parents weren't there still needed saving, and there was no way she was ever letting Penny out of her sight again, ever.

"What's it going to be, dickhead?" Rachael said. "You ever have kids? Is this what you'd want for them?"

The guy dropped his gun.

Rachael nodded. "Start putting them in the truck. And where's Aella?"

"She was here," the suit said. "I don't know."

Sarah climbed back over the side of the military truck and sit Penny on the long bench at her side. Kneeling next to her daughter, Sarah received the kids the guy in the suit passed over the splintered rail.

"Gotta go!" Sarah's father called from the front. Sarah could see the chaos around them devolving, becoming more of whatever it was, be it violent, or gluttonous, or depraved.

"I am a God!" the President managed to make it back to the microphone.

No one seemed to listen. No one but Rachael.

She held up her pistol and pointed it right at the President's head.

The two guys in suits stopped handing kids across and went for their guns.

"Don't," Sarah said, drawing down on them. She didn't say a word to Rachael. Everything had already been said. The speeches delivered. The sermons, the metaphors. If Rachael was going to kill for revenge, this was her moment. Certainly, the President was the commander of the forces that killed Cassie.

"I am the most tremendous President in the history of the United States. Of the world!"

Rachael lowered her gun. "Idiot." She turned to Sarah. "What are we going to do about Jamie?"

"We have to go," Sarah said. Rachael nodded. She jumped into the truck, then cupped her hands to her mouth. "Jamie, we have to go! Now!"

Jamie stood looking from one side to the other. Then, she ran to the podium and pushed the President aside.

"Hey lady, what the fu—" the President started.

"Aella!" Jamie shouted into the microphone. "Aella, honey, go home. I'll wait for you there. You hear me, Aella? Go home!" Jamie ran for the truck.

"Dogs, come!" Sarah yelled.

They did. Dickens almost missed.

Sarah grabbed the panting Lab and hauled him in.

A dozen terrified kids aged two to ten screamed and cried amid the chaos and carnage.

"Don't look kids," Jamie said. "Sit on the floor with me."

Some of the kids climbed down off the benches.

"Come on," Jamie insisted. "Down here."

Sarah wanted to sit down there with Penny. She didn't want to see. But she knew they needed her gun right now. She settled for putting Penny down on the floor and wrapping the girl around her leg while she knelt on the bench with the other and looked for trouble.

It didn't take her long to find it.

Chapter 48

Mike

As Sarah and the others loaded the kids into the truck, Mike looked for trouble. And right behind the stage, he found it. Dale and Vic stared around, wide-eyed at the chaos. Running soldiers. Knights bashing vomit-covered lunatics with the butts of their rifles.

Mike's hand dropped to the gun in his pocket. Wounded arm or no, he could brace the gun on the side of the door. Terminate Dale's command.

Mike brought the gun out of his pocket.

Dale planned to bludgeon Penny in a half-baked attempt to create another freak like Vic. Another human with Vic's gift of the touch. It couldn't stand. He couldn't be allowed to live.

The rational part of Mike's brain told him that with the stage on the other side of them, if Mike missed, he could hit someone innocent

He scanned the scene, seeking out Jonathan. It didn't take long to spot the man's massive form running to the stage, just on the edge of Mike's vision.

No one was taking this truck. Not right now. Not in the middle of whatever weirdness was happening on the stage.

Mike opened the door and stepped down from the truck, then crossed the distance toward Vic and Dale.

"Dad!" Sarah shouted. "Where are you going?"

The burned-out cornstalks crunched under his feet. His blood pumped faster. The pistol grip etched its waffle pattern into his squeezing palm.

"Dale!" Mike shouted.

Dale turned.

Vic whipped his bound hands over Dale's head and pulled back hard.

Dale's eyes bulged.

Mike brought the gun up. Two birds. One stone.

Except he couldn't do it. Vic was a tragic figure, not evil. And Mike's veneer of civilization hadn't entirely cracked away.

"I'm not your fucking slave anymore!" Vic hissed through clenched teeth. "You superior son-of-a-bitch."

Dale elbowed Vic savagely in the gut. At the same time, he whipped his head back, cracking Vic in the face.

Blood burst from Vic's nose. He howled in pain.

Dale ducked out of Vic's chokehold.

"Don't move, Dale," Mike yelled. His arm hurt from the effort of holding the gun up.

"What are you going to do, Mike, shoot me in cold blood?"

"You kidnapped my granddaughter. You were going to beat her head in, trying to make another Vic." Mike said. He kept advancing. Slowly. One slippery step at a time. Falling on a patch of snow would be a disaster.

"Hey!" someone shouted. "US Army! Put down the gun!"

"I'm going to stick my dick in you!" another voice yelled.

And then Jonathan was there, pushing Mike's gun down. "You gotta go back and get those kids outta here!"

Shit. Of course he did. He raised the gun again, putting slight pressure on the trigger.

"This ain't you," Jonathan said. "Go protect your family."

"Yeah, right." He lowered the gun and headed for the truck.

"Oh thank God," Dale said. "Jonathan."

"Fuck you," the giant said behind him.

Jonathan's gun barked once.

"What about me?" Vic complained.

"Good luck," Jonathan said. His feet crunched the snowy ground as he caught up to Mike.

"Aella!" Jamie yelled. She moved frantically from one side of the truck to the other, leaning over the rail and screaming. "Aella!"

Mike climbed into the driver's seat.

"Jamie," Jonathan called up. "I'll find her!"

"She won't trust you," Jamie called back.

In his rear-view mirror, Jamie jumped down. She and Jonathan disappeared amid the running figures.

"Jamie!" Rachael screamed. "No!"

No time to wait around and sort this out. They had to go. Jamie and Jonathan were on their own now.

The whole world of human depravity unfolded through the windshield of the M35. He needed every bit of the unstoppable ten-wheel drive to get over what was going on outside.

People were chopping each other up. Eating each other, going to the bathroom on each other. Cutting themselves up. Fucking each other while doing any of the other things. His stomach did angry flips in his belly. He didn't want any of it. And he didn't want to run people down, no matter how twisted their minds had become in the last few minutes.

A severed hand bounced off the windshield, leaving a bloody splatter mark. Mike steered further from the crowd, aiming the nose of the truck on a curve that ended at the house where they'd parked the Humvee.

In his mirror, Mike could see the beginnings of real trouble. It was hard to tell with the gray sky, and the gray ground, and the ash-covered lunatics, but it looked like maybe the crowd had started following the truck.

"Fuck!" Mike ground the gears, coaxing a little more speed out of the engine, but honestly, the ground was so rough, speed wasn't the limiting factor. It was the well-being of the kids in the back. Any faster and he'd end up launching one of them into the crowd of maniacs.

Sarah banged on the roof. "Stop the truck!"

"Now?!"

"Dad!"

Mike stopped, front bumper in the corn just behind the house. "What?!"

"No time to explain," Sarah said.

"I'll get the radio," Rachael said, leaping from the truck.

Sarah cast an eye toward the figures running toward them across the field. "Go to the house!" Sarah yelled.

Mike jammed the truck back into gear. They bumped through the corn and pulled up at the barn.

Rachael came running up to meet the truck holding the radio. She looked up at Sarah. "Do we make the call? Jamie's still out there."

Sarah squinted into the distance.

Mike followed her gaze. Some in the crowd were running toward them. "We don't have much time. The crazies will be here soon."

"Shit," Sarah said. "We've gotta save these kids." She nodded to Rachael.

Rachael keyed the radio. "This is Street Gang to Almighty. Do you copy?"

"5-by-5 Street Gang, what's your status?"

"We are at the Hargrave farm in Destination, Idaho. There are two thousand unrecovered in stage two, but the children are secure at the house." Rachael said.

"We have fast movers on station," the radio crackled. "Get undercover. The ordnance is going to come in danger close."

"Shit!" Mike cursed, climbing down from the cab. "They were waiting for you. Run! Get the kids inside! Look!" he pointed at the crowd racing across the cornfield. They couldn't be allowed to get the kids.

They had time, but not a lot. It would take the crowd a few minutes to get there.

The frightened screams of the children in the back clawed at Mike's nerves over the engine noise. But another cloying sound rose, one all but forgotten. The approach of jets.

Mike eyed the sky. "Go, Sarah. Take Penny. Get safe."

"Dad, you have to come too."

"I have to give you time to button up in there. I have to lead this crowd away, so the jets don't target the house."

The sound of the jets grew closer.

"Sarah, let's go!" Rachael shouted.

"Rachael..." Sarah held up a finger. "Dad.... I just found you. I... need you to be there."

Mike put his hands on her shoulders, the pain in his arm all but forgotten. "Sarah, don't you see, drawing them away to get blown up? That's how I show up for you." His voice hitched. He swallowed. "I'm so proud of you, Sarah. So proud. Now get out of here and take care of that little girl!"

He didn't turn. Didn't see Sarah's tears, or whether she got inside before he jammed the truck into gear one last time and spun around, heading back out into the field. He hoped that whatever had possessed the unrecovered to chase the truck in the first place still held.

It seemed to. They turned and followed Mike, the Pied Piper, in a deuce-and-a-half.

Mike swung away from the farm, bumping across the furrows of burned corn, leading the crowd toward the center of the field.

The jets streaked in from the west, low and straight at Mike. One, two, three flights of fighters that didn't exist in his Vietnam days. But the ordnance they dropped, it was terribly familiar. The tumbling cylinders with tapered ends hurtled toward him.

Napalm.

Fucking ghastly. They hadn't come up with anything better in fifty years? These poor, unfortunate bastards behind Mike were going to burn.

The hell of it was, Mike couldn't swerve. He couldn't stop. He couldn't disengage. If he pulled off, the bombs might miss the unrecovered.

Another fast mover released its payload. And another. A forest of twirling, tapered death bore down on Mike.

The first bomb hit right in front of the truck.

Chapter 49

Rachael

The kids huddled together in the storm cellar. They sat on the bunks in threes and fours. Sarah sat on the edge, holding Penny. Rocking her. But somehow, Sarah and I were the only adults.

Sarah looked up. "Asim?"

I squashed the impulse to stamp my foot and turned for the door.

"Rachael," Sarah said. "You can't. They're on their own. You can't go, Rachael. You're part of this family now, and you're needed here. Safe. Alive."

"No...." I stopped. And felt at once the soft-hearted joy of being part of a family again, and like a total shithead coward for not going after my friends.

A deep, rumbling thud shook the storm cellar.

"I always thought bombs would be louder...." The ceiling had no cracks, but staring at it while more explosions hit the ground made me feel like a submarine commander in an old movie. And then my thoughts turned to Asim and his daughter, and Jamie and Aella.... The world spun at that hard angle, like the beginning of the pandemic. People dying. Despair. Loneliness — preemptive this time. This wasn't the first family of mine the smiling flu could wipe out. Shelter or no.

"Almighty, come in?" Sarah said into the radio.

Only static came back.

"Must be the storm cellar," Sarah said.

It was hard for me to think of the people out there. Just regular people who once had the smiling flu and now lost everything because of it. They weren't evil or bad people. Just people. Flawed people. Now, dead people.

The bombing lasted fifteen heart-sickening minutes. Wave after wave.

And after five minutes of silence, the waiting was killing me. "I'm going to look."

"Rachael!" Sarah reached out.

"I have to *know*."

I pushed down on the air with my hand. The gesture wasn't meant to placate Sarah, just annoy her into thinking about something else. "I'm just going to peek through the scope."

Sarah frowned.

I like to use my powers of manipulation for *good*. Right now, Sarah was thinking about how annoying and condescending I'd just been, and not the fate of our friends and their children.

The steel cylinder revealed nothing, just thick, heavy snow filling the air in a white cloud, obscuring everything. I'd never heard of a snowstorm moving in that fast.

"Can't see anything," I said, reaching for the door.

"Rachael!" Sarah called.

"I'm just going to peek and come right back."

"Rachael, NO!"

I opened the steel door leading to the wooden stairs and the overhead hatch.

Some white shit that looked like instant potato flakes fell through the cracks along the sides of the trapdoor.

I dropped it. Not because of the flakes, but the sharp chemical smell in the air. I ran back into the shelter and closed the door. "I bet a prepper like Ed has gas masks in here somewhere," I said.

He did.

"Come on, Rachael," Sarah said as I put on the mask. "You're not going out there."

"How long do you want to wait?" I asked. If something happened to Jamie or Asim, no one would know we were there. No one was coming. Sarah had to know that, right?

Sarah took a hand from around Penny and pointed at me. "Longer."

"I have to *know*," I said. My words were muffled by the rubber barrier between them and the free air.

Sarah started to say something else, but I was already closing the door. Not an airlock, but enough. I lifted the hatch. The window above the stall showed snow. The flakes that drifted in on the breeze weren't snow, though.

I closed the hatch behind me and scattered some hay over it. Then stepped out of the barn into a different world. White flakes drifted down from the sky. It was snow, and, it wasn't. Like some kind of weird powder.

There were no fires. No burned-out vehicles, houses or corn. Instead, white flakes puffed underfoot, making a cloud that followed me. And there were people.

They stood in knots. Any blood, or puke, or who knew what else on them, was covered in white powder.

It was a world of ghosts.

And instead of savagely indulging in their most primal and atavistic urges, they just stood and stared at one another. At the wounds they'd inflicted. The harms they'd committed. They stared at the animal versions of themselves, come up across the millennia of evolution for a visit.

A track in the corn led toward the clearing where the crowd had stood. Along that track were hundreds of ghost people. Some just sat where they'd fallen. Some cried quietly and pressed hands to their wounds.

Until I knew what this white shit was, or what these fuckers were going to do next, I decided to avoid them.

Three figures emerged from the corn, their heads and shoulders covered in white powder. The rest of their clothes bore traces of color where the leaves of the corn had scraped away the powder, or deposited it. I wasn't sure how that worked exactly. The first two were Jamie and Aella. The third figure, a big man, stumbled, walking backward, pointing a machine gun, covering Jamie and Aella's back-trail.

They trudged toward me, not looking up.

"Hey," I called. "Jamie...."

She walked past me without saying anything. Like I wasn't there. Like she didn't know me. Maybe she didn't hear me through the rubber mask?

"What happened?" I called louder.

"Aella needs a bath," Jamie said so quietly I almost didn't hear it.

They kept walking toward the house. Their house, I realized.

The big man turned, stumbled again, and fell to his knees. His coat flapped open, revealing a knife in his chest.

Jesus.

"Got to keep them safe..." the giant wheezed.

"Jonathan!"

I turned toward the new voice.

A figure covered in white powder approached. "Jesus, big man...."

Jonathan raised his eyes... and the gun.

I drew my pistol.

He waved our guns down. "It's alright." Mike Sampson's eyes turned back to Jonathan. "It's me."

We lowered our guns.

"Sarah and Penny?" Mike asked.

"They're safe," I said.

Mike smiled. His shoulders dropped. "Jamie and Aella?"

I smiled behind my mask. "They're safe too. You did it."

He sagged with relief and nodded. "Thank you," he said, fighting back tears.

Jonathan turned his eyes to me. "They're safe?"

I nodded.

He collapsed, dropping the gun, clawing at the knife handle in his chest. The sudden realization that his mission was complete gave him permission to feel his own pain again.

Mike limped to his side and knelt down in the dust.

I knelt too. "You can't take it out," I said. "You'll bleed out."

Mike took the big man's hand from the knife and clasped it in his own.

Jonathan looked up at Mike with wide, watery eyes. "I found Aella in the field. She... Aella... she had a bag."

"Don't talk," I said, the rubber gas mask muffling my words. "Rest easy. Help is coming." I *hoped* help was coming.

"...It was full of severed hands," Jonathan gasped. "Fists, with the thumbs up. She said...." He coughed, then grimaced. "She said, look at all the likes I got...." He wheezed for a moment. "I threw her over my shoulder, tried to get her the fuck out of there."

"Shhh, it's okay," Mike said. "You did get—"

"Aella didn't understand. Because of who I am. She thought I was... I was... It's her knife."

Shit. I would have done the same thing. The anger boiled up inside me again. Anger at this stupid, fucked-up world. "Shit."

He reached up, grabbed Mike's coat, and pulled the old man close. I could barely hear him whisper, "Am I... Am I one of the good guys?"

Mike sniffed. "Yeah. Yeah, Jonathan, you are. You're one of the good guys."

Jonathan's hands fell limp at his sides. He stared up at the sky, unseeing.

Mike reached out a trembling hand and closed Jonathan's eyes. Then stood beside me.

I got to my feet.

I couldn't wait any longer. I needed to know. "What is this shit?" I asked, brushing the white powder from my coat.

"I don't know," Mike said. "But it stopped the carnage." He pointed to my gas mask. "I don't think you need that."

I peeled the mask off. "What happened?"

Mike looked stricken. He shook his head and swallowed. "They had those tumblers, like they used for napalm in Vietnam. But these were full of that white powder. They hit the ground and bounced up and away, over and over, spraying that white powder everywhere. And some airburst shells. Once it got to the unrecovered, they just stopped. Like... clockwork toys winding down." His eyes, which had turned cloudy and looked at a point somewhere over my shoulder, honed back in on mine. "Take me to my family."

I took a step back. "Let's make sure you're okay and...."

Mike nodded. "The last time I was here, they dosed me with something that put me in a coma for fifty years." He looked at the ground, his lips drawn into a thin line.

"Fuuucck," I said.

"Have you seen Doctor Parks?" Mike asked, still looking down.

"No," I said. "How 'bout Asim?"

"I don't know who that is."

"I guess not," I said. "A guy we met along the road. A good-guy. Had a daughter here."

"Seems like everyone did," Mike said.

Huh. True. "Every woman is someone's daughter. Sarah and Penny are in the storm cellar, in the barn," I said. "I've got to tell Sarah what's happening."

"Take me to my family," Mike said again. "Please." His chin crinkled up, and his eyes threatened tears.

I smiled.

He smiled back. "I didn't think I'd ever see them again." Silent tears cut tracks in the white powder covering his face.

Something blocked my throat. "Yeah," I choked, turning away. It wasn't about being tough, or what Mike thought of me. He was part of my family now, too, I supposed. It was about having work to do. Finding Asim. Figuring out if this white shit was safe enough for Sarah and the kids to come out. No time for emotions now. When I used to spar with Cassie, she told me to 'feel the pain later.' And when *I'd* hit *her*, she'd said kind of the same thing: 'celebrate later.'

"Let's go see our family," I said.

Chapter 50

Everyone

Sarah stood, staring at the closed hatch to the storm cellar. Her belly churned. Every noise made her start. Penny had fallen asleep in her arms, and she rocked the child, feeling the warmth of Penny's little body against her. Penny's soft hair tickled her cheek. The warmth of relief radiated through every part of Sarah's body. Penny was finally where she belonged.

Dickens put his head on her thigh next to Penny's and wouldn't be moved. Koontz and King sat sentinel on either side of her. It filled Sarah's heart with a sense of rightness. Yet the sensation wasn't complete without Nate and her father.

The trapdoor opened with a bang.

The outline of Rachael's head appeared, silhouetted in the gray light spilling from the barn window behind her. "Someone to see you." The shadows hid her features, but there was an unmistakable smile in her voice.

A figure in an ill-fitting army coat eased himself down the stairs. "Hey, little monster."

"Oh, my God!" The wail forced its way past Sarah's lips before she could stop it. "Dad!" He'd called her that when she was little. She'd forgotten. But the words touched a bone-deep memory. Yes, he'd called her that.

Penny stirred.

"Shhhh," Sarah whispered, as her tears wetted Penny's hair.

"It's okay, Sarah. I'm here now. And I'm almost me again," her father's voice caught. He swallowed. "And I love you."

Another sharp cry, this one more powerful than the last, packed with fifty years of longing and wondering, burst from her.

"Mommy?" Penny asked.

"Hey, it's okay. Mommy's here," Sarah said through the tears. "So is Grampy."

Mike

As he sat on the splintered wooden steps gazing down into the storm cellar at Sarah, he saw her differently. Gone was the estranged, tough, guarded woman. In her place was his little monster. All grown up. A strong, beautiful, loving mother. The lump in his throat threatened to cut off his words. "I'm so proud of you," was all he could manage.

Tears streamed down Sarah's face, yet she had a thin, quiet smile. She motioned him down to join her.

"I don't dare," he motioned to himself, and instantly regretted it. The stitches sent a stab of pain up his arm. "We don't know what this shi—" he glanced at his granddaughter and checked himself, "uh—stuff does. I think I should keep away from the kids until I can get cleaned up."

Sarah nodded. Still smiling.

"I hate to break up this party," Dr. Parks said behind him. "But we've got to get these kids somewhere decent. They need warm clothes, beds, and a hot meal."

"Who doesn't?" Rachael put in from somewhere behind the doctor.

Mike stood. After all he'd been through, he somehow felt stronger and more fit than he had since waking up from the coma, screaming into the void.

He climbed the steps and stood aside for Dr. Parks and an army medic to descend. A Middle Eastern man and a somber-faced Army Colonel with the name 'Harding' on his breast stood just inside the barn door.

When Sarah emerged holding Penny, Mike sidestepped to avoid getting any of the white powder that covered him on his granddaughter.

"You!" Sarah said, pointing at the Colonel. "Better late than never, I guess." Mike resisted the urge to take her clenched fist and lace her fingers in his.

"Miss Sampson," the Colonel said, patting the air with his hands. "I came here personally as soon as I learned about the operation. I came to make safe the citizens under our protection."

"Protection!" Sarah hissed through clenched teeth.

The German Shepherd at Sarah's side let out a low growl.

"We're doing the best we can," Harding said. "We've still got all those nuclear and chemical plants to secure, plus logistics for what's left of the population."

"And this?" Sarah pointed to Mike's powder-covered sleeve.

"As soon as we learned about the second stage, every doctor, every med tech, everyone started working on it. Laetanol was the key. We started with that, since the majority of people who took it before the pandemic never got sick. Otherwise, it might have taken years. As it is, we're still not sure about it. There were no trials. No studies of long-term effects. It seemed to work, so we deployed...."

Mike understood all that, but the scare they'd given him... "Man those napalm tumblers, what the hell! I thought I was dead."

Colonel Harding shrugged. "I'm sorry about that. We needed a delivery vehicle we could build and deploy in a matter of days. Wooden bombs were easy. We made them in the back of a hardware store."

"Yeah," Mike let out a breath. "Jesus."

Carl ascended the stairs. A line of children climbed up behind him.

"This way," the army medic said, leading the children away.

Colonel Harding nodded to Carl. "We'll want to do a full debrief on your work with tau on the unrecovered. Your research could be instrumental in improving our response to stage two of the smiling flu. Together with our Laetanol-based compound..." he trailed off.

"Of course," Carl smiled. "I'm looking forward to it."

Mike hadn't seen Carl smile like that in a long time. It felt good. And just the simple warmth in his gut, feeling good, made Mike realize how much Dr. Parks had helped him.

"Carl," Mike said, risking a white-powdered hand on the doctor's shoulder. "Thank you, for everything."

Carl's face reddened. But before he could say anything, Rachael's shout cut the atmosphere.

"Asim!" Rachael ran up and threw her arms around him. "I was so worried about you!"

The old man smiled and wrapped his arms around Rachael, still clutching his cane. "As you say." The old man's voice wavered.

"Did you find her?" Rachael asked.

"We're still looking," he said.

"We?" Rachael pulled away and looked at Asim.

"We're conducting a search and rescue for the unrecovered who fled before we dropped the antidote," Harding said. "Mr. El-Shaer is assisting with that operation."

"They need comfort, not commandos," Asim said. "I will talk to them, comfort them, allow them to get the cure quietly, peacefully. And... hopefully find Ghada."

"I'm so glad you're okay, Asim," Sarah said.

"And I am also glad your family is finally together," Asim said. "Go take care of them."

Sarah brushed a tear from her eye. "Yes. Thank you. For everything." She turned to Mike. "Come on Dad, let's get you cleaned up and check on Jamie and Aella."

Dad. She'd called him that a few times that day, and it still sent a thrill through him.

The cold bit into Mike as they approached the house. The smell of wood smoke filled the air. A thin plume rose into the sky from the farmhouse chimney. Inside by the fire, Jamie and Aella sat, holding each other.

"Hey," Mike said, crouching down beside them. "How are you holding up?"

"About how you'd expect," Jamie said. "I've got my baby back."

Mike laid a hand on each of their shoulders. "Truly and finally back. No more despair. We're all finally out from under the black water."

Rachael

They flew us home. I was honestly surprised they burned the fuel on us. Though I'd never ridden in a prop-propelled plane before. The army guys said it was more fuel-efficient.

When we got home, I stayed with Sarah, Mike, and Penny. I couldn't face going back to Cassie's apartment on the Fort Walters army base. Not yet.

After Destination, my rage and my quest for vengeance evaporated. That was enough violence for a lifetime. Several lifetimes. Now, I just lay in my bed.

Sarah tried to get me to go back to work at the library.

"Come on," she said. "There's a lot of new history to write."

I just turned over and faced away. I couldn't. Not without thinking about Cassie, and that hurt too much. Still. But that was the story I had to write. Her dedication to this world, to me, to the kidnapped children she gave her life to save... needed to go down in the history of the smiling flu.

"Maybe after the funeral," Sarah said, closing the door.

The army had waited until the members of Cassie's unit had all returned from their temporary duty assignments to have a funeral for everyone who'd fallen.

I stood by the row of flag-draped coffins in scrounged black clothes. The words and prayers of the ceremony flowed past my ears without seeping in.

She was in there. In that rough pine box. I just wanted her to hold me one more time. Laugh with me. Punch me in the arm for being sassy.

"I'm so sorry," I whispered. "If I hadn't let Vic touch me in that jail...."

"It would have happened anyway," Mike said, putting his arm over my shoulder. "This isn't your fault."

I bit my lip, holding back a sob.

Sarah put a hand on my shoulder.

The gunshots of the salute made me flinch into Mike's side. Then they played Taps on a bugle. I tried so hard not to cry as they took the flag from Cassie's coffin. But tears ran down my cheeks when the soldiers in dress uniforms laid that folded American flag in my arms.

The Smiling Flu Series

Book 1 – *The Unrecovered*
Book 2 – *Rachael's Apocalypse Diary*
Book 3 – *Beneath the Dark Water*

Also by Len M. Ruth

The Pull
Tales of the Doomed

Stay Connected

Get updates, behind-the-scenes notes, and bonus reads in Len's monthly newsletter:
lenmruth.com

Len M. Ruth writes character-first horror with a literary edge—stories about grief, resilience, and what people become when the world stops making sense. His work includes *The Pull*, *The Unrecovered*, *Rachael's Apocalypse Diary*, *Beneath the Dark Water*, and *Tales of the Doomed*.

He also co-authors the **Spectral Seduction** series with Devora Gray, blending paranormal heat with eerie mystery and dark humor.

Len's fiction leans into found family, hard choices, and the thin line between survival and surrender—books for readers who like their fear with heart, and their endings earned. He lives in Las Vegas with his partner, Emory, and their dog, Cooper. Find him at lenmruth.com

www.ingramcontent.com/pod-product-compliance
Lightning Source LLC
LaVergne TN
LVHW041112080826
845145LV00007B/1784